Sky Lanterns Over Nether Ides

A Redferne Family Adventure

Pattison Telford

This novel's story and characters are fictitious.
Certain long-standing institutions, agencies, and
public offices are mentioned, but the characters
involved are wholly imaginary.

ACKNOWLEDGEMENTS

Thanks to my advance readers! Samuel Alfrey (dragonfly magic), Brady Burkett (love the *Chekhov's Guns* reference), Yvette Caradonna, Claire Edwards, Norm Finlayson, Pia Fransen, Milo Griffin (the book is not suitable for a five-year-old), Rob Hannah, Audrey Jacques ('Vine' chapter), Deb Livingstone, Mary O'Neill (Newton's superpower, coming soon), Karen Papadopoulos (map), Matthew Pittman, Audrey Platteel, Ethan Wood.

Impeccable editing by vickybrewstereditor.com

Cover design by Darin Morrison-Beer

REDFERNE FAMILY ADVENTURES

You can find out more at www.pattisontelford.com

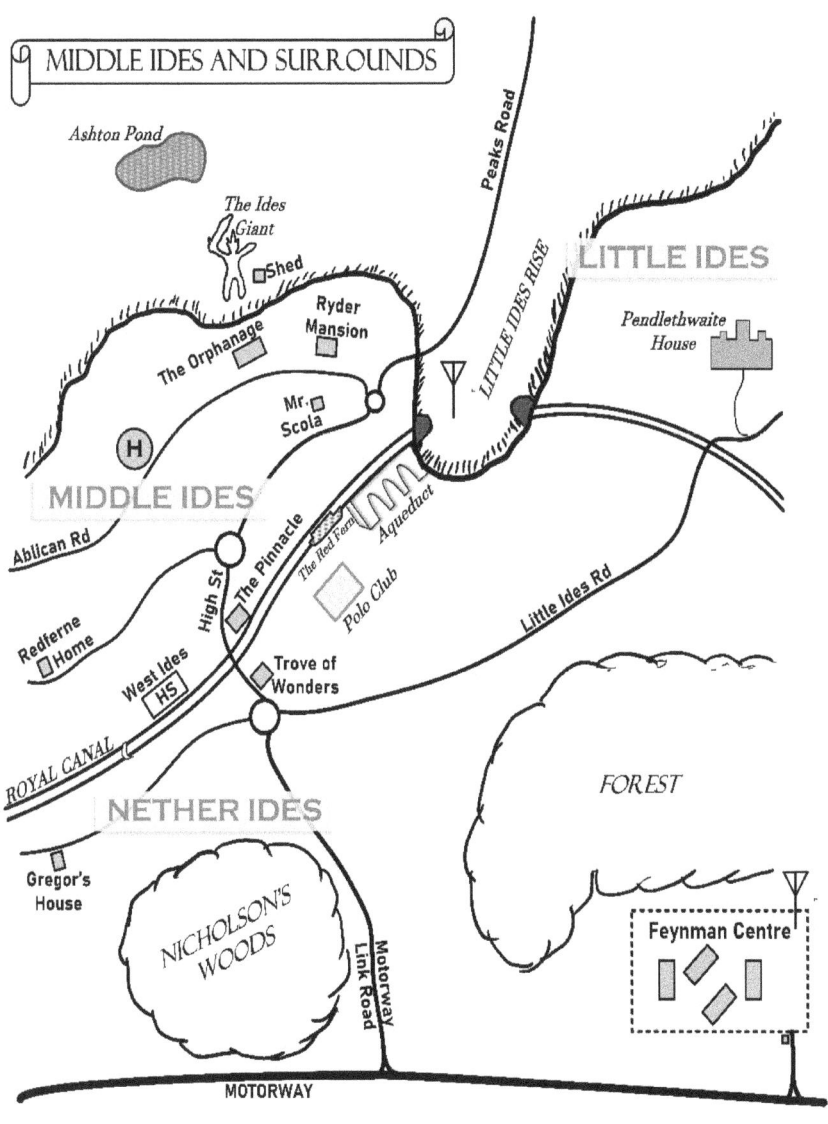

Sky Lanterns Over Nether Ides

.

CHAPTER 1 - ORPHANS

Higgs

My brother Faraday's primal instincts solved the helicopter crash at the fringe of Nicholson's Woods. He stood a touch too close to the blazing wreckage and used his obsessive attention to detail to point out to Newton and the other police officers what had happened.

I had my own strange experience that same night. With everyone in the family snarled up in the aftermath, it felt awkward to mention what had happened to me. I cut those conversations short, not wanting to be the pest distracting my brother's protectors. At fifteen, I'm his baby sister by a little more than a year, but he will always have an inner child that needs every source of guidance available.

Here's what happened. That evening, I could hear my eldest brother Newton talking to my parents from the kitchen, which was directly below my bedroom. I felt I could almost touch him, the rich tones of his voice a comforting vibration emanating through the floorboards. But I was ensnared by the nightmarish black smoke that glowed orange underneath from the still burning helicopter, visible from my bedroom window. Leaning through the screenless frame, the breeze on my face and hands was not unpleasant. However, when my grandmother's voice whispered from the back garden, every fine hair on my body stood on end, as if there was a prize for the straightest-looking strand.

"Higgs!" The voice was dreamy. "Higgs! You are a tree." I could hear her as if she stood in front of me, but she wasn't visible, though nobody had bothered to turn off the string of bulbs that ran suspended over the garden's length. But it couldn't be her out there, could it? She was in a medical care home up by the hills—an unthinkable meander away, especially at night.

I dared to call out to her tentatively, although I did not believe she was there. "Granny?"

No direct answer came, but her distinctive, musical voice spoke once more, this time at full volume. "A tree."

Although it felt like one, this wasn't a dream. She said nothing more and my hairs settled. My palms started to itch, and when I turned them over for inspection, tiny shoots of vegetation sprang from them. It seemed like a dream that the shoots erupted into leaves, green at first and then crinkling into autumn reds and oranges. But I know it wasn't a dream— although my palms had returned to their normal girlish state in the morning, fallen autumn leaves littered my bed. It was springtime.

I was in denial, like a polar explorer looking at blackened, frozen toes and figuring they'll recover after a nice soak in warm water. An unscratchable itch had formed in a deep crevasse of my brain, but I refused to acknowledge it. I resolved not to tell anyone the whole story, lest they think me unhinged. Only later would I understand what happened to me that night, though I puzzled over it often.

Muted family conversations continued downstairs late into that night, a soothing soundtrack as I calmed myself, and in the morning, only my father and I were awake as I prepared for school. It was often hard to tell if he had brushed his antenna-field of hair, bristling grey with the odd remnant of red. Today, it appeared he was trying to absorb maximum signal from the world through his untameable mane.

"Dad? Last night I was looking across the back garden, and I swear I heard Granny speaking to me. Could I be going crazy or something?"

He raised an eyebrow as unkempt as the hair above. "No, it's nothing like that. What did she say?"

"Not much. Something about me being a tree."

"Huh." He paused and fiddled with his earlobe. "Sometimes I hear her voice too, but probably everyone hears their own mother's voice from time to time. Usually instructing you to pull up your pants or keep your shoulders back and down. But the tree thing does sound like something she would say—you should ask her about it when you catch her in a moment of clarity. And you do somehow remind me of a tree. Maybe she's onto something."

"Why? Because my skin looks like bark and if you cut me open you'd count fifteen rings?"

He laughed at that. Sometimes being a smart arse was helpful. "Well, yeah, those things … but mostly because you are tough. You bend, but virtually nothing can break you. Plus, you have powerful roots."

I shrugged off the sentiment, the slightest of smiles toying with the outer realms of my lips. Strange that Granny's voice coming from nowhere hadn't surprised him.

Backpack shouldered, I placed a tented post-it-note at my brother's habitual breakfast table position. Dad looked at it. "I'm guessing Faraday will crack this in two seconds flat, but you'd better decipher it for me or else I'll waste the next thirty minutes on it."

I had jotted CHASED SALARY FAVORS.

"That anagram unscrambles to '*Faraday solved crash*'. And yeah, he'll make quick work of it."

"Nice one! Anyway, do you want a ride to school?"

I nodded. "Jag or Jeep?"

* * *

The crash investigation elevated Faraday to minor local celebrity status for a time. The night before, his hair wafted traces of smoke, and he still smelled of aviation fuel as the first reporters and prying neighbours appeared at our house. My parents politely turned them away, but in town for the next few days, Faraday's walks were brisk and anxious. His shoulders would hunch and his pace quicken rather than accept the praise and earnest interest expressed by the people accosting him. His bedroom became more of a haven than usual.

But four days after that, everything changed. Mum died of an aneurism.

She was working in her lab at the Feynman Centre for Nanotechnology. A slump, and then she was gone. Our lives became a waking, walking hell of arrangements, well-wishers, and emptiness. I didn't help my father with any of the ten thousand little things he was attempting to organise, forever tarnishing the part of my mind responsible for regret. Each of us felt the uncomfortable spotlight of well-meaning attention, with no apparent way to slink off-stage.

A wedge hammered and hammered its way between Newton, Faraday, my father, and me. It was fabricated from silence, wall punching, and comments like, "You wouldn't have done that if Mum was here!" There was no logic to such a shared loss separating us, but it became harder to communicate at the time we most needed to.

After four months, it was time to break my sequence of sullen breakfast silences. "Dad? Thanks for making me breakfast every morning and driving me to school, even when I never say anything."

He looked up from his newspaper at me, a wistful smile flickering across his tired face. "You don't need to say anything, Higgs. I can hear what you're thinking. I'm not so

4

attuned to your brothers, especially Faraday, but as long as I can sit with you, we're harmonised."

"It's not fair! And I'm not just being selfish, either. It's not fair to you, not to Faraday, not to Newton." I gestured to the dog bed's snoozing resident, warmed by the early morning sunbeams flooding through the back door. "It's not even fair to Disco. She probably thinks Mum will walk through the door with a treat any moment now."

He looked at me with a glance of surprising penetration. Although it sounded like a simple reassurance, what he said that morning would keep returning to me. "No, it's definitely not fair. When you misplace something, it's an annoyance, but if that same thing gets snatched from you, that's something entirely different."

As events led me to unmask the Knights of the Drowned Cabal, I thought back to that morning, wondering if my father was trying to tell me something about Mum's death. Did he mean that her death wasn't simply the end of her thread of life, but that someone had cut it short somehow? But there would be no chance to dissect that thought with him—they pronounced him dead at the scene of the car accident that same evening.

* * *

In Middle Ides, a town hurled like a damp towel at the base of the hills and then forgotten by the main roads and rail lines of northern England, we Redferne children were always treated as off-kilter. Until their deaths, my parents kept us accepted by and connected to the town's fabric. Middle Ides was big enough that they weren't part of the public consciousness, but they had a wide circle of friends.

They were woven into events ranging from the polo club party to the fundraisers for the upkeep of the Ides Giant—a looming limestone outline of a primitive figure cut by inspired but unknown ancients into the rising hills overlooking the town. Undoubtedly, the social connections of our parents brought a thousand little kindnesses as we worked through the chaos of their absence. And we needed every iota of help, with my brother Newton our home's elder at twenty-two, struggling to know whether to parent fifteen and seventeen-year-olds, or to just be our brother.

Naming us after famous scientists didn't help us blend in as we grew up, but my mother was a nanotechnologist, so that wasn't particularly surprising. Newton might be forgivable—it sounded like a proper first name, and he often got called Newt. But Higgs? And Faraday? Giving my already weird brother the name of the pioneer of electromagnetism didn't strike our teenaged schoolmates as a good reason to stop making fun of him. I spent many afternoons waiting to see the headmaster after lashing out on his behalf. If you asked me, Jordan Franklin deserved to have a permanent blue mark deep under the skin on his forearm where my pen point made landfall. I may be short, but I make up for my lack of strength with determination and a side order of vicious.

Only our scholarly names, the fleetingly coherent Granny Redferne, and our dog Disco kept us tethered to the time when our parents were alive. Faraday and my grandmother found Disco as a stray puppy, up by the canal tunnel, and boy and dog have been inseparable ever since. She came to us with a triangular rip in one silky-soft ear and an unregulated eyeball that tends to get bored with what the other eye is observing and rove off to find its own superior viewpoint. Perhaps Disco, a scrawny whippet with snaggly teeth, sees Faraday as a fellow misfit.

Disco

Humans are such idiots sometimes. I'm no steak surgeon, but sheesh. I'm not even the smartest dog in the neighbourhood. There's a French bulldog that lives around the corner. She looks dumber than a sheep, with her comical under-bite. Still, she somehow outsmarts me every time. But dogs are rarely wrong about the basics. We don't overthink things. We never let analysis defeat instinct. We protect the pack.

Check out that human that visited our house with Higgs after school a few times. He was always chatting and getting closer than she seemed to like. I don't know his name. Just like I don't know almost everyone else's name. He smelled like raspberry leaves, talcum powder, and faintly of frying bacon. That guy. I knew he was concealing something, from Higgs and from everyone else. Without a reason to think that, I still knew it. It was my mission to find out what he was hiding. If only I could persuade the kids to take me to the right investigation spots. I could protect the pack.

CHAPTER 2 -   BROTHERS

Faraday

I think my sniffer was broken. It's not that I couldn't smell anything, but that the smells lacked all emotional connection. They didn't seem to register anywhere in the range from offensive to delightful. I was more like Disco than a proper human. We would both sniff a dead badger, a fallen slate roof shingle basking in the summer sunshine, or the blooms of a lavender bush with enthusiasm, but with no real reaction. She might get more emotional about a smell than I do. I guess you smell with your mind, not your nose, so maybe it's another sign that whoever put my brain in my cranium gave it a quarter turn before insertion.

Sadly, my sniffing quirks didn't help me avoid the allergic sneezing that seemed to be affecting everybody. The tiny miracle of fully formed tree leaves emerging in the space of two days from rust-coloured buds, erupting rose petals, and wisteria blooms were nature's way of distracting you from eyes that demanded gentle clawing. Droplets of nearly pure water falling from your nose into your lunch are off-putting. Even Disco was in a pattern of sniff, sneeze, sniff, sneeze.

I still didn't have a job, although I graduated early from high school. I applied and gained admission to several universities, but I couldn't bear the thought of being thrown in with a bigger throng of students. West Ides School was enough chaos for me—maybe later I could face university. I was gradually warming up to my father's efforts to nudge me into finding a job, but that incentive evaporated. I was trying to focus on being helpful during the unending organisation needed to run a household with three people and a dog. None of us had a practical sense of how that worked. It was a relief, because of the helicopter crash, that I could persuade Newt to take me along with him sometimes when he went to work. I know it was hard for him to justify that, and I could see the scowls from other officers when I appeared alongside him, but he always managed some sort of excuse. That's the kind of brother he was.

Newt wasn't on duty on the foggy evening when he got the urgent call to get to Nicholson's Woods. He and I were enjoying some fine dining—pre-packaged sandwiches and half a Toblerone each—in the front seat of the car, parked up overlooking the canal. It was Mum's car, so of course, her choice was an electric vehicle. It was a well-kept BMW i3 with a stunted red body and black roof as if it wanted to be a fire engine when it grew up.

Well, not so well-kept this week. Newton had been using the car for the past two weeks because Mum was on holiday, puttering around the house and spending significant time on maintenance work at the Ides Giant. The car had quickly lost its sparkle. There were the remains of several previous dining experiences in the footwell behind the passenger seat, and almost enough of Disco's hairs back there to construct a whole new dog. I added car clean-up to my mental list of things to do to prove helpful.

At first, we didn't know it was a helicopter accident. We figured it was a high-speed crash because Nicholson's Woods flanked the motorway link road. Newt reached out his window and clamped the magnetic blue police light to the car's roof. We sped off, zipping through the turns to the link road with the blue light pulsing into the fog. Although it's challenging to eat an egg salad sandwich as a car lurches around corners, I managed it without staining my clothing and also polished off the remains of Newt's sandwich. The Toblerone would have to wait.

As a supplement to my insatiable need to count things, I also like to time everything. We made it from the town centre to the motorway link road's accident scene in 6 minutes and 34 seconds, which was quick, but I'm sure we can break that record if we really push.

It was only in the last 30 seconds as we approached that we realised it wasn't an ordinary car crash. There was a cave-shaped gash in the side of Nicholson's Woods that faced the link road. The closely packed ash and poplar trees looked like someone had taken a giant ice cream scoop to them and then lit the resulting scoop-hole on fire. Black, oily smoke rose out and up from the site, a dark smear on the overhanging but dissipating fog. We approached two marked police cars that were blocking off traffic as we decelerated along the hard shoulder. A fire engine had made it through the roadside ditch's bottom and stopped in a precarious-looking position on the far bank. The fire crew were frantic, reeling out hose to get within squirting distance of the blaze.

There is something that I don't understand the working of, but it happens to me occasionally. It was obvious we were confronted with a problem that needed some focus to solve. I also had a strong impulse to solve it. As Newt stopped the car and said something to an attending police officer, I descended into a focused place in my mind. It was like a thick but invisible tent sprung up around me, sheltering me from distraction.

The conversation between Newt and the other officer shrank to something muffled and indistinct, but other sounds sprang to the foreground. Crackling and popping from the fire informed me of numerous live trees that didn't want to burn struggling against the rage of ignited aviation fuel. I looked around and noticed several things that shouldn't be obvious, but it was like I peered down a tunnel and saw only the scene's relevant parts.

I left the car door ajar as I stepped out and scanned the scene. The helicopter was not a place for survivors, but I ignored that. I could see the helicopter's rippling silhouette as a darker part of the flaming hole in the woods. Its full side profile was visible—it must have crashed while drifting sideways. That pulled my attention to the tail rotor which is what keeps the helicopter from spinning around the axis of its main rotor. The helicopter's tail was visible, and its rotor was absent. Many helicopters use an arrangement called NOTAR, which is an abbreviation of No Tail Rotor, but the tail ducts of that system were not to be found on this model. I knew the tail rotor was missing. An image sprang into my head of the helicopter rotating out of control in a dizzying spiral, with the pilot struggling to find a place to land.

The next two things my eyes flicked to were a slash in the turf near where the fire engine perched, and then a piece of metal debris further forward on the motorway. I imagined the helicopter pilot, attempting a landing, catching the main rotor blade's tip in the grass at the embankment's summit, slicing a long, arc-shaped divot from the bank, and snapping the rotor at the same time. Between the slashed turf and what I identified as a rotor shard on the roadway, lay a green and brown accordion of dislodged grass and soil.

But how had the helicopter got into this frantic situation? Sprinting through the gulley and up its other side, next to the fire engine, I stood directly between the flaming wreck and the slashed-out embankment section. The fire crew shouted at me to get away, but that was an annoyance I automatically ignored. Turning so that the blaze's heat warmed the back of my jacket, I imagined the helicopter's presumed path.

Spending summer evenings on the gently sloped slate roof outside my bedroom window, I knew every point of light that surrounded Middle Ides. The sentinel light on the maintenance shed where Mum kept the tools she used in maintaining Ides

Giant's crisp outline. The ugly radio broadcasting tower on the peaks beyond Ashton Pond. Canalside overhead lamps on the aqueduct before the Royal Canal passed into the tunnel to Little Ides under the cell tower's watchful arrogance. And the signal antenna at the Feynman Nanotechnology Centre, with its red-limned stalk. It should have been straight ahead of me where the helicopter had come from, blinking red through the light fog in the evening sky. But I couldn't see it.

Newton

"Newt! Newt!" Faraday was yelling to me. Somehow, he'd run from the car over to the fire engine while I was trying to get a situational assessment from the other officers at the roadside. He was beckoning like a human-windmill hybrid.

I ignored the questions from the other officers about what he was doing here and ran across to Faraday. Although I would do anything for him, at times like this when I was just supposed to be supporting the team at the scene, his refusal to adhere to police procedural rules was annoying and a potential career hazard. I could feel the intense heat, but it got cooler as I faced Faraday with him positioned between me and the fire. My eyes struggled to focus on his shaded face with the raging brightness surging around his silhouette, but I could see the animation coursing across his face.

He blurted out that somebody needed to go to the Feynman Centre immediately. That made no sense to me. I put my palm on his chest and told him to take three of his deepest breaths; this was a long-standing technique to draw him out from wherever he goes at times like this, and he responded without question. Taking those breaths, his eyes stopped darting around, and he composed himself to speak in a less frantic fashion. He explained what he thought had happened, and I jogged back to get on the police radio and send someone over to inspect the tower at the Feynman Centre.

Everything Faraday told me in the five minutes after arriving at the crash scene was borne out by the air accident investigators. The helicopter, carrying the owner of a prominent football club, flew too low and too close to the mast at the Feynman Centre. Tail rotor clipped off, it failed an emergency landing on the motorway link road. Although I dodged media interviews, my Detective Chief Inspector found my rapid identification of the crash's significant details impressive. He mentioned me several times both at internal police meetings and in statements to the media.

I was a local hero for the week, thanks to Faraday. Although I didn't go into details, everyone at the scene knew that Faraday had helped me somehow. This meant that fewer raised eyebrows appeared when I let him tag along with me subsequently, and that proved useful as he helped me decipher details during subsequent investigations.

My fame faded over the following weeks, but I was consumed with Mum's death, and this didn't register. The police investigation in Middle Ides returned to its more peaceful state, and I drifted along numbly. The next investigation of significance to me would be my father's fatal car accident, after which things both sped up and became chaotic.

It was only because of my father that I joined the police as a detective. During the day, I'm officially Detective Constable Newton Redferne, but I still feel like an imposter that should work at a coffee shop or a grocery store. When he wrangled it, he must have thought it was a safe starter job—how much detective work could a place like Middle Ides need? And the first few months were incident-free. I spent a lot of time in over-warm rooms, sitting on uncomfortable plastic chairs in training sessions and learning police operational procedures.

I rode along to a few traffic accidents and worked with the Birmingham police when a gang ripped an ATM from a grocery store's wall using a stolen dump truck. There was another comical incident, reprimanding some teenaged graffiti artists who were foolish enough to buy their selection of spray paints at the only paint shop in town, where they were known to the owner. My first missing persons case resolved itself when Srinivas Patel returned home after a camping weekend he failed to mention to his mother.

It was only a few weeks after Dad's accident when five separate incidents arrived in a flurry. I needed a bit of Faraday's expertise for the first one, so I picked him up from our house on the way to the scene of an accident on the motorway. We would also need to stop by the Feynman Nanotechnology Centre and visit Chronos at The Pinnacle. From there, we would follow up on a complaint about a swarm of sky lanterns launched the previous evening.

CHAPTER 3 - HEDGEHOGS

Faraday

Humans have a natural talent called a sense of number. It's your ability to view a set of objects and know, without counting them, how many items are present. But only up to 4 or 5 objects—more than that and you have to count them individually. Technically, this ability's name is the parallel individuation system, but the term 'sense of number' is more descriptive. A second ability, called the approximate number system, complements this. It's for estimating rough quantities of objects—you can look at a jar and guess it contains 25 pickles.

My ability to estimate large quantities is terrible. With too many items, I have a physical reaction and flick my eyes away—lingering glances would unavoidably lead to counting. But my sense of number far outstrips other people's. Looking at a field of sheep or a tray of appetisers, I know instantly and with certainty that there are 22 sheep or 34 mini bruschetta slices. It works for me up to 40 objects.

I used this ability at the motorway accident scene. Debris lay scattered on the rain-slicked road like Lego on a playroom floor. A confetti of computer parts, a cornucopia of technology had spewed from the bent-open rear doors of the toppled and jackknifed PC Factory lorry and blocked all 3 motorway lanes. The jumble was too random to support counting items in the wreckage, but as Newt stopped the car beside the overturned trailer, I looked back along the motorway and could see 36 thorny wooden objects scattered. That was interesting!

I jumped out, jogged the 40 metres to the first object and retrieved it. Newt would undoubtedly have told me to touch nothing—preserving the crime scene—but his suggestions mostly boomeranged past me and hit sometime during their return flight.

The wooden object filled my outstretched hand, with six bristling points. It balanced on 3 of its points, with the other 3 angling skyward. My brain whizzed. It couldn't proceed without naming this new object. It was reminiscent of the obstacles placed on the beaches of northern France during the Second World War to prevent invasion craft from making landfall. Those barriers were called Czech hedgehogs, so these wooden miniatures became oak hedgehogs in my internal catalogue.

I picked up another and compared them. Although of the same design, they bore quirks in their pointiness and the angles between the arms, hallmarks of hand production. Their fabricator crafted them with care. I carried 2 back to Newt at the crash site and showed him. "Someone threw these on the road to cause an accident," I said. "And look at the tires—I count 7 more of these embedded there."

The driver's eyes swivelled lazily, slow to centre on Newton as he spoke. A cut at the outer corner of his eyebrow bled a trickle around his eye, striping his cheek. With punctured tires, the cab had whipped around, vainly trying to follow the lorry's trailer section, and the driver's head had struck and snapped off the rear-view mirror. As the ambulance paramedic fastened a Steri-Strip to close up the cut, the driver said he glimpsed a man dressed in black with a wide-brimmed hat pulled low over his face, retreating into the trees of Nicholson's Woods shortly before he lost control.

It felt wrong to trudge along the middle of a motorway where traffic in normal circumstances would have coursed toward us, but a trio of angled police cars dammed the tide of cars ahead. Stopped traffic snaked around the next bend. We reached the point where the oak hedgehogs lay scattered. The urban planners had adjusted the contours of Nicholson's Woods, distancing the tree line from the road to discourage deer from bolting across multiple lanes of high-speed traffic. Exploring the periphery of the woods, there were no signs of lurkers—unsurprisingly, whoever had caused the crash was long gone. A path was visible as a recent disturbance in the damp grass. Someone had approached the motorway and retreated to the woods, but once under the forest canopy, the man in the black hat's movements were not discernable. There was no sign of any vehicle—if he had left on a dirt bike or any other form of transport that could navigate the forest, I would have expected signs of passage like tracks in the leaf-strewn forest floor or a channel of churned earth.

I paused, letting Newton proceed with the detailed search that he was so good at. With upraised face and palms, I greeted the light rain which I had all but forgotten and glanced idly around the forest's edge. I didn't want him to think I was abandoning him to the painstaking work of looking for missed details.

As usual, his patience paid off. He called me over to look at a spot where our suspect had likely lingered. Fallen leaves were disturbed, and he pointed to a granola bar wrapper peeking from the leaf debris. It had been dropped only recently, based on its cleanliness. I leaned in for a nosey look while Newton snapped a photo before he put on latex gloves and slipped the wrapper into an evidence bag—he rarely left home without plastic bags and cable ties in his pocket.

He made two other noteworthy observations to me. Near the wrapper were three nub-ends of raw parsnip. I shone my torch on them and could tell they had been gnawed on by either a person or an animal. They deserved their own evidence bag. And the last oddity suggested that the person had waited here a while—there was an unusual symbol crudely engraved into the prune-veined ripples of ash bark.

"Faraday? What planet has six moons?" he said.

I guess to him it resembled a sad face emoji inscribed on a planet with the encircling trails of six orbiting moons.

I laughed. To myself, I thought, but it must have squeaked out because Newton glared at me. I shrugged.

"It's not a planet. If it was, the moons would orbit around the same axis, not have orbits spaced symmetrically at multiple angles around it."

He raised an eyebrow, awaiting my inevitable conclusion in silence.

"You always think too big. No wonder Mum despaired of trying to explain nanotechnology to you." I meant that only as a fact, not as an insult, but I watched his features scrunch up at the mention of Mother. A feeling of loss I hadn't expected cascaded over me too. I let it pass.

Unable to remain deadpan, Newton's eyes brightened, crinkling at the corners. "So … it's something smaller than a planet?"

I laughed, properly this time. "It's a carbon atom. Well, a sad carbon atom. Those are electrons, not moons. No idea why the frowny face was added."

Newt took several photos of the bark etching with his phone and spun a web of crime scene tape delineating the spot of interest. We walked back to the car in silent contemplation, where he radioed for a forensic team to perform a proper sweep.

The oak hedgehogs cast spiky shadows on the roadway in a threatening pattern. Newton asked the attending uniformed officers to collect them before the clean-up crew and heavy towing team started the mammoth task of clearing the lorry and its debris. Only two real questions remained: who threw the hedgehogs, and why?

We had a more personal way to tackle the second question, with a visit to the mansion of Alan Ryder. Alan was both a family friend and owner of the very successful national chain of PC Factory shops. It was one of his shipments that lay scattered. Maybe this was a targeted attack against his business. First, we had two other stops.

CHAPTER 4 -   PULSE

Newton

Our first stop combined business and social elements. I had known James McCann since my memories were an indistinct jumble of sensations and emotions. The same age, we advanced together through school and shared several first experiences, setbacks, and heartbreaks, not to mention a few incidents that remained unreported to our parents. But almost nobody called him by his real name. To most, he wasn't McCann, but 'Canny' because of his practical streak that could look vicious when you saw him in decisive action. To our family, he had always been Chronos. A tower, casting a shadow over everyone else our age—first in height and later, strength, my father suggested that he was a descendent of Greek Titans. A godly sized child. So the name Chronos, from the most prominent of Titans, had stuck. I'm unsure if nicknaming him after the god of time was what obligated him to continually arrive late, or if it was his frequent tardiness that made the nickname stick, but late he often was. Including that day. The late James McCann.

This was likely another boring and routine detail-gathering mission that got added to my slate as the junior investigator. Faraday and I waited nearly fifteen minutes in our car outside The Pinnacle—the club Chronos managed—before he arrived.

Faraday would have told you it was thirteen minutes and eight seconds, but sometimes his precision added little value.

We dawdled. The quiet goings-on of Middle Ides would hardly raise the pulse of a city-dweller, but we revelled in its reassuring small details. The sound of rubber on cobblestone as a car emerged from a side alley onto the smoothly paved high street. The views to the hills, visible everywhere because there were no buildings taller than three storeys. Our local oddball, tattooed neck and white-boy dreads swinging as he walked his ferret on a long lead and harness. Or was it a mink? Who knew? Although we might sometimes have wished for more than one cinema or a fancy French restaurant, the number of Idesians that were born, raised, and stayed here was a testament to the quality of life that was the sum of every little pleasantness.

Eventually, Chronos pulled up on his motorcycle. It was a full-sized motorbike, but it looked like a moped under his massive frame. He wore the obligatory club manager outfit: black jeans and a leather jacket. A tufted mess of hair erupted as he pulled off his helmet, but he didn't care to straighten it. When you are six foot seven tall and similar in breadth, with hands suitable for transplanting onto a grizzly bear, people don't notice your hair. Or if they disapprove, they don't mention it. His leather jacket still appeared to be travelling at high speed, a sail filled with wind, but it was his muscles straining the stitching.

"Newt, come and get some." Chronos laughed, placing his helmet astride the bike and dropping into a caricature of a wrestler's stance.

I said, "Leave it out, man. I'm here on official business." I smiled enough as I got closer to make him laugh in return and swap his attack pose for an offer of a handshake. That was my cue to charge. I had tried tactics like this before, but this time I added more gusto than usual and left my feet as I flew at him. My face was at the same level as his, despite my being eight inches off the sidewalk. This just might work. I even shouted,

"For Narnia!" as an added attempt to distract him, but as usual, I failed to faze him.

This was no cat and mouse fight that might continue for several minutes. It was headed for either a surprise victory or another casual defeat. Chronos opened his mouth but found no sensible retort, then swatted me out of mid-air to the ground. I scraped my palm as I landed—a slight snagging in the thigh of my trousers accompanied by a ripping sound. I came up laughing.

"Someday. Someday!" I promised, not believing it.

Chronos hauled me up from my sprawl. "It's a good thing your trousers didn't rip higher up, or we would have been treated to the spectacle of your police-issue Y-fronts."

"Oh—hey, hey, Faraday!" My brother exchanged with Chronos the 'secret handshake', which amounted to closing to within millimetres of each other without any clasp. Their actual secret handshake was so secret, they did it only when there were only the two of them, without observers. Or so they claimed. Maybe they never shook hands. Chronos may have known me since our earliest school days, but he had known Faraday and Higgs since they were babies. He loomed large over their lives in every way.

But this wasn't a total social call. We were there on police business. Something unusual had happened the previous night at The Pinnacle.

Chronos unlocked the side door and flicked on banks of overhead lights as we entered. Some flickered, and many failed to illuminate. It looked less glamourous under the fluorescent lights than it would in the surreptitious evening lighting. Scuffs from heels of both high and Doctor Marten varieties marked the floor, applied by dancing, prancing, and excited feet. The railings separating the dance floor from the elevated bar would normally have LED lights illuminating them from within but, unlit, we saw them for what they were: clear plastic tubes, worn and scratched. The elevated DJ booth looked less like a place for worshipful, shouted requests, and more like a shelter to protect yourself from unknown substances that might drift from the spray-foamed rafters.

"At about eleven-thirty," Chronos said, "things went haywire. Every till at the elevated bar malfunctioned—only the ones at the satellite bar closer to the main entrance stayed up. The computers and handheld scanners were all screwed. Priti, one of my bartenders, dropped a handheld scanner that erupted in sparks and smoke. And the four desktop computers back there in the office died completely. I haven't been able to turn them on since, but I can't turn off their monitors. It's like they're taunting me, and you know I don't take taunting very well. The DJ equipment went berserk, flicking every few seconds between Ed Sheeran, Skepta, and Donna Summer."

Faraday was looking around at the various malfunctions as Chronos pointed them out. I looked at him, waiting for a pronouncement, and he did not disappoint.

"I was really wishing I was here for the incident until you started mentioning the music. Anyway, it looks like the work of a flux compression generator," he said. "Let's check the alley behind the building."

I didn't move, but glanced at him sidelong. "A flux compression generator? Isn't that a *Back to the Future* thing?"

Faraday laughed for maybe ten seconds. "No—that was a flux capacitor—it's fictional. A flux compression generator is a real thing."

Faraday

Many people already know what an EMP is. An electromagnetic pulse. It's a nasty effect occurring near a nuclear explosion if you don't get vapourised by the giant fireball. An expanding ripple of strong electric and magnetic energy bursts from the explosion, and will knock out electronics and communications equipment over a wide radius.

A flux compression generator is a portable device that can produce a directed EMP burst. It's nowhere near as technically demanding as making a workable nuke, and can be built using a thousand pounds' worth of parts. Not everyday parts, mind you—the pulse gets kicked off by a small charge of high-explosives, so you need to get your hands on C4 or something similar. And the device is one-shot, destroyed in the minor explosion that creates the pulse.

Know why this device was familiar to me? I didn't learn it in school, but I stumbled upon mentions of its potential military (or terrorist) use when reading about protecting sensitive equipment. You can deflect interference with a surrounding mesh of metal. That's called a Faraday cage.

Judging by the equipment affected, the pulse was more powerful in the club's rear section, so the three of us ducked out back to look for traces. Stepping out via the emergency exit into the back alley, we saw that my guess looked correct. One big-wheeled bin that held recycling from the club had a sizeable hole blasted through the side facing the club's rear wall. It had abandoned its sister bins and skittered to the alley's other side. An impressive, glittering mass of beer-bottle glass splinters clung to the cement block construction of the club's wall, and a sizeable patch of black paint had been blasted off, revealing a substrate of coarse cement.

Yes, there were a few remains of a flux compression generator still discernable in the wheeled bin. And yes, forensics would find traces of C4 used in the detonation. Chronos would have to replace every damaged electronic device and close the club for a few days while the electricians did their work. He peered through the jagged and fused bin hole with boyish curiosity.

But Newt and I ignored that.

Instead, we froze momentarily, looking up at the electrons swirling in their spray-painted tracks around the carbon atom nucleus. It had been drawn in haste but loomed two storeys high on the windowless wall across the alley. The sad face in this drawing's centre was as tall as Chronos, and it set Newton and me on edge.

CHAPTER 5 -   WIZARD

Higgs

I had known Dot Pendlethwaite since we toddled like misshapen pinballs at mothers' group meet-ups. Although we shared the same outlook on life, onlookers would only pick out our differences. Dot appeared insubstantial, belying surprising wiry strength, with her reflective dark hair often half-drawn curtains across her pale face. I was a pixie compared to her, with the tufty peaks of my blonde crop reaching no higher than her chin when we stood close in conspiring conversation.

There was also a newcomer to our circle, Lars Janssen. He arrived at West Ides School only last year and lived in a small, cluttered apartment in the town centre with his mother who ran the Trove of Wonders consignment shop at the High Street's less glamorous canal end. His English still had a Swedish lilt to it, and he sprinted his lightweight frame from home to shop to school with little care for the state of his shoes. Friendly and unpretentious, he found Dot and me in his first week and has been a permanent fixture ever since.

The West Ides School doesn't know what it wants to be when it grows up. You pay fees to go there, but I don't think it's outrageous—Newton attends to the finances now. It has pleasant, manicured lawns, a long run of wrought-iron fencing painted in a charcoal grey with fine cracks from several seasons of sun, and four strategically placed willows stretching out, up, and back to the lawn. But it backs onto the Royal Canal, where the overgrown towpath is a magnet for abandoned shopping trolleys and plastic bags gusting along like urban tumbleweeds. We refer to it as the 'banal canal' because of its lack of any endearing qualities. Most teachers at West Ides were fantastic, but the shortage of supplies and general upkeep implied a budget problem.

I was admitted because my parents prioritized education and preferred to pay for us to enrol there instead of riding the educational roulette wheel of Middle Ides High School. But not all students were there by their parents' grace—there were several spots reserved for high performance on the entry exams. That's how smarty-pants Lars was accepted. The result was a mix of privilege and intelligence in the halls. Many of my classmates distanced themselves from me—a combination of not knowing what to say after my parents died, my oddball brother who graduated only last year, and over-enthusiastic attempts on my part to be social.

Dot, Lars, and I had our own territory at the back of Miss Grey's history class. It was a zone of continual distraction, characterised by running side chat amongst ourselves, although Emeline Grey was among the most interesting teachers at West Ides. One of the youngest teachers, she had a stylish sophistication that gave her both kinship and set her apart from the students. Although only in her twenties, her hair was pure grey, but lustrous and well-cut. She wore high boots and an array of belts, bangles, and zippers. Dangling earrings offset her slim frame. I could see why she dazzled Newton at school meetings, where he now participated as my surrogate parent. Despite her appearance, Dot nicknamed her 'Gandalf' because of her grey hair and Grey name.

Her voice pierced a whispered side conversation with Dot. "Miss Redferne? Could you share your expertise on the reasons for the Reformation of the Church of England under Henry VIII?"

"Probably because, like me, he didn't enjoy going to church?" I smirked.

Miss Grey's eyes creased slightly, with maybe a hint of a twinkle. "He was more like my own mother. King Henry regretted his marriage, and he fumed at a Roman bigwig telling him what he could or couldn't do. Plus, if you're king, and you need to start a whole new church just to get divorced, why not?"

This devolved into a class discussion on missed opportunities for additional reform in the Church's founding principles. Lars tried to give an impromptu introduction to the Swedish royal family, but it did not go well. When you mention to a bunch of British teenagers that the heir to the throne is the Duchess of Västergötland, the educational aspect fades into a sea of voices making up new Swedish words. One of our classmates coined the new word 'phonenflöster', which described the awkward attempts to silence your phone during class without drawing attention to yourself.

At the end of class, I told Dot and Lars to go ahead while I stayed behind to talk to Miss Grey.

"It's a struggle to come up with a topic for my 17th century project," I said, approaching her battered, varnished desk.

She aligned her hair behind one earlobe and peered at me sidelong. "You should talk to your grandmother and see what she suggests."

"Um … Granny isn't *that* old." I chuckled. "And she's not very with it these days. It's hard to get any sensible conversation about today's lunch, so I'm not sure she'll be much help for a history project."

"Try it," she said. "She may surprise you. And come through for you, now that your father can't."

Although I tried to hide it, I'm sure she realised something had surfaced that I wanted to submerge. It came in a crushing wave—how much I missed my father, my mother, and everything I should have said or done with them while I had the chance.

"Oh, Higgs, I'm so sorry," she said, holding my hand in a not very successful attempt to share my grief. "Your father and I may not have seen eye-to-eye on many things, but I hope you can look back on this time as both a great tragedy but also a source of inner strength and growth. Talk to your grandmother. In particular about the 1600s. It will help. Really!"

I choked back a full-on flood of tears, staying at the level of a few snotty sleeve wipes. The only thing that restrained me was the strange realization that Emeline Grey not only knew my grandmother—who had been in a care home for several years now—but also seemed to have had dealings with my father. Did he visit the school concerning me? More likely visits regarding Faraday. I'm sure there was a weekly call from the school discussing how to cope with him. But he never took history, did he? It didn't seem likely he would have had Miss Grey as a teacher, and Newt graduated before she arrived at the school.

I wiped away the final tears and traces of distress and forced a smile. "Oh, and if you felt like keeping me back for detention, I'm sure Newton would be overjoyed with a school request to come and talk to you."

With a faux scowl, she let out a low chuckle. "Run along now, Higgs. Your friends are probably waiting."

CHAPTER 6 -   DISCO DIVERSION

Higgs

I caught up with Dot on the manicured school lawn. She was dawdling, her gangly legs swinging a mesmerising pattern as she sat atop the ramshackle brick wall abutting the walkway to the school's front doors. Lars had just left. I heard him sneeze twice as he started his sprint off toward the centre of town, where he worked at his mother's shop. Dot had to finish her history project too, so I told her what Gandalf had said about visiting my grandmother. We would pit stop at my place, pick up bicycles (she could use Faraday's), and go over to see my grandmother together.

Our house was a short walk from the school—no need to cross the canal—with a vantage point overlooking most of the town from the verge of the hills. It was tall and skinny, attached on the left to a mirror-image Victorian brick home, with three storeys and a rough basement each. Unlike most of the homes in town, which were a mix of semi-detached and row houses, our pair stood oddly aloof from the neighbours, featuring generous gaps on each margin. Dot and I scooted across the expanse of side lawn to the back garden and the normally unlocked back door. Neither brother was home when we arrived, so we grabbed a quick drink of juice from the almost completely evacuated fridge, then leashed up Disco and mounted the bicycles.

Granny Redferne was at the Orphanage. It wasn't an orphanage anymore but had been converted into a seniors' care home. It always seemed like a bit of a cruel name to keep, especially when you considered that some residents rarely had visiting family. Some were reverse orphans, abandoned by their youngers. When built in the early 1800s, the orphanage had been outside of town, on the last strip of level ground before the looming hillside. Now, the town had snuck up on it, with the mansions along the hill's skirt maintaining a respectable distance.

We set off. With Disco in tow, we wouldn't ride full pelt, but she could keep up with us or even outpace us for a medium-distance ride like the one to the Orphanage without exhausting herself. Her whippety legs whirled, and our ride was accompanied by the clicking of claws on pavement and a good deal of tongue lolling. We skirted the town centre, but in a stroke of good planning, we cruised to a stop outside Blondie's Bakery, where we pooled our pocket change for a muffin each. The girl at the till added a free home-baked dog biscuit since she could see Disco standing on her hind legs peering through the shop's front window.

We opted for one blueberry and one raspberry muffin, which we halved and shared in unspoken consensus, but I noticed a new addition to the baked good display. "*Parsnip* muffins?" I remarked, crinkling my nose in the universal facial expression for 'ew, really?'

The girl at the till said, "Yeah, I don't get it either. I tried one, and it wasn't very appealing, but we've already sold over ten dozen today. Want to have a taste?"

I laughed and shook my head, looking over to Dot to see if she dared try any. When she saw me turn to her, she glanced away and pretended to inspect the cherry turnovers. Normally, the situation would have cued a smirk or at the very least an eye roll, but not this time for some reason. Strange. I would remember this later, but it quickly left the forefront of my mind as we returned to our bikes and started to divide up the spoils while Disco created a small deposit of crumbs and drool on the cement. The baked treasures devoured, we sped up the rise toward the Orphanage.

It was always satisfying to feel the transition of bike tires from the perforated hum of riding across pavement slabs onto the crunch of a gravel drive, which was one charming feature of the Orphanage. As we made the sharp turn, of course at a speed that added the thrill of occasional wobbles, we could see the Ryder mansion, which was four of five mansion-widths along the boulevard from the Orphanage. We were due to see Alan Ryder at the polo club anniversary party—I seemed to remember it was fast approaching.

I was a known visitor at the Orphanage, so Dot and I strolled in through the main doors and up the grand staircase to Granny's room.

Disco

Templeton would take me right into the building to see his mother. That was Higgs's father. I liked Angelina Redferne. She always had treats for me. I could curl up in her lap indefinitely while she stroked my back in a rhythm that soothed us both. It was strange. I am often antsy sitting with anyone else. Have to get up and pace around frequently.

But Higgs didn't think about me that much. Up the gravel drive to the Orphanage. Leaned her bike by the door. She let me off the leash. Headed in with her backpack. With that other dark-haired one. The one from the *really* big house. I loved going there. They had *cats*.

The grass had been cut. Deep green blades clung to my paws. I sneezed twice. Smelled like rabbits. I rested under my favourite bush. Legs tired, so I took a slow wander behind the building.

Wait! I could see the section of hill above where Alison used to take me. The part with the white paths on it. Where was Alison? She hadn't taken me for a walk for a long, long time now. Neither had Templeton. Maybe she was up there.

There was a path around here somewhere. Not one of the white paths. A normal path. The white paths were only higher up, by the shed. There. The path up.

When I got near to the shed, I could smell Alison. I think. A little. The shed door's rotting wooden bottom smelled like her shoes. I lay down, nestling at the door. Waiting for her to let me in. She didn't. But I heard something in there. Yes. Nearly silent. A faint scritching sound, like a baby flea marching inside my ear.

CHAPTER 7 - ANGELINA

Higgs

My grandmother, Angelina Redferne, had been in residence at the Orphanage for at least ten years. Long enough for me to not remember her living anywhere else. She could manoeuvre herself around using a cane, but she tended to drift in and out of conversation and maybe in and out of reality. Most often she recognised us, but talking to her was an exercise in confusion, guesswork, and interpretation.

Today, she looked sharp in a purple blouse and a black skirt. Wisps of grey hair rose from the top of her head in effortless style. She wore several rings and a brooch that were probably worth a fortune, but I had seen them so many times they were part of my mental image of her. She sat in a grandly upholstered chair positioned side-on to the window that looked out to the rear of the Orphanage. A commanding view of the Ides Giant's ghostly outline filled the room's oversized rear-facing window, its thick-fingered hands held over its head, either threatening or beckoning to the sky above.

Granny's visitors were limited to our family, with an occasional friend thrown in. My father was her only child, so my brothers and I were her only grandchildren. Since Mum and Dad died, visiting Granny was a comforting thing to do. I often brought my homework up here, spread it out on the table and worked away in silence beside Granny, her presence stable in the confusing meat grinder of the world we had been flung into. Sometimes I would chat—mostly at her, not with her since she was often lost in her own waking dreams.

So it was a surprise when Dot and I arrived at the open door to her room to find the afternoon sun slanting in from behind us onto a visitor preparing to leave. He was a man of around my father's age. Dressed in a waistcoat, he looked dapper, a pocket watch on a gold chain beneath a tweed suit jacket. He held Granny's hand as we arrived, and was concluding their conversation, saying, "… I really think we can bring them in, Angelina. Just give it a little time. It's a good step toward healing this silly family feud."

I couldn't place how I knew this man at first, but as he turned and I noticed his oval glasses and a tangle of blond and grey eyebrows, I recognised him as a frequenter of the polo club where my parents socialised. My siblings and I attended occasional events there, and I was sure he was part of that circle.

His head shape was remarkable. It appeared to have been carved by a lazy and somewhat careless totem pole artist, almost as if the minimum number of chisel strikes were used to form the facial features from the raw material of a tree trunk. But the mostly missing left ear jostled my memory; the arm of his glasses teetered on the remaining nub which looked like it was a remnant from a clean slice, long ago. Or maybe the totem artist lopped the ear from his creation with a careless swing of the hatchet.

He also recognised me, somehow. As he turned and saw us, he smiled and addressed both Dot and me by name. "I'm so sorry for the tragic loss of your father. And your mother too, of course. I can't imagine what it must be like."

I had heard outpourings of genuine sympathy so many times now that they no longer stirred the same intensity of grief. After each death, the merest mention of my parents would turn my inner eye back on myself and produce a surge of hard-to-describe emotions. Other triggers ranged from eating familiar foods to watching an animal on a nature show go limp in the jaws of a predator. They would bring on the same feelings and inevitable tears. But over the time since my father's death, my immunity to these triggers was on the rise.

The visitor gave a final wave to my grandmother and strode off toward the staircase. I made a note to ask Dot who that man was, since he seemed to know her too, but Granny's hug beckoned. Bouncing across to her chair, I fell into a long, lavender-scented embrace. "You brought Miss Pendlethwaite with you," she said after she had released me. She appeared to be in a phase of clear-headedness.

"Yes, we're going to work on our history projects," Dot said.

I added, "And I wanted to ask you a bit about my topic. Gandalf told me I should ask you for some advice."

"Gandalf?" Granny raised an eyebrow.

"Sorry, I mean Miss Grey, our history teacher. Do you know her somehow?"

My grandmother failed to hide a roll of her eyes and nodded, but did not elaborate. Instead, she asked, "What's your project?"

I explained that I could choose my own topic, but that it had to be about some event in British history from the 1600s. She thought for a while, long enough that I wondered whether we had lost her to her own thoughts, but she eventually turned and asked, "Did Templeton ever tell you about Pendle Hill?"

It didn't sound familiar, so I asked her to elaborate.

"Most of it will be in the library. But after the hangings at York, a priest believed it his duty to prevent the witches' evil spirits from returning to haunt Pendle Hill. It meant carting the bodies away, binding them in iron chains and metal crosses, and sinking them into a pond up there in the hills." Granny waved toward the window, toward a pond only her mind's eye could see.

Peering to see if there was a pond visible out there, all I noticed was Disco sniffing around the maintenance hut up by the Ides Giant.

"From York to Middle Ides? That's like seventy-five miles! A long trip to dump some bodies, especially in those days."

"Ahh, yes, my girl. But even priests in those days dared not doubt witchcraft. I've heard stories that the location of this particular pond was renowned for being a source of protective magic. Maybe he was trying to cleanse Pendle Hill of the taint and brought them South here. Get those evil spirits away from the locals to a place where, if there is such a thing as magic, maybe a good cleansing would happen."

Granny wanted to help me with my topic, but as usual, she had jumped into the middle of a story that she could envision but was hard to follow. Scribbled notes would let me figure out the details later. Pendle Hill. Witches. Priest. Pond.

"How do you know about something from the 1600s that won't be in the library" I asked.

"Your father will tell you." She paused for a short while, and I could tell she was drifting. "The Redfernes all know. Always watching grey devices. It's still happening. Can I have a cup of tea, please?"

Well, that was confusing, apart from wanting a cup of tea. "I'll get you some tea," Dot volunteered.

"Who's that girl?" asked Granny, squinting at Dot. She fumbled a little to open her ornate, gold-framed glasses and get a better look. Glasses in place, she looked startled for a moment. After a short pause, she said, "Oh. Pendlethwaite. Definitely a Pendlethwaite."

By the time Dot had made her way back up from the kitchen with cups of tea for us all, Granny was silent, peering out the window at the Giant, the dog, and maybe the pond beyond.

Dot and I worked away at our notebooks, with an occasional half-intelligible murmur from Granny while she gazed out at Disco investigating the hillside. After a while, we packed up, and I kissed Granny goodbye. She hugged me and said goodbye, but called me Alison. I was going to ask her about the man that was leaving when we arrived, and why he referred to a blood feud, but experience told me any questions would need to be saved for another visit.

Dot unlocked our bikes, and I called for Disco, who wheeled around the building's carved masonry corner, tongue flapping to the side. As the crunching of bike tires on gravel accelerated, a muffled boom sounded from our left. We slowed to a stop outside the gates and saw a cloud of dust rising to the east along Ablican Road.

"Let's go look." I stood up for a few pedal turns, gaining speed. Dot soon overtook me, her hair streaming behind her and her helmet dangling forgotten from her left handlebar. Disco's ears rippled a rhythm in her steady jog beside me.

Over her shoulder, Dot called, "Hey! Something happened out front of the Ryder mansion. Look!"

There was a convergence on the dissipating cloud from three directions. Dot, Disco, and I skidded to a stop as we completed the short ride from the Orphanage. My parents' longstanding friend Alan Ryder jogged up his driveway to survey the chaos at its end, and the tweed-jacketed man that had been visiting my grandmother arrived a few moments later. He was walking from the opposite direction to us, reaching the Ryder mansion from further east.

The raggedness of Alan's breathing was a sign of the distance from his front door to the road. He slapped his palm to the expanse of forehead between his tufty eyebrows and receding regal grey hairline. "Lord! What happened here? Did you see?"

It wasn't obvious what had happened, but what was once a posh yellow-brick wall supporting wrought-iron gates had been reduced to rubble on one side of the drive. The gate hung askew on a single hinge. Bricks lay scattered and ejected by the explosion. Chips and slivers of brick had flown and skittered clear across the roadway, resting in the grass like a smattering of popcorn.

"We didn't see it happen. We heard the thump as we were leaving Granny's place and pedalled down here."

Ryder turned to the man rubbing his ear stump, whose brow furrowed as he emitted muted coughs in the lingering brick dust. "Beauregarde, did you see the explosion?"

"I was starting my walk when I heard the sound and saw the cloud. I noticed a kid in a black hoodie pulled way down over his face running the other direction, but I didn't get a proper look. Not very tall, so it could have been a girl, I guess. It's too bad you two weren't cycling from the other direction, kids. You would have done a better job at identifying them than I ever could."

Ryder had regained his breath. He flung his arms wide, palms up. "But how could a kid, on foot, do all this damage? And why me? In the middle of the afternoon!"

"Alan, you'd better call the police," I said. "They won't catch the guy now, but they need to get out here and tape off the area. Lots of sharp bits on the road, too."

"Good point, Higgs. But come here first. This isn't a proper way to meet." He was all about manners. Failing at social graces, even in the face of an exploding wall, said something about his anxiety.

I dismounted and cast my bike aside gracelessly, striding to him for our usual greeting hug. "And hello, Dot." She got a two-fingered salute from his brow line. "Say a big hello to your father for me." Alan fished out his mobile phone. "Should I call Newton? No, I'll call into the emergency services, I guess."

He began to dial but paused. "Oh, how rude of me. Dot, Higgs, this is my neighbour, Beauregarde Device. Beau, this is my virtual daughter Higgs Redferne, and her friend Dot Pendlethwaite."

The one-eared man smiled enough to show a gold molar. "Ha, yes. We just met up at Angelina's place."

Ryder nodded. "Oh yes, yes, I forgot you are a friend of Angelina's too. Okay, introductions done. Let me call the police."

After the call and some incredulous inspection of the jumbled destruction, Dot and I remounted and began to pedal.

Nice to meet you, Mr Device." I called back.

"Twice!" he replied.

CHAPTER 8 -   SKY LANTERNS

Faraday

There are many angles to explore when investigating a car accident. I can tell you how far a vehicle can travel, depending on its speed, during the time it takes a person to react to something on the road. I have seen the studies on how reaction time gets dangerously battered by distractions like mobile phones.

A car moving at only 35 mile per hour will take at least an extra 8 metres to stop with a distracted driver. The stopping distance when driving 60 miles per hour, after you have already taken 50 metres to react, is a little over 50 metres on a dry road, but 140 metres if it's wet. And I always carry a multi-tool that can measure tire tread depth. If your tires wear down from 8 millimetres when new to a nearly worn-out 2 millimetres, water on the road has very little space to shift into, so your tires remain in touch with the road. Stopping distance when wet will double with shallow treads. I often inspect the brake pads too, because brake pad wear and brake rotor composition are factors.

None of my accident assessment techniques helped me calculate the distance a sky lantern can fly. Was there a way to estimate when the paper shell would ignite, or its total burn time? I figured this was a field without any experts, but I had an advantage. Disco and I were on the roof outside my bedroom when the sky lanterns launched—prompting Mr Scola's complaint—so we had an unobstructed view as they floated up. They drifted through the night sky over Middle Ides like a cloud of fiery dandelion fluff, eventually winking out in a series of brief blazes.

Now illegal because of the fire hazard and because the wire skeletons of burnt-out lanterns entangle curious small mammals, these candle-powered paper lanterns can be home made or bought on the grey market. The complaint about the sky lanterns was the next stop for Newton and me. Mr Scola, who lived east of the town centre, verging on the canal's first tentative steps onto the aqueduct, called about the lanterns that passed overhead last night.

* * *

My brother's eyes rolled at most of the tasks that got assigned to him. I think he found them boring, and he wished for more responsibility, but I found the gathering of every little detail fascinating, especially when they pointed somewhere unexpected. We rolled up to Mr Scola's house in Eastern Middle Ides. I turned to Newton, smiling, and said, "Hey— we're in the Middle East!"

It was a traditional stone cottage, single-storey, and we parked on the grassy verge alongside the layered stone wall, mottled with green and blue lichens. Presumably, that was Mr Scola battering a set of wind chimes that hung from a tree in the front garden using a rake handle. Because the electric car crept up in silence, he continued the thrashing until he was startled by the car doors thunking shut. He turned and flicked the rake away, feigning innocence. It landed at the foot of the tree.

"Oh, sorry. My wife is in town just now, so I took the opportunity to deliver some justice on those damned chimes. One of them sounds like an incoming text message and I keep needlessly checking my phone on breezy days. And the other four keep me awake at night. Good riddance, I say!"

Mr Scola met us on the path from his front door. "Come to the field and have a look," he said. "I could see these lights in the sky on Sunday night, lifting off from Little Ides Rise." He indicated, with a vague gesture, the hill that separated Middle Ides from Little Ides. "They floated up, right over the canal tunnel, and one crashed here in my back field. I didn't report it until now because it seemed unimportant, but then I realised it could have started a fire somewhere, so it's a dangerous thing for them to do."

"What time was that?" Newton asked.

Both Mr Scola and I answered, almost in unison. Mr Scola said, "About nine-thirty," and I said, "Nine-thirty-six, the first one was launched."

Newt raised an eyebrow in my direction. "Disco and I were relaxing on the roof outside my room," I explained.

He sighed and chastised me. He probably knew he would never control my excursions onto the slanting slice of roof outside my window, so he said, "You shouldn't be taking Disco out there. You know her claws slide on the slates. How many of these lights did you see?"

"Forty-seven."

"And did they all come down?"

Mr Scola carried on from here, although I gave a more detailed description of their flight later. The floating lights had appeared from the hilltop at Little Ides Rise, and ascended slowly. They caught in the light evening breeze, drifting with laconic intention in a tight fan formation above Middle Ides. After somewhere between 5 and 15 minutes, each one burned with momentary intensity, then disappeared. One winked out above the grassy field behind Mr Scola's house.

Mr Scola grumbled. "It's probably some hush-hush science experiment conducted by the government. I don't trust the things that go on up at the radio tower." He nodded dismissively toward the tower on the hills behind the point where the sky lanterns had been launched.

Mr Scola led us to the field, with its wild grasses well-maintained, but still reaching up to tickle our calves. His foot nudged the debris that had fallen from the sky. It was a frame of very thin wires, forming a ten-panelled balloon shape with a circular opening at what would have been the bottom. A hook descended from the bottom opening, but it held nothing. In a circle around the landing point were traces of ash. Tatters of browned paper fluttered from the frame.

It was obvious to me what this was. But Newton said, "It's one of those Chinese flying lantern things that gets powered by a small candle."

"A sky lantern," I replied matter-of-factly.

"Yeah, that's it. I think they're illegal now."

"They haven't been legal for several years, but you can still make your own without much planning. It's not rocket science." I grinned. "Well, not *advanced* rocket science."

"Thanks for calling us in," Newton said to Mr Scola, "We'll look into it."

He walked us back around the house and half-turned to us as we skirted it. "I just cooked up a snack—maple-glazed parsnips. Would you like a few to take with you?"

"Parsnips?" I blurted out. Hearing my tone of voice, I felt Newton's critical gaze boring into my skull because of his sense of civility. I dared not turn my head to face him. I tried a subtle correction. "No thanks. We already had lunch."

* * *

Newt said it was likely the work of bored but somewhat inventive teenagers. He hadn't heard of any fires starting Sunday night as a result, so he decided to write up the report and forget it.

"Maybe we should have taken some parsnips," he said, once we were both inside the car. "We haven't eaten since breakfast, despite what you told Mr Scola about our invisible lunch. Let's go home, grab an early dinner, and then do our last visits after."

Cooking wasn't something we had figured out yet. It's not that we couldn't cook basic meals, but the whole process was broken for us. We were so scattered that grocery shopping was infrequent and largely unplanned. Without enough ingredients to satisfy a recipe, ongoing learned hopelessness infused our mealtimes. We had exhausted the stocks of home-made dishes that family friends had brought after our parents' deaths, and we'd eaten enough frozen packaged meals to last us a lifetime. There was way too much sandwich and cereal eating in our house. The only thing we were diligent at was keeping Disco well fed. It didn't make sense that we could shop for her but not for ourselves, but almost everything failed to make sense.

Newton echoed my thoughts. "Remember when we used to ask Mum or Dad what was for dinner, and they would say 'fuffy'?"

Our parents started out by saying 'fend for yourself', then shortened it to 'FFY', and ultimately 'fuffy'. Part randomness and part a life skills lesson, they'd pull it out on a different day each week, like a surprise attack where our dinner was the victim.

"Yeah – I hated that. When I have kids, I'm going to have a long list of ways to confuse them. But for now, I promise to look at Granny's recipe book and plan our shop for next week."

In keeping with this new tradition of poor planning, we pulled up at our local takeaway favourite, Codforsaken Fish and Chips, just as the dinner rush was starting. Newt waited in the car while I dashed in to order. I greeted the cheerful-looking, apron-adorned man behind the counter. "Hey, Vish, fish and chips three times. And two portions of bread and butter too, please."

"Want to try Fish and 'Snips instead?" he asked. "I came up with the idea of using parsnips instead of potatoes on Monday, and I think I've perfected the recipe now. It's been a big seller. You should try them!"

I glanced around at the customers scattered between the counter, with its high chrome stools facing the street, and the small conspiracy of bistro tables clustered in the side room. I could see they were popular. Almost everyone here was indeed munching away at pointy, deep-fried parsnips instead of traditional chips. "I'm even working on a new batter made from parsnip flour, but I haven't got it to crisp up as much as I would like yet."

"Um ... Maybe I'll try them next time. Just the usual for now, please, Vish."

CHAPTER 9 - GOLDFISH

Higgs

My bicycle wheels slowed to a stop in our drive, and Disco was still breathless when Newt and Faraday parked alongside us. I released Disco's leash, surmising the boys had brought takeaway dinner home from the way that she pogoed against the passenger door. Sure enough, Faraday emerged with a telltale takeaway bag from Codforsaken. Nice.

With a cursory handwash, we each seized a Styrofoam container and opened the bread and butter between us on the worn maple dining table that dominated the open-plan kitchen and dining area. With fish and chips, you need to eat while it's still hot. Newton scouted the barren cavern that was our fridge and poured us glasses of pomegranate juice. An interesting pairing of food and beverage, but I guess that's how new classic combinations get discovered!

I pulled back the fourth chair for Disco, who fretted if she couldn't see what delicacies might soon be leftovers. She posed majestically and ranged her gaze across the three of us, trying to divine who might be the best candidate for scrap donations. We rushed to dissect the fish and chips, using the flimsy plastic cutlery from the open takeaway bag, not bothering to get proper cutlery, although Faraday was within touching distance of the drawer without leaving his chair.

As I munched, I recounted the explosion that Dot and I had heard and the scene of destruction at Alan Ryder's mansion. Despite my storytelling, I made more progress through my dinner than Faraday. He was an advocate of Fletcherism, the Victorian fad of chewing each mouthful twenty times before swallowing as a digestive aid.

Newt described the sky lanterns' launch over Middle Ides. I hadn't seen the glowing armada, but Lars had mentioned them yesterday. One had landed beside his mother's shop in the town centre.

Then I remembered the one-eared man.

"Hey, I went to the Orphanage, and a man I didn't recognise was visiting Granny. He was Dad's age, well-dressed, and he had one mangled ear. Well, probably mangled. It was missing. It's a long-disintegrated piece of gristle by now. He lives near the Ryder place—Alan said his name was Beauregarde. Sound familiar?"

Faraday said, "They normally can't reattach severed ears because blood flow is poor around the cartilage. That's why ear piercings are slow to heal."

"Thanks for that tip. I'll keep it in mind next time I'm performing recreational surgery. But do you know who he is? He sure recognised Dot and me. It seemed like he was asking Granny to do something for him or with him, and mentioned a family dispute or bad blood."

That puzzled them both, but Granny had a few visitors we didn't know, so it wasn't too surprising.

Changing topics, I described my school project. Neither of my brothers knew anything about my topic, the Pendle Hill Witches, but Faraday laughed when I mentioned that Granny seemed to be familiar with the story and added her own details of the corpses.

"Ha! She's always trying to tell me witchy stories when I visit. Especially when I was a little kid." Faraday seemed to have an array of Granny tales to choose from. "Did you ever

52

hear about the two-headed monster in the canal over near Little Ides?"

"She still says those things to you?" asked Newton. "I remember she told me a couple of stories a long time ago, but she never mentions them now."

Faraday pointed a plastic fork at Newt. "Probably because I don't believe in them, and you're gullible enough that she thinks you're already indoctrinated!" They both laughed. But knowing him, Newton likely conceded that was true. Faraday dwelled in a fact-based world, but Newton had always been more open to others' beliefs.

Newt's pager beeped from his pocket. I wasn't not sure why anyone needed a pager any more, but it was a police thing, apparently. "As expected, I need to visit Alan Ryder and see what's up with your explosion. I swear they only send me on jobs where I know the person or it's too boring for my sergeant to lift a finger."

I used my best Cockney police suspect accent. "Well, it aint *my* explosion, gov'. I was with me China Dot, down the oldies' home when it all 'appened. You're barking up the wrong tree, mate."

"Okay, okay, I've eliminated you from my list of suspects. But there is something strange going on. One of Alan's lorries was sabotaged on the motorway this morning. Someone wrecked the electronics at Chronos' club using some kind of weird home-made device—"

"A flux compression generator," Faraday said.

"—and now this. Two attacks aimed in Alan Ryder's direction on the same day is worrying. He should come and stay with us for a while."

That seemed sensible, while the police double-checked things. And I was glad that the boys had seen Chronos, even if it was in strange circumstances. He was a good influence on them and eased their brooding with the brightness of their shared histories.

A scattering of chips remained, so it was chip butty time. Lining several vinegar-soaked chips onto his bread, Newton mentioned the new menu item at Codforsaken that Vish was peddling.

"Fish and 'snips?" asked Faraday. His nose crinkled as if he could smell the odd concoction. "And that Mr Scola we visited about the sky lanterns was making parsnips too. Maybe he's trying to perfect the recipe."

But this was strange. I had seen how popular the new parsnip muffins had been at the bakery this afternoon. Describing what Dot and I had experienced, I shook my head at the bizarreness. "This is just a strange dream and Mum will nudge me awake for school any minute now, right? Anyway, I'd be overjoyed to never eat another parsnip, so let's talk about something else. I made up two new anagrams for you on the ride home, Faraday."

I was good at unscrambling anagrams, but nowhere near Faraday's ability. It was another of his useless superpowers, but we made good use of it by playing our little game.

I started. "I was thinking about school. *RAFTS SNARL US.*"

Newt pulled a pen out of his pocket in a display of professional police efficiency and scrawled *RAFTSSNARLUS* on the lid of a Styrofoam container. He lived in the vain hope that someday he would figure out an anagram before Faraday.

But Faraday got this one right away. He leaned back in his chair, and after Newt had finished writing out the letters, he called out, "Lars runs fast!"

I continued. "Okay, I have a second one. Use your supernatural witching powers on this: *DEAFENING LEARNER.*"

Newt jotted *LEARNERDEAFENING.* I scoffed internally at his hope that writing the words in the other order might help him.

Faraday closed his eyes again. Newton scribbled a few letter combinations. Disco eyed the remaining slices of bread, and a glimmering strand of drool sneaked from the snaggly side of her mouth onto the table. This was taking Faraday longer than usual.

Newton jumped up and shouted "*Angelina Redferne*! Ha!" After hundreds of consecutive defeats, he had finally jumped to the answer ahead of Faraday.

Disco took the opportunity and grabbed a slice of already-buttered bread. She took off at high speed to an instinctive place of shelter deeper in the house. We laughed, deep abstraining guffaws. The most intense laugh we had had together since our father died.

* * *

After dinner, I had to hustle across the street to where I had a regular babysitting gig. Our neighbours were going out for dinner while I attended their angular four-year-old daughter Jasmine. I ruffled her angel-fine blonde hair, resulting in enough static build-up to make twenty strands float on an invisible current above her smiling, flushed face. "Hey, Jazzy. What are we going to play tonight?"

Her parents said rushed goodbyes and hurried off to their car, and Jasmine sauntered to her room to get materials for our activity. There was a rustling and a couple of thumps as toys hit the floor. Then she called out to me in a quizzical tone. "Higgs? What's Mrs Juice doing?"

Mrs Juice was her pet goldfish, so I strolled to the bedroom, hoping to witness a triple backflip through a flaming hoop. Instead, Mrs Juice was floating belly-up on the surface. "Oh no! Let me check her."

I swear that parents have a special switch hidden behind the coats in the hall closet marked 'babysitter chaos' that they flick right as they leave. It's unavoidable that something goes wrong when you babysit.

Could I bear the discussion about death with Jasmine? The Redferne bloodline and Granny's disembodied voice rose within me, and stirring powers told me a goldfish death was something I could reverse.

I stared at Mrs Juice's lifeless form, burning an image of her into my mind's eye. Taking as deep a breath as I could muster, I closed my eyes, placing my hands flat on the desk, astride the goldfish bowl.

With deep focus, I listened for my grandmother's voice. I thought of my mother's funeral, hands on her casket, imagining I might open it and find her stretching and yawning, ready to get out. I felt again the eyes on me—my father, my brothers, Granny, Lars, Dot, my parents' friends. There was another layer of mourners beyond that—her lab technician, Iain Vanderkamp; my father's boss, the athletic-looking Icelander Scarlett Thorisdottir, with her delicate upturned nose; a throng of familiar faces from the polo club and her peers at the Feynman Centre.

I channelled their sympathy into the task at hand, imagining Granny's voice repeating, "Higgs—you are a healer!"

There was no tingling. Forcing an even more intense focus, I mumbled to myself. "You are a healer ..."

The little splash from the goldfish bowl beneath my nose made my eyes pop open with anticipation. A shiver fluttered at the back of my memory—the leaves growing from my palms.

My aspirations to have magical powers faded as I saw the Lego brick floating next to the still-dead Mrs Juice. Jasmine prepared to drop a second one.

* * *

I thought again of my mother as Jazzy and I painted an emptied cardboard toothpick box, preparing it as the goldfish's final resting place. We planned a burial ceremony for the back garden. I tried to explain Mum's work to my painting partner.

"Do you know what my mother used to do Jazzy? She was a nanotechnologist."

"What's a nanu-macologist?"

"It's a special kind of scientist. My mother invented tiny machines. And those tiny machines made other, *really tiny* machines. And those machines made other machines so small you can't see them. They're smaller than a grain of sand."

"What can a machine that small do?"

"Well, they do things which seem like magic. Imagine if this paint had lots of invisible machines added, and they could spread the paint across the whole box if you put a big blob on the top? Or maybe later, if paint got scratched off, the machines could move the paint around, like tiny little diggers, and smooth the paint over again so the scratch disappeared. Wouldn't that be amazing?"

"So your mum made magic paint?"

It was true. She was her own kind of magician. "Yeah. She could do a lot of things."

"Can she come over and put the magic into Mrs Juice's paint?"

I struggled to reply. "Um ... not really. See, my mother is like Mrs Juice. She's dead too, and she won't come back to me."

Jasmine was silent. We placed the goldfish into the painted box and buried her in the garden using a small trowel. I was unsure if I should attempt a short speech, but even a few words would have devolved to tears and blubbering. Fortunately, Jasmine saved me from that task. Softening the impact of the first pet death using the painted coffin and burial rituals was wasted on a four-year-old. She still held my hand as she asked, "Why didn't we just feed Mrs Juice to the cats?"

CHAPTER 10 -   TEMPLETON

Higgs

In our town, nobody lived on the wrong side of the tracks. There were no tracks to get onto the wrong side of, because the train planners that had criss-crossed England with rail lines must have used a map with Middle Ides under the sign showing 'here be dragons'. But you can live on the wrong side of the canal.

Which one is the wrong side depends on who you ask. Since you're asking me, I can assure you that the proper side of the canal is the northern side—the Middle Ides side. The other side, where Nether Ides nestles, is clearly the wrong side, if for no other reason than the fact that our house is north.

The canal was now a barrier to be crossed, a conduit for leisurely boat trips, or a fishing spot. Once it was the lifeblood of the weaving trade whose factory floors have gradually been converted into flats. But as our town was slowly outclassed by bigger industrial centres with richer backers, Middle Ides has faded from a place of distinction to a quaint Cheshire residential area.

One of my classmates, Gregor Radzinski, lived in Nether Ides. His house crouched close enough to the canal's southern edge to overhear the anglers chatting on a sunny afternoon as they lifted their fishing rods to allow an occasional narrowboat to ease past. His walk to school was short—a pedestrian bridge rusted its way over the canal. This led to a hedge-lined pathway that spewed West Ides students scurrying schoolwards as the nine o'clock bell rang every weekday morning. But if you were to drive from his place to school, it would involve an excursion through the town centre or a meandering expedition through laneways to the west of town before you could find a bridge willing to let you cross the almost-jumpable width of the canal.

Although Gregor had been a classmate off and on since we first started school, he had only recently taken a more serious interest in talking to me. He was social, known for his elaborate embraces and secret handshake routines in the hallways between classes, or for pranks like spraying deodorant onto boys' backs as they changed after PE.

Like a butterfly, he fluttered from one squad of schoolmates to the next, from one conversation to another, without intruding or lingering overlong. With this flitting, it seemed unusual that he would spend any time chatting to or walking home with me, but both became regular occurrences. It was a particular surprise because he would walk with me, or sometimes with Dot and me, to my house, despite having to then double back over the bridge to Nether Ides to get home.

I glimpsed our shadows one afternoon as we strolled home. Dot's slender spectre strode beside my small bristly outline, both contrasting with the striking breadth of Gregor's shoulders. Nobody would describe him as handsome, but there was nothing unattractive about him either. His appeal sprang not from his physical plainness—it was personality driven. He could insinuate himself without friction into any discussion, and was a gifted topic-starter. Gregor triggered a lengthy, laughter-filled debate about who would win a fistfight between various celebrities, with Taylor Swift versus Elton John being too close to call.

I think my father would have been suspicious of Gregor. Or maybe imagining Dad's disapproval was how my subconscious surfaced my own feelings of suspicion, without having to admit them to myself. And Disco had obvious feelings about Gregor too. She wouldn't outright bark at him, but her ears flattened back when she saw him with me, and she would emit pre-bark heavy breaths. I had an odd trust in her instincts, knowing that she had been enamoured from first contact with many of our family's deepest friends.

I wished he could still guide me—my father. Even a glance over at him if I was questioning my feelings would be enough to give me the confidence and reinforcement I craved. Wordlessly, he communicated with me using the merest wrinkling around the eyes, encouraging or warning. He was a listener and analyzer, my father. This was both in his nature and, I assume, part of what gave him success in his always vaguely described government job.

He remained unseen in our last encounter. I lay in bed, still awake, on the night he died. I heard his muffled telephone conversation downstairs. He got louder, culminating in, "I'm going to Feynman to have a look for myself!" The front door clicked closed, and there was a spray of gravel as he left our driveway at pace in the Jaguar. Maybe because that was my last sensation of him, I continue to think I hear him sometimes, trying to send me a message, undecipherable in the same partially distinguishable telephone language that rose through the floor that fatal night.

Newton

There's unerasable guilt that I had more years with our parents than either Faraday or Higgs. Their loss stabs me more keenly than my own. Despite the extra time I had, significant holes in my understanding of my father's story remained unfulfilled. As a child, you have a built-in expectation that your parents will always be there, so you don't rush to find out everything about them. It's only once they are gone that you pry details from their friends and colleagues, and uncover an unknown layer of their existence. Gaps appear where unasked questions have left ragged holes.

Still, I knew more about Templeton Redferne than either of my siblings. I had more chance to have adult discussions with him, being a fledgeling adult myself. He was born and bred in Middle Ides. My grandmother used that exact phrase to describe him, although at the time I was very young, and thought she said he was 'borne on bread'. Whenever I hear that expression now, I cannot help but imagine the person being carried in on a gigantic slice of toast, hoisted by a platoon of mythological creatures.

My grandmother grew up in Middle Ides too, although her history was less substantial in my mind—raising questions for the next time I visited the Orphanage. Her maiden name was Templeton, and that's how my father got lumbered with two surnames instead of a proper first and last name.

Templeton was an Idesian. He attended university at Imperial College in London where he studied something at the intersection of medicine, philosophy, and psychology. Not a formal scientist, he poked around the edges of science, picking away at the fringes, trying to separate reality from superstition.

Luckily for us, he frequently mixed with science majors, including an Alison Descartes, who pursued dual interests in medicine and engineering. In one of their first real discussions, those two students, who would become my parents, discussed Alison's descent from the French philosopher Rene Descartes. In traditional Greek philosophy, the focus was on only the inputs provided by one's senses. Descartes realised there were ways to prove hypotheses that lay beyond our direct perceptions.

This first discussion framed their explorations after that. My mother specialised in the realm of nanotechnology—systems undetectably small for our normal senses. And my father searched for examples of forces in this world beyond science that could be detected only faintly and only when properly attuned.

The hard science and ephemeral wisps of magic allowed my parents to thrive and intertwine. I saw it in their storytelling, their informal experiments around the home, and their careers. And us! After hearing my father and grandmother alluding to someone who seemed to have extra luck or an unusual influence over people, animals, or the environment, I would believe that if you tried hard enough, you could move to another level of consciousness and experience minor superpowers.

A shred of belief would last for a while, and then my mother would explain to me how her lab was building machines that were building tiny machines, that in turn were fabricating microscopic machines that would create nanotechnology to do amazing things on a scale almost too small to comprehend. It was science wrapped up in disappearingly small packages like a set of high tech Russian dolls.

After Templeton graduated from Imperial College, he had to wait for Alison to finish her much more involved studies, so he worked several different jobs in London. Ultimately he landed in the only career we ever saw him in. It was a government agency, but somehow the exact department, his job title, and what he did daily were a mystery to us. I didn't realise this until after his death—how few details we knew about his work. He never exactly shunned questions about it, but he must have been brilliant at gliding the conversation elsewhere, leaving the questioner satisfied but not much wiser.

Fortunate circumstances would return them to Middle Ides. Already a nanotechnology expert from her studies and having gained a follow-on research fellowship at Imperial College, it was a natural move for Mum to come to the newly opened Feynman Centre for Nanotech just outside Middle Ides. With a demonstrable talent in the field, three births later she won promotion to Chief Scientist.

If you were acquainted with Templeton, you might jump to the conclusion that he was a spy. And on reflection, I'm confident he worked alongside the government intelligence services, but I don't think he worked as a spy in the classical sense. Yes, he would go on work trips to exotic places, but not typical locations for intelligence-gathering. Spies go to hot spots like the Middle East, the former Soviet republics, or to foreign competitors like China. But Dad visited places out of the spotlight, like Romania, Haiti, or Nepal. Then again, maybe his legacy as a true spy was fooling his family the whole time, and I bought into the story wholeheartedly.

Faraday

I struggled to forgive him for leaving us. He was supposed to take on both halves of the responsibility once shared with my mother. And yes, it was a car accident. Everyone has a deep understanding that people get killed in car accidents through no fault of their own. But he didn't bother fastening the seat belt. Speeding along the motorway link road, he would have survived if he had buckled in. But when you get thrown through the windshield of a classic Jaguar—tumbling along the highway like a floppy doll—it's game over.

Newton and I saw the accident scene, but thankfully we arrived only after they had taken Dad's body away in an ambulance. When rumours of the crash victim crackled over the police radio, a patrol car had whipped by our house to pick up Newton, thinking he might want to be with Dad for the ambulance ride, and I jumped in with him. Tragically, that collegial instinct was too late and of no use. Dad was already being zipped into a bag as we were driven to the scene. The accident investigation was underway, but compulsion drove me to do something on my own, while Newt slumped in the back of his colleague's police car. I took my own pictures and measurements. I checked out the relevant car parts myself and noted nothing unusual. If I could do nothing else to control things, at least I could accurately document them. Some of the officers made half-hearted attempts to keep me away from the scene, but I intentionally didn't give them a glance, and they let me pass.

My father loved to drive that green Jaguar, even though repairing it from various niggles had become an almost monthly occurrence. It halted only a fraction askew in its lane as if caught and frozen, ambling over to smell a patch of wildflowers on the verge. The only signs that something horrid had happened were the glittering path of windshield shards lancing from the car and the four parallel skid marks trailing from its now stationary tires.

I measured the skid marks—89 metres—meaning Dad was travelling faster than allowed on this road. But the surface was completely dry, and the sky was clear, so it didn't seem weather played a part. Possibly a deer ran across the road and made him slam on the brakes? But the whole accident still didn't sit right with me. He always wore his seat belt. Always. Why not this time?

I re-checked the usual car components again after it had been towed to the police recovery yard. None of us could bear to drive it home, even though the only things wrong with it were the windshield and the worn-down brake pads. The brakes were fine, although battered from the long skid. The steering was fine. Because of the car's age, there were no computerised parts to inspect. Everything seemed in proper order, and orderliness is my life.

Deer. I can't see one now, looking all innocent in wide-eyed attention, without accusing it of being the one that surprised my father and took him away from us.

CHAPTER 11 -   MANSION

Newton

Well-fed, we had more enthusiasm to conduct our last two visits. The sunbeams slanted across the hills, with the extra light and warmth that springtime affords. For variety, we took Dad's jeep for this trip. I grabbed the mag-mount beacon light. I rarely require it, because the bulk of my investigations are gathering details, not responding to emergencies. But you never know when the flashing blues may be useful.

The jeep was an interesting vehicle—military surplus that Dad acquired through a connection from work. It was a traditional model from after the Second World War, maybe the 1950s. Its original paintwork would have been camouflage colours or a uniform drab olive green, but its recent re-painting featured a more modern forest green. It had a detachable hard-top roof and removable doors. With the weather warming up for the summer, we had the roof on—resting on the wide threaded pins at the windshield's top and at four points around the rear bench—but we hadn't bothered to attach the nuts that would normally secure it.

We awaited a fine sunny day when we could winch off the roof and ride into the countryside, pretending to be much more carefree than recent events would allow. Wind whipping your hair into shapes that might appeal to birds of prey looking for a safe place to lay their eggs ramped up the feeling of freedom. And the bugs arriving at high speed to your mouth and eyeballs help you forget your general troubles and focus on more immediate sensations. In a token tribute to bare-bones driving, we detached the removable doors, leaving the sides open for rushing scenery alongside. As always,we kept our seat belts pulled tight.

Instead of a normal car stereo, the only thing to amuse yourself with during a journey was the high-powered radio that made us jump every time it crackled into occasional life. It was a military-grade Clansman radio set, and an antenna erupted from the jeep's back corner. It would have reached to double the vehicle's height if not bent in an arc, attached by a short length of chain to an eye built into the front bumper. We looked proper military when we drove it, and we felt it too. The shock absorbers were more concerned with pushing the wheels into ruts and keeping traction than considerate of passenger comfort. The hard rubber seats forgave less than the suspension. After many years of our Dad roaring around town in the Jeep, it was no longer a novelty meriting a second glance around town.

I let Faraday drive. I could tell he felt some attachment to our missing father when he assumed the driver's seat. If I looked over as he drove, he often looked entranced, a hand caressing the steering wheel and head tilted back, letting him peer at the road along the length of his nose. I thought about earlier times as a passenger, running errands with Dad. Or even earlier, strapped in the back seat with Higgs and Faraday, with our mother sitting in my current seat.

Faraday turned the ignition, and the engine produced the satisfying rumble that lacked every advancement in engine design and sound insulation found in modern cars. He took full advantage of the small turning radius, and we spun on the gravel drive to face the road. With a lurch, we left home.

We went to the Ryder mansion first, because the security supervisor at the Feynman Centre was on the late shift and said we could visit any time before midnight. The jeep grumbled through the town centre. Faraday geared down as we ascended the foothills of Peaks Road, exiting left before it wound its way into the hills. The warm air flowed through the doorless jeep as the town centre's glare and activity faded into dappled shadows, the late afternoon light slanting in from the west.

Although Higgs had described the situation, the damage was enough of a surprise that Faraday slowed the jeep to a crawl as we approached. Considerable tidying had already taken place. The dusty veil on the roadway and adorning the row of small evergreen trees at the opposite neighbours' place illustrated the explosion's power. The jeep's tires made popping sounds as we drove across brick fragments and turned to stop on the long driveway. We left the jeep running, but both jumped out to have a closer look at the crumbling wall and the damaged gates.

The wall that separated the Ryder mansion from the road was a low blonde brick barrier, rising to double its height at the driveway to support two ornate wrought-iron gates. Well, it formerly supported two gates, but now the brick curve that had arched up gracefully to support the right-hand gate was a jagged wreck, with a pile of brick fragments at the foot of what looked like a crudely constructed porcupine sculpture. Bricks splayed from the gate support's remains at improbable angles, and a small section of wall nearby had also collapsed, spilling on to the lawn behind, faded yellow lumps backed by dusty green grass. At first, I thought the right-hand gate was missing, but then I spotted it, further back on the lawn, as if it had been in a furious argument with the other gate and had thrown itself to the floor in a fit of tears. The left gate was still attached, but only by the top hinge, so it leaned out menacingly. Luckily the gates were broad enough that opening only one would admit even a large car, and driving up to the mansion was still possible. The epicentre of the explosion was apparent, even without Faraday's likely forthcoming analysis of the debris scatter. It was an arm's reach right of the missing gate.

We had visited the mansion many times as a family, and I had vivid memories of a mailbox set into that stretch of wall. It seemed likely that whoever did this had planted the explosives into the mailbox. I didn't know the first thing about explosives, but the forensics team had been here earlier, and they would soon report on the substance used.

"Faraday," I called over to my brother, smiling. "What do you call an explosion that blows up a brick wall?" He shook his head slowly, knowing a bad pun was forthcoming. "A masonic boom! Get it? Bricks, masonry?"

I crossed the main road and clambered atop a bus shelter to better survey the damage. I was rewarded with the glint of red-painted metal in the grass on this side of the road. Sauntering over and turning it over with a booted toe, it turned out to be the Royal Mail red I had imagined. The hinged mailbox face that had formerly been the barrier between Alan Ryder's mail and the weather was now a warped remnant, burnt and pitted on the inside but still recognisable.

"Faraday! Look familiar?" Scratched into the red paint was a more primitive version of the atom and frowning face that we had seen twice today already.

Faraday

I was unnerved. What did this scrawled symbol mean? I typed 'carbon atom frown emoji' into a web search on my phone, but didn't trigger the search, knowing I would get lost in a lengthy and likely fruitless browse. Pocketing the phone, I instead turned to the part of my brain that churned out deep logic. Was there any sign that the attack on the motorway, the electromagnetic pulse at Chronos' club, and now this extreme vandalism at Alan's house could be the devilish work of the same person? It seemed like a lot of work for one person on one day, but I struggled to imagine that multiple people would commit these acts independently or in any kind of planned fashion. It was too bizarre.

I started wondering about whether there were other related incidents. What about at Mr Scola's place? Had we missed seeing the strange insignia there somewhere? And what about my parents' deaths? Had I missed some clue suggesting they were not just the unrelated incidents they seemed? I desperately wanted to point the flaming anger of blame for their deaths on something other than bad luck. But I couldn't make sense of this. My logic was failing me.

It felt like the tendons all over my body were shrinking, making every muscle tense in response. My hands cramped like they were trying and failing to complete some intricate task while I looked in a mirror—something that only dentists could accomplish. The Jeep keys slipped from my fingers to the driveway gravel. I inadvertently imitated the Tin Woodman of Oz with a stiff stoop to gather them, and handed them to Newt. I was finished driving.

The gears in his head were probably spinning too, so we wordlessly eased into the Jeep, and he crept us along the considerable length of driveway to the main house. Although pointless, I reflexively buckled my seat belt.

By the time we rolled to a stop next to four other cars on the open gravel fronting the mansion, Alan Ryder was waving to us from the doorway. The cars were all his, and despite their various exotic natures, didn't look out of place in front of his house. It was a beautiful yet imposing Georgian construction, flat-fronted with a central doorway at the top of three stone steps. Weather-beaten red tiles sloped away from chimney stubs at the roof's ends, with a pair of dormer windows marking the Ryder boys' bedrooms. We had spent many an afternoon as children and teenagers within before they left for university. The ground floor's face featured five large 12-paned windows, separated by the large stone blocks typical of the period's architecture, each a different texture and hue of quarried grey.

A more vivid grey, Alan Ryder's stylishly unkempt crop of thick hair defied a flat cap. Although he wore casual clothes, they did not come from shops many Idesians could afford. They possessed a quality and fit that went beyond high street purchases, with no ostentatious branding. But initial thoughts of him being snobbish dissolved when anyone met him. With a genuine interest in everyone he encountered, no one would guess he was the head of a successful nationwide chain of computer retail shops. He seemed more like a country gentleman who thrived on having guests for lively dinners or someone who might offer you a sip from his flask if you encountered him hiking the trails of the local peaks.

But we didn't need any first impressions. He was almost as familiar to the two of us as we were to him. With well-mannered restraint, he didn't get right to talking about the gate explosion when we greeted him at the door with handshakes and hugs. He was keen to make sure we were doing okay, since he had as close a view as anyone of the chaos following our parents' death. "How's Higgs doing? I saw her and Dot this afternoon. Are you keeping a good watch over her?"

We assured him we were muddling through okay, that Higgs seemed angry but coping, and that yes, we would let him know how he could help us. Alan was the Middle Ides Polo Club's president—he reminded us we were welcome at any polo match, and that he fully expected us at the fast-approaching polo club annual ball. "Since Thomas and Johnson won't be back from Oxford for this year's ball, you must attend as my surrogate children."

"Of course we'll be there—and Higgs. We haven't missed a year ever, I don't think," Newt replied.

It was only Alan at home. His wife June was visiting her sister in Edinburgh. He hadn't reported the gate explosion to her yet, not wanting her to rush home, but frowning browlines betrayed his consternation.

We had settled in the living room with cups of tea that he carried from the kitchen on a small silver tray, adorned with sugar tongs and a curvaceous miniature milk jug. His eyes twinkled as he braved a first scalding sip. "By tradition, I suppose I should have made myself an extra sweet tea. Isn't that the British solution to soothe any shock?"

"Ha—yes, stiff upper lip, old chap!" I said.

Ryder turned to Newton. "Where do you think someone would get their hands on explosives to do something like this? From one of the quarries in the hills?"

Newt said, "To me, that's a secondary question. I'm concerned about co-ordinated action against you personally. It looked like a planned attack on your lorry this morning, and now this."

Ryder hadn't realised that one of his PC Factory lorries had crashed, and as I filled him in, he squeezed three fingers with his other hand and looked down and away as he thought.

Newt asked, "Is there any reason for someone to come after you or your business?"

"Whoa, no! Everything is going smoothly at PC Factory as far as I know, although I don't have too much day-to-day involvement currently. And I can't see why anyone would have a silent beef with me personally. Maybe it's someone from the Manchester Polo Association that's upset that we keep trouncing them," he joked.

I always travelled with a pocket-sized hard-backed black notebook and at least two pens. I took out the book and sketched out a good replica of the symbol we had seen in the tree at the motorway, on the wall outside The Pinnacle, and just now scratched onto the twisted wreckage of his mailbox. "Recognise this?"

He stared at it for a moment but didn't instantly identify it. "It looks like a logo for some planet where everyone is sad."

Newton chuckled. "I thought it was a planet too, but Faraday tells me it's a carbon atom. We don't know what the frowny-face means, though."

"I don't see what carbon has to do with me. Could it be an eco-warrior group? I'm not sure why they would target me specifically."

"It's a struggle to see any connections here, but there's something decidedly sinister happening. Can I recommend that you stay someplace else for a few days, to make sure you are safe from any further threats." Newton's tone was low and serious. The links and threats of today were piling up in Alan's lap.

I nodded. "Yeah, you should come and stay with us. Or you could even spend a few days on the Redferne narrowboat, Mr Ryder. It's still moored near the viaduct."

He laughed. "First, I keep telling you to stop calling me Mr Ryder. It makes me feel old. I only want to hear 'Alan' from now on. And second, I've been on that narrowboat before. The beds aren't suited to a person of my advanced width, and as I recall from our trip to Wales when you two were still arguing over Lego, you practically have to stick your arse into the corridor while taking a shower. But yes, maybe I should spend a few days at your place until this gets figured out. I am a bit spooked now."

Agreeing this was a good idea, the three of us went back outside and walked the perimeter of his property looking for any other signs of illicit activity, but found nothing unusual. Alan planned to drive himself to our place, where he could stay in our spare room. I called Higgs to let her know. Our parents' room would have been more comfortable, but we didn't pause to consider that. It seemed so foreign. Newton and I had one last stop—the Feynman Centre.

CHAPTER 12 - PROWLERS

Newton

The jeep rattled down the motorway link road, past the scarred part of Nicholson's Woods, where the helicopter crashed what seemed like a lifetime ago. The sun had crept behind the hills, cloaking us in shadow, but the blackened hollow was still eerily visible.

The almost complete lack of suspension and the breeze rushing past like a warm caress prompted parental memories. Now I was almost a parent. Luckily, the considerable insurance policies were kicking in now, so it wasn't money problems that we faced, it was the unwanted responsibility thrust upon us all that seemed insurmountable. As the eldest, it seemed more my burden to bear than my siblings'. But I had to snap out of my reverie and attend to the task at hand.

"I don't get it, Faraday. What's with this same strange inscription at three different incidents on the same day? It's got to be some gang or conspiracy, doesn't it? But is there any other common thread between the three, or even a motive, other than to wreck things?"

Faraday agreed. "Yeah, I can't make the connection either. It seems so juvenile but sophisticated at the same time. Making those oak hedgehogs took time and care. Building a flux compression generator is not trivial. And where would a random vandal get explosives powerful enough to demolish a solid brick wall? Is it possible that one person was responsible for everything and has taken care planning this?"

"It would have needed precise planning. Three different parts of town. The wall graffiti at the club was hasty, but large scale—it needed a ladder. You'd think someone must have noticed that. I'll ask around."

"A timer on the explosives?" ventured Faraday.

"Possibly, yeah. Maybe the explosives were planted last night, before triggering the EMP at Chronos' club. Although that could have been on a timer too. And then the oak hedgehogs this morning. Seems like they were planted in person given the driver mentioned our mysterious loiterer."

"Beauregarde also saw someone scurrying away from the explosion," Faraday said.

"True. Curiosity would draw people toward the explosion, not away from it—unless they fled because it was their handiwork. I guess we don't really know much at all, aside from the oddness of the whole series of events."

Flummoxed, we turned our attention to the complaint from the Feynman Centre that we were to investigate. The security team there had reported occasional prowlers around the perimeter fence becoming more frequent over the last few days. It didn't seem like anything illegal had happened yet, but the remoteness of the Feynman Centre made it unusual to see anyone in the vicinity other than those visiting on business.

It would be odd returning to the Feynman Centre for Nanotechnology. Not because the place was strange, but because it was where our mother drew her last breath.

Looking like a typical high technology campus, the Centre consisted of four newly built, low-rise glass and steel buildings, architected in different but complementary angular shapes. In the broad, grassy space between them wandered meandering paths, covered pagodas and spaces for outdoor activities. A running track ran in an oval around the four buildings, and beyond that were several car parks. A chain-link fence set the whole campus in a tidy square, with only a single entrance from the Centre's dedicated motorway exit.

I showed my warrant card at the gatehouse, and Faraday used his driving permit when signing in. A solitary guard manned the post, the murmur of a radio audible behind him. We were expected. Both Faraday and I had been frequent visitors with our mother, so we knew where to park and the location of the security office. A smattering of cars inhabited the car park; the scientists and technicians here often worked odd hours or lost track of time when absorbed in demanding research or testing. We grabbed a pair of flashlights from the jeep's glove box, expecting a walk around the site.

As we approached the door to the main reception area, a man emerged with a grey messenger-style bag slung over his left shoulder. He wore jeans, a collared shirt, and a light outdoor jacket, and we recognised him before he even noticed us.

"Iain!" I called as we approached. This was Iain Vanderkamp, the lead technician who worked with our mother. He organised the technical work that she selected and pursued in her role as chief scientist at the Centre.

It took him two blinks and a reflexive shunt of his glasses up his nose to recognise us in the dim outdoor lighting. He let the door close behind him, and we met a few steps outside the building. He looked tired, more like a general, grinding exhaustion than the sleepiness of a single long day. We hadn't seen him in the months since our mother's funeral, and he looked a lot older now than he had then, though he was only in his mid-thirties.

After a quick handshake, he motioned us further away from the door, and we huddled with hushed voices. "I'm sorry. I should have talked to you about this earlier, but even now it feels awkward because I'm not sure exactly what to tell you. You know I was there when your mother had her aneurism, right?" We both knew that, so I nodded and he continued.

"Did anyone tell you someone else died there at the same time? In the same room?"

That was a real surprise to both of us. "What? Who was it? Why wasn't that in the autopsy report? That puts a whole different slant on things!" I was shocked, confused, and angry all at the same time. I could feel a nervous quiver from Faraday beside me, and I squeezed his elbow firmly to stop him from unhinging.

"That's the thing. He was some special visitor who came to see Alison. They met in her nanotech lab space, which is where she collapsed. I went to the lab to ask her a few questions about an experiment I was conducting, and I found them both collapsed on the floor on opposite sides of her conference table. Within three minutes of me shouting for help, two men came in, zipped him into a body bag, and between them, dragged him through the emergency exit from the lab to a waiting car that had pulled up, right on the grass. They sped off before the ambulance arrived for your mother."

I reverted to detective mode. "Wait, what was on the table between them? Could he have killed her and the autopsy was somehow forged?"

Iain continued, signalling us to keep the volume down, my voice a crescendo while my mind raced. "I took a good look. Alison had her notebook open but had written nothing. She had a selection of her nanotech models on the table. She often used them to explain our research using props visible to the human eye. I keep replaying the scene, and there was nothing strange at all, no signs of abnormal activity, other than that they both died at the same time."

Several obvious questions hung in the silence, unasked, so he pre-empted them. "Nobody was talking about the visitor. Not many people knew Alison was meeting him, but the visit went entirely unmentioned, even by the security staff who responded to my call and who saw the lab before it was closed off. All anyone else would have seen was Alison being taken away on a stretcher to the ambulance, and maybe a car pulling up onto the grass for a couple of minutes."

He lowered his voice to a whisper. "So I did some low-key investigations myself. I'm friends with a gatehouse guard. I took him out a mug of tea one night and got him to show me the visitor log. I'm sure I found the sign-in notes for the unknown visitor and his two colleagues. Not likely their real names, because they signed in as Alfred, Brian, and Charles England, and they sure didn't look like brothers to me. But the guard wrote 'UPDA' beside their names, although like me, he didn't know what UPDA stood for."

The building's main door opened again, and we saw the Head of Security emerging to meet us. The gatehouse must have notified him of our arrival.

Iain Vanderkamp took a quick sideways glance. He whispered that we could talk more later, then said in a louder voice, "Good to see you again, guys." He gave us quick pats on the back and walked off toward the car park.

Faraday

Newton would of course do the talking with the approaching head of security. I was here as an unofficial sidekick, and hoped I wouldn't get called out on attending police business, as sometimes happens. I could almost hear Newt's mind racing as much as mine, but I trusted him to act rationally more than I trusted myself. The news that Iain had given us might mean that security at the Feynman Centre was involved in some sort of cover-up. I silently re-examined every angle of my mother's death to find any anomaly, but was left unrewarded.

Chase Cooper had been Head of Security for 6 years, and both Newt and I had met him several times. He wore standard security garb: black pants and a dark nylon jacket with an insignia, intended to lend an air of serious authority. A thick belt from which dangled an explosion of keys, an electronic passcard on an extendible lanyard, and a torch attached by a carabiner completed his outfit.

"Officer Redferne, Faraday. Glad you could come."

He offered a firm handshake to each of us. I noticed that his blond, close-cropped hair was thinner and wispier than the last time I saw him. It was time to admit defeat on the hair front and go for a clean shave. Confoundingly common for a balding man, he sported a thick, red-tinted beard. I imagined a mischievous goblin yanking it, making the blond hairs on his head retract and appear instead in a ginger glory below his chin, never to return up top.

I returned to pondering what he knew about the day of my mother's death that he might have concealed from us. Damn. Unlike my father's car accident—the unresolved details of which gnawed at the back of my consciousness—I had almost reached the point where I could accept Mother's death as sudden and tragic, nothing more. Now that too was unexpectedly yanked back onto the list of things I must obsess over.

While the analytic engine in the back of my mind worked on this problem, I remained on full alert, waiting to see what Newt could find out about that fateful day, while investigating the current matter.

"Good evening, sir," Newton said. "I heard there have been suspicious sightings outside the perimeter fences here. What's been occurring?"

"Yes, it's pretty odd," Chase said, motioning us through the glass doors that reflected the rising moon behind us. We eased into comfortable seats, arranged around a low table in the deserted reception waiting area. "And my apologies for not arranging this sooner. There have been so many people calling in sick this week we've run ragged. But I guess overworked is better than having everyone sneezing on you;

I've used so much hand sanitizer, I smell like I've been pickled in vodka. Anyway, you both get how isolated we are here at the Centre. It's not like anyone would walk around outside the fence by chance. But the security staff have seen people—or maybe the same person repeatedly—walking outside the fence peering in. Twice just after dawn, and three or four times at dusk. They may prowl at night too, but we have little illumination out there, so I can't say. Before this week, you might see a group of walkers once a year going past, and occasionally staff having a walk around at lunchtime. All very strange."

Newt nodded. "And have you noticed anything else? Unusual activity *inside* the Centre, for example?"

I could tell what Newt was thinking by the way he phrased that question. I watched Chase blink. Nothing was revealed, but I had started counting. He had blinked 27 times so far since we sat down. I knew that people blinked more often when stressed and fewer times when they concentrated, but I didn't know the average number of times per minute.

"Well ..." Chase paused for a moment as if he half-expected a drum solo to break out and punctuate his thoughts. Maybe he was considering telling us more about what had happened on the day of my mother's death, or what the term 'UPDA' on the security logbook meant. Or maybe this was a legitimate pause while he tried to recall any other noteworthy events. "I can't think of anything else that might be related. It's not like they've *done* anything, but it makes me nervous that these might be reconnaissance passes for something nasty coming soon. It'd be great to hear your opinion."

I wanted to observe Chase more—could he be involved in a conspiracy? Maybe we could persuade him to be sympathetic to us and provide more details about the day of Mum's death. "Can we walk the perimeter fence, see if we can spot anything?"

Torches in hand, we followed Chase through the main gate and began a circuit around the grounds. As we reached the run of fence furthest from the gate, Chase halted and flung his arms out to signal us not to pass him. He pointed to a section of the fence wire that was snipped from ground level to the height of an adult. It would be simple to pull back the slit fence and slip onto the grounds, unnoticed by the gatekeeper. A smattering of severed links littered the leafy grass near the cut, but the torch beams didn't reveal any other signs of intrusion.

I turned to shine my torch toward the darkened tree line. It was about 8 metres from the fence, only dimly visible in the scattering of reflected light from the Feynman Centre. It sprang into focus as Chase swivelled his much more high-powered beam to supplement my dim ray. I imagined Newt was anticipating a sighting of the same carbon atom sign we had seen elsewhere. The three of us advanced across the dewy grass to the split in the fence, shining our lights in concert at the forest's edge.

I was sure we would spot a similar sign here, etched into tree bark, burnt into the leaf-strewn forest floor, or on a sheet of parchment nailed to a tree. But for the last year, every time I had been sure of something, it crumbled into uncertainty like a burnt-out log, leaving a mess of loss and regret. I never dreamed that I would lose even one parent, and now I had neither. I thought I knew what happened to my mother, and now that was unravelling. And I still harboured suspicions about my father's accident, but could not flag anything conclusive. Our torch beams searched the treeline. There was no sign of the frowny atom logo that had preceded us everywhere else today.

I put a hand to the cut section of the fence, eager to shimmy my way through and have a closer look amongst the trees. But something else was out of place. A strip of grass cuttings extended in a ridge from the tree line through the snipped gap in the fence and across the grounds to the closest building's edge. It was like someone had detached the bag from a lawnmower and carried it from the forest through the fence and right up to the wall, leaving a tidy trail of clippings in a path behind them. But why would anyone leave a trail like that?

CHAPTER 13 -   BLOOM

Faraday

I lit up the grassy trail with my torch. "What the heck is that?"

Newton traced the line too. "Looks like some gardener's mess, but on both sides of the fence? Right here where the snip is? I don't get it."

Chase knelt and followed the line with his more powerful torchlight, its beam snaking across the grass and the short stretch of cement tile walkway to the wall. "It's too orderly to be an accident. It looks like a mix of grass cuttings and green leaf mulch. Obviously deliber—"

A sharp crack, like an axe splitting a log, halted his thinking mid-sentence. We swivelled to orientate ourselves toward the sound. It came from the forest—somewhere beyond our lights' penetration.

More cracking sounds followed in quick succession, and then we saw something so beyond normal experience that we froze like a trio of perplexed statues. Along the trail of clippings, a row of saplings sprang up in a crackling furor. The ones at the forest's edge were already as tall as I and growing unchecked. The height decreased along the line toward us, with sprouts erupting from the raised trail where it traversed the fence.

Branches exploded from the growing trees as the sprouts became knee-high—then waist-high—saplings, advancing in a sinister line across the Feynman Centre lawn.

I gestured at the tree line, where I thought I detected subtle movement near the tree growth's volcanic origin. "Newton, there's someone in there!"

He was already in action, scrambling to pull back the fence and wrestle his way through the torrent of blossoming leaves clogging the split. I gave him a dose of brotherly encouragement in the form of a double-handed shove that sprung him free on the other side and allowed me to squeeze through in his wake.

"There he goes!" Newton's torch caught the glint of a bespectacled eye throwing an over-the-shoulder glance as its owner fled deeper into the woods. The line of fresh trees continued to pop and thrust out branches as we gave chase.

Footfalls ahead of us guided us when we couldn't catch glimpses of him in the crazy beams of our twin torches. We wove our way through tanglesome undergrowth and snatching branches. Thistles clung to the shin of my trouser leg.

We arrived at a small clearing and paused. The sounds of scrambling escape had ceased, replaced by a stillness punctuated only by the continued tree growth behind us. The beams of our torches ricocheted off each other as we swept in widening arcs, trying to detect any signs of our mysterious quarry. I focussed on minimizing the breath of my exertion, so we could listen for hints.

Nothing. No rustling. No disturbed leaf litter on the ground. It was as if we pursued a person who arrived in the clearing and then lifted off into the ragged circle of sky overhead, leaving behind two confused Redfernes, a smattering of fallen twigs and leaves, and an ancient tree stump snapped off at head height.

My brother and I spent several minutes peering into the surrounding undergrowth, finding nothing new. The evidence was contradictory—a path of disturbed vegetation led directly to this miniature clearing, with no realistic exit for anyone running at speed without leaving some telltale sign. Could he have doubled back without us seeing him? But we were almost within touching distance of him when we hit the clearing. How could this have happened, losing contact when we were nearly upon our prey?

"Not possible. Not possible!" I looked at the moonlit break in the canopy above us and shouted in frustration. In my mind, I had connected this mystery to the apparent conspiracy surrounding Mum's death. The injustice was too much. In a fit of frustration, I nodded my head against the stump but instantly regretted it. My head collided with a gnarly bark outcrop perched like an ear right at forehead level. Circling to the stump's other side before being enraged would have been a cleverer way to do something stupid—this tree had only one lump at my eye level, and I managed to head-butt it in that most damaging place.

"I'm calling it," Newton said, and headed back along the path we had carved through the woods.

Stamping in annoyance after Newton, I rubbed along my brow to diffuse the pain. When we arrived back at the fence, the fresh trees had grown to double or triple my height and had trunks as thick as elephant legs. The ferocious sprouting and whipping noises from the unnatural growth spurt were replaced with the silence of our astonishment. The trees appeared to have ceased growing.

The crowded new line of mature-looking aspens and maples stopped a branch-length shy of the building. We could no longer wriggle through the gap in the fence—trunks and straining boughs filled and expanded the slice, breaking the fence and preventing our return passage. I hooked my fingers through the fence links and pressed my face up against its diamond pattern as Chase approached from the opposite side.

Chase brandished a leaf blower. "I grabbed this from the gardener's cart over there and blew away the last metre of clippings before it could turn into these demon trees."

Small expressions of incredulity punctuated the long trudge around the perimeter fence and back through the main gate. Chase paced us inside of the fence, and after a while, Newton reeled off official police guidance about next steps. I relegated both sides of that conversation to the garage of my consciousness—a place where I put stuff that was unwanted and likely to never reappear. Instead, I tried to organise the events into any kind of sensible relationship. Was this a rogue nanotech experiment gone wrong? Maybe Iain could explain it. Could it relate to the mysterious guests marked UPDA? Maybe we should be suspicious of Chase, although he seemed as rattled as us.

How did we end up in the middle of this muddle with no parental guidance available?

Disco

I heard it arrive. The Jeep. I leapt up several times to see who was in it because I am too short to see through the window in the front door. Faraday and Newton. I felt glad they were home, so I barked a few times to let them know. That other man was already asleep upstairs, but I forgot. Higgs too. I hope I didn't wake either of them.

When the boys unlocked the door and entered, I felt their exhaustion more than normal. They kicked off their shoes, which smelled of damp grass and wind. They talked to each other in quiet voices, but I didn't know any of the big words. Newt was tough and okay, just tired. But Faraday radiated pain and confusion.

I followed him to his bed. He took off his trousers but not his shirt before he slid under the duvet. I lifted the bottom edge with my nose. Climbed in too. Snuggled up beside him. I knew the feel of my fur would make him feel better. He was part of the pack.

CHAPTER 14 -   LUDDITE

Higgs

I had a private chuckle about the disastrous situation last night with Mrs Juice as I slung my backpack over one shoulder and headed to school. A colossal figure on a rumbling motorbike passed me going in the other direction, then spun around and came to a stop beside me. Even before he took off his helmet, I could tell by his massive shoulders and familiar leathers that it was Chronos.

"Higgledy Piggledy! What's occurring?"

"Well, you know how it is, Chronos. I had to wake up early, do a bit of work on my best-selling memoirs, make packed lunches for the boys, and take a few calls about my new plan for world peace from the United Nations. How about you? Save any lives yet today?"

"Ha! I slept through my alarm, so I'm a tad behind on my life-saving today. But I could save you a walk to school? Slap on the spare helmet back there and let's ride."

I slid onto the extended saddle behind him and tried my best to hold on to him—a tall order when my wingspan was nowhere close to his torso's circumference. I love banking around the bends when I am confident in the rider's skills as I am with Chronos.

As we slowed and glided to the school gate, it was quiet enough to shout the question I had been pondering during the ride. "I'm never sure whether Faraday should be tagging along with Newt. Do you think he's up to it?"

"I get your concern. He's still fragile, but I think keeping him as busy as possible will help prevent him from sinking into a funk of over-analysing."

I nodded, considering that. It seemed like a good nugget of wisdom. From the corner of my eye, some unusual movement made me look across the lawns to the corner of the school building. Two pink-shirted horse riders paced their mounts gracefully into view. I remembered that two of the Argentinian players from Alan Ryder's Middle Ides Polo Team were visiting the school today to take questions and show off their skills— and their fancy uniforms by the look of things. They beamed at the students drawn to them like magnets, revelling like peacocks in the soft morning sunshine.

"Look at those skinny South Americans on their ponies, Chronos. If you tried to ride one of those, it would probably—"

Both of our gazes swivelled in raw instinct to the school building, where fire alarm bells sprang to life. Chronos popped the kickstand, and we removed our helmets with accidentally mirrored precision worthy of a synchronised swimming team. Was it a false alarm? No. Wisps of smoke streamed from the open windows of a ground floor classroom.

Fire! I heard Chronos' helmet strike the pavement as he set off at a sprint across the lawn toward the affected classroom.

My science teacher Mr Shinoto appeared at a back-lit window, wreathed in flames and cloaked in dark grey clouds of smoke. He was on fire. It took a second or two for the reverberations of his anguished screams to reach me and register.

Mr Shinoto fully opened the window and ejected himself into the bank of low shrubs outside at the same time as the blast of a fire extinguisher smothered him briefly, obscuring him from my view. Dot's silhouette appeared in the window behind him, open-mouthed, preparing to douse him a second time.

Mr Shinoto was smouldering, jacket emitting plumes of smoke and half of his hair aflame. His jacket burst into flames again just as Chronos reached him, bundling him in the biker jacket he had removed as he ran and tackling him into an extended drop-and-roll on the school lawn.

Dot half-turned to survey the classroom and directed two fire extinguisher blasts behind her.

"Dot! Jump out!" I screamed.

She couldn't be thinking of heading back through the classroom—she was smarter than that. She proved me right as she edged arse-first out the window, still producing a gratuitous cloud of fire retardant, and plopped unceremoniously into the shrubs.

To say this spurred me into action would be an understatement. I sped across the lawn and arrived in time to help disentangle her from the bushes as a crowd gathered, full of anxious questions. Dot was shaking with the adrenaline rush and croaked out, "I'm going to be sick," as I hauled her away from the belching window.

Chronos tended to Mr Shinoto, whose blackened face had crisped on one side but whose clothes were no longer alight. Several other students had their mobile phones out, and I heard the ululation of an ambulance siren.

"Dot. Holy crow—are you okay?"

She looked at me, wild-eyed, barely tousled hair somehow remaining a tribute to modern grooming. Several clinging scraps of shrub adorned her dress. "Uh, yeah. I think so. My butt hurts where you pulled me out of that cozy bush onto the stony ground, but I know who to blame for that."

"What happened in there?"

"Something went wrong with Mr Shinoto. I was passing his classroom door, and he had every Bunsen burner gas tap open and hissing. He was about to light a match. There was a second when I thought nothing would happen—he was standing there with the lit match, and I could smell the gas, even out in the hall. Then there was a whoosh, and the fireball shot along the hallway. It passed over me. I felt the heat, but it passed in an instant and didn't light me on fire, luckily. But the whole room started to burn—all the papers, the curtains, and Mr S. too. His hair was on fire, and his clothes. He started screaming and ran to the window."

"Wait, what about the gas taps? And how did you end up with the fire extinguisher?"

"There must be some safety system. After that first blast, the gas somehow turned itself off. Or at least they stopped spewing flames. Only the stuff in the room continued to burn. And I felt guilty, so I ran in and grabbed the fire extinguisher from its bracket inside the door and started going to town trying to put him out."

The sound of more fire extinguishers being sprayed came from the windows, and the smoke reduced to just an occasional emerging wisp. Dot readily accepted a water bottle offered from the throng surrounding us. I watched Chronos taking advantage of several more bottles as he doused Mr Shinoto, who was gasping and whimpering with his eyes closed on the lawn nearby.

An ambulance left divot tracks across the school lawn, and its doors burst open revealing a pair of women armed with their paramedic kits. Teachers cleared some space around Mr Shinoto, and Chronos retreated to let them work.

I realised the scent intruding into my subsiding panic was the soothing smell of horses, and without thinking, I stroked the shoulder of the dappled brown polo pony that had sidled up to me during the commotion. My eyes followed the length of my arm, snatching it away after discovering I verged on caressing the polo player's knee and not the horse.

The pink-clad rider spoke with a Spanish accent that tinkled with amusement. "It's okay, senorita, this horse is very friendly. Here comes Miss Pendlethwaite, she will agree with me."

Dot stumbled over, looking drained of what little colour she normally possessed, but managing a slight smile and nod at the polo player.

"Hi Gabriel. Hola Faustino," Dot said.

I peered around the bulging chest of the horse next to me and only then noticed the second polo player standing in his stirrups alongside his teammate.

I aimed a raised eyebrow in Dot's direction. "My dad sponsors Gabriel to play for Middle Ides. All four of the team have been round to our house for dinner."

Life with Dot was a series of small surprises. She looked like she needed a hug, so I made a good attempt at smothering her with concern.

Chronos approached us, shaking his head. "Well girls, that was slightly more excitement than I bargained for at school drop-off. And I think my jacket needs a trip to the cleaners now." His brow furrowed. "When I was dousing him with water, he kept saying, 'No more science, no more science'. Something's clearly snapped with that guy."

Dot twitched, adding, "Yeah. Something. It's all gone wrong."

Chronos inspected us, a hint of a smile at the corners of his mouth. "One of you looks like you've been dragged through a hedge backwards, which in this case is literally true, and neither of you is getting in that school until they pronounce it safe. I'd give you a ride back to your place, Higgs, but three on a bike isn't a good look."

I rose to my tiptoes and slung an arm as best I could over Dot's shoulders. "Come on, hero. I'll make tea and toast at home. Let's hike."

"Oh, but no, Senoritas, we can offer you a better way to get home," said Gabriel, saluting from his helmet-line in a show of chivalry. "Hop up, one with each of us."

Dot and I exchanged amused glances, shrugged, and accepted the assured grips of the polo players as they helped us to the saddles while they stood tall in the stirrups. It was a bumpy but entertaining ride back home.

CHAPTER 15 -   FAVOUR

Newton

Incidents in the last few days in Middle Ides surpassed the normal vandalism, missing cats, and break-in cases. They rolled over me like an overwhelming wave. Fortune shone dimly on us—a burnt science teacher was a horror, but the PC Factory lorry driver could easily have been hurt or killed, and the explosion at the Ryder mansion was outrageously destructive. The EMP and the unnatural tree growth attack were also distressing, even if they didn't directly affect people. Mum had shown me some amazing nanotech solutions before, but could something accidentally released from the lab have spurred those cuttings into rapidly sprouting trees? I couldn't see how to link everything together and would blame myself if anyone else suffered in this chain of events. This was already well beyond normal police work and it seemed like somebody more senior should be taking the reins from me. Why did these seemingly trivial cases keep weaving into such complex webs?

The whole school must be traumatised. With the pull of the polo players enticing more early arrivals than usual, many students witnessed Mr Shinoto's alarming arrival on the lawn. I wondered if I should pay a visit to the school, to see if there was anything the police could do to reassure the kids. But I still felt like a kid myself. Even so, a meeting with Higgs' teacher, Emeline Grey would be a pleasant diversion. Maybe I would encounter her if I went to talk to the headmaster. There was something whimsical yet intense about her.

Could this be terrorist activity? It seemed insane to link all these events together, let alone think that a terrorist cell performed them, but they were clearly related. Was there even a purpose behind any of this? If I couldn't ask my superiors in the police force without looking like a candidate for nutter of the year award, maybe there was another avenue I could take.

Scarlett Thorisdottir had been my father's boss. Though I wasn't sure what she did, I knew she was a good friend of his and would know how to directly navigate the government agencies so I could ask some discrete questions. She had mentioned to me at the funeral that if I ever needed to talk to someone privately about anything, she would gladly be the receiving ear. It was time to take advantage of that offer.

I found the number buried in my phone's contact list and called. "Hi, Ms Thorisdottir, it's Newton Redferne. Templeton's son."

Her voice was cool but not unfriendly—a matter-of-fact Scandinavian directness flowed through her. "Ah, Newton. I'm very glad to hear from you. How are you? How is the family managing after—well, you know?"

"We're struggling through. Not enough attention to laundry. We run out of groceries on the regular. But Higgs is doing really well at school, and I keep an eye on Faraday. Once in a while, I forget for a moment that our parents are gone."

"It's hard. I know that very well. Can I help with something? Anything?"

"Maybe. It's not about the family. It's police-related. Several really strange things have happened recently in town—several attacks where we have seen the same symbol left at the scene. A lorry was knocked over by some spikes thrown in its path on the motorway, a wall was blown up by someone planting explosives in a mailbox, and someone built what Faraday tells me is an electromagnetic pulse device that frazzled the electronics at a nightclub in town."

"Wow. That's a lot—too much to be a coincidence."

"And that's not everything. Faraday and I saw first-hand someone try to do something to the nanotech centre on the edge of town where Mum worked. I don't even know whether to call it an attack. It involved a line of trees growing from nothing to full-sized in a matter of minutes. Maybe it was some sort of nanotech experiment gone wrong. Also, the science teacher at Higgs' school set his classroom on fire, and kids keep setting off these floating candle lanterns that fly over the town."

"I thought Templeton told me he lived in Middle Ides because it was pleasantly quiet. Anyway, I know just the people who can help investigate. Let me get in touch with your Detective Chief Inspector, and we'll get a team up there to take the lead on the investigation."

"That's a relief. I wasn't sure you could really help, but you said I could always call you. But can you keep me out of it? I'm sure there will be noses out of joint in the local force if they find out it was me that got outsiders to swoop in as if we're all incompetent."

"Understood. Now that I think of it, this was just a social phone call. The team I organise will have heard about these events from reading the local news, right?"

"Ha—yes, of course. So little happens here that the *Ides Reporter* has been all over it. Thanks for this, Ms Thorisdottir. It will really help."

"My pleasure, Newton. And it's Scarlett. Just Scarlett is fine."

* * *

Things progress quickly when the right powers are brought into play, and Scarlett clearly knew the right people. Late the next morning, a general meeting was called at the police station, and we were introduced to the leaders of a government agency team brought in to deal with potential terrorist-related events. Although it wasn't made explicit, the underlying message was that the National Counter Terrorism Security Office was running the show now. Every police force was acutely aware of NaCTSO, the special police unit that supports the 'protect and prepare' strands of the government's counter-terrorism strategy.

My DCI, making the announcement, also suggested it was his choice to bring in the special team as he thanked us all for our work over the past few days. That part wasn't true, but it suited me perfectly. The new team would be taking over the motorway incident, the pulse attack, the Ryder explosion, and the Feynman Centre intruder. I was happy to be left to track down the sky lantern launchers while my Seargant would handle the follow-ups at the school. A bunch of kids messing around up at Little Ides Rise seemed more like the proper scale of investigation for me.

In less than two weeks, NaCTSO collected enough compelling forensic detail to come to a conclusion that shocked the town and particularly the West Ides School. There were DNA traces, mobile phone records, and personal diary entries that put Higgs' science teacher, Calvin Shinoto, in all the right places at all the right times. He had apparently been waging a one-man anti-technology war. They whisked him away to London from the hospital ward where he remained in recovery from the third-degree burns to his head and arms.

In his diaries and interviews, Mr Shinoto confessed to a psychotic disillusionment with the modern world's reliance on technology, indicating he used his skills to start a campaign of sabotage against the local PC Factory business. In parallel, he planned to set off a series of EMP pulses across the country, following the successful trial run at The Pinnacle. His mental state deteriorated, and he torched his own science lab at the school. It remained unclear if this was part of a larger terrorist network trying to damage British technical infrastructure, or if it was a lone-wolf attack.

On the day that these announcements rang out across the police information network, I arrived home to find my siblings, Chronos, Dot, and Lars at our house.

"Breaking news! Chronos and Dot, you are now responsible for apprehending an international terrorist."

I was greeted, as expected, by uncomprehending expressions. "Um, I've broken up several terrorist rings this week," Chronos said. "Which one exactly are you talking about?"

We all laughed.

I filled them in on the details that NaCTSO found, under a promise they wouldn't spread information until it was made public, probably tomorrow.

Higgs expressed the natural first question. "Why would he do all that?"

"He was on an anti-technology spree. Apparently, he was planning a series of attacks across the country before he torched himself while setting fire to the science lab at the school."

Dot wrinkled up her face as if a bad taste lingered at the back of her mouth. "I still feel sorry for him. He must have been lonely or had some sort of mental problems to do those things. Seems hard to believe—he was such a cheerful teacher. Especially setting himself on fire like that. I'll never forget that smell when his hair was burning."

Faraday glanced at me without fully turning his head from Dot's face. "And he did that thing at the Feynman Centre, too?"

I raised my eyebrows and gave a tentative nod. "Yeah, apparently. I asked for more details, but it's an anti-terrorism agency responsibility, and they don't share much. Dad's old boss brings a heck of a lot of firepower to bear on cases like this. It's impossible for regular police to match the powers they have been granted."

Faraday rested his chin in his hand, elbow on the table. "Hmm," was all he said. I liked him thinking deeply about things, but this was headed somewhere I knew I wouldn't enjoy. I tried not to allow it to gnaw at me.

CHAPTER 16 -   GIANT

Disco

Faraday grabbed my leash from the corner cabinet, where they always leave it. It excited me to be going somewhere. Maybe I could investigate the suspicious boy that followed Higgs. My claws slid and clicked on the kitchen tiles as I ran a few circles around Faraday as he pulled at his shoelaces. Alison always trimmed my nails. I wondered when she was coming back.

I looked at the keys that Faraday retrieved from the key hooks beside the door. Jeep. As soon as he opened the door, I sprinted out. I did one lap around the Jeep, then hopped in through the unfilled opening left by the detached door. I waited. Faraday placed my leash beside me and started the Jeep. I spread my legs wider. I hunkered a little lower. I didn't want to slide out the door if we turned sharply.

Lots of smells as we drove. Spring smells, but new summer smells were creeping in too. Tree blossoms. Mud. Pollen. Was that the whiff of a baby pine marten? Faint house smells drifted through open windows. Fresh feathers as birds whispered in flight overhead. Maybe I oversniffed. I sneezed four times. And parsnips. Several bursts of raw and cooked parsnips as we passed houses and shops. Unusual. They smelled *good*. Vegetables smelled good? I mean, I eat vegetables but only in a meat shortage.

We drove higher. I looked out the side door and pointed my head toward our house. I knew where it was, but I couldn't see that far. It didn't matter. We must be near Faraday's Granny's house. And yes, I recognised her building as the Jeep edged onto the grounds and parked. I thought we would go in to see Angelina, but instead, Faraday attached my leash, and we navigated around the building and up the hill. My investigation of that boy would have to wait. But I could sniff for whatever made that scritching sound I heard here last time.

Faraday

I wished I could talk to my mother. There had to be a scientific explanation for the things happening around us, but I seemed incapable of grasping it. The erupting tree line at the Feynman Centre presented a conundrum. Perhaps I could try to channel some of her insightfulness if I immersed myself in one of her former pastimes.

That's why Disco and I trudged the hill behind the Orphanage to fulfil one of her regular commitments. The key to the maintenance shed at the Ides Giant dangled from the same ring as the Jeep key, and that's where we headed. Maybe I could quieten my overwrought mind with the physical work of keeping the Giant's outline sharp by cutting back the grasses. Sometimes the best thoughts come when you aren't thinking, like an inspiration that arrives at waking or at the end of a physical workout.

As we approached the hut, Disco surged forward to the end of her leash, and it looked like she pressed her ear against the door as if listening for activity inside. She's silly sometimes. She jumped and scratched at the door as I turned the key in the padlock.

My mother had petitioned to extend the town's electricity up here. It powered an array of downlighters that basked the

Giant in varying colours of light on special occasions, making its vivid outlines visible from town at night. But it also meant proper light inside the hut. I flicked the switch beside the nondescript electrical box mounted on the wall inside the door and chased away the gloom.

The interior flickered into view; it was relatively modern, and more cavernous than was needed to house the small collection of gardening tools. The floor was finished with large, square rubberised tiles, sloping lazily to the rear where a drainage slot allowed for spraying down the floor for cleaning. The peaked ceiling was graceless; all exposed rafters and nails from the shingles winking through at occasional spots in the plywood. An array of hooks, shelves, and hanging trays held various groundskeeping tools. A pair of poster-sized framed photographs of the Ides Giant decorated one wall, to either side of a window offering a glimpse of the carved white outline of a colossal leg. One photograph had been taken from a drone on a sunny summer day. The other was a nighttime photograph taken from the roof of the Orphanage of the blue-lit silhouette. It was fractionally askew, so I had no choice but to level it.

I released Disco from her leash and picked up a long-handled, flat-faced spade and a pair of heavy-duty garden shears. These were the main tools of Giant maintenance. Disco leapt from one rubber tile to the next, pausing on each one in a fit of whippetness. She wouldn't stray too far, so I left the light on for her and emerged to inspect the Giant.

I performed the traditional first ritual. The implements aligned on the grass, I paced the Giant's outline. It took 9 and a half minutes and 957 steps to walk the circuit. He was drawn using a single line, so I travelled his left leg, navigated around his left arm and crown-adorned, misshapen noggin, circumnavigating his raised right arm and the club it held. By this point, I felt like slowing pace as my breathing became laboured—the slope was steep in many places. But the remainder was downhill. I descended his right side and around both legs to my starting point. Along the way, I evicted intrusions into the line's purity—a desiccated bird's nest, a few clumps of hay, and an occasional sharp-edged rock borne by storms into the outline. The head needed the most tidying. I felt a kinship with this monstrous cranium.

Returning to my starting point, I hefted the tools and walked across the Giant's body toward the neck area. I glanced at the hut from my position mid-torso and noticed Disco engrossed in a slow circumnavigation of the shed, pausing to sniff at its outskirts at regular intervals. She returned inside, so I carried on to the junction of the Giant's shoulder and neck.

The rut forming the outline allowed the underlying limestone's natural greys and whites to provide contrast against the mixed hill grasses' greens and yellows. It formed a shallow trench, wide enough to amble along the outline and to pass someone coming in the other direction with only moderate awkwardness.

The main act of maintenance involved slicing and clipping away the grasses that grew to overhang the outline—like a balding man desperate to comb his remaining patches of hair over a deforested scalp. I set to work, slicing off the most egregious sections of encroaching vegetation with the spade but mostly stooping with the shears to prune the verges. Falling into the pleasant rhythm drew me from my normal analytical thinking into more sensory experiences—the whiff of the cut grasses, the stretching back muscles as I stooped, and the spade tip hitting rock with a sharp clack.

I reached the head's crown, both calmed and sweaty with the effort, when I heard Disco barking in the distance. She scanned the horizon from beside the shed, and when she saw me, she pelted in my direction. Soon, her ears flapped in a full sprint, which is impressive when a whippet is involved. I smiled as I watched her race feverishly up the outline of the torso and around the left arm. It would have been an easy shortcut across the shoulder, but she seemed to relish running on the trough's hard base and completed the circuitous route.

She skidded to a stop in front of me, panting with her dripping tongue lolling to one side, and bowed to me, her head sinking for a moment to her outstretched front paws. Catching her breath, she barked twice and backed up 2 paces. I was shown her narrow back for three steps down the Giant's head, then received a glance thrown over a dark grey shoulder, beckoning me to follow. She barked again impatiently and took two more steps. I laughed and said, "Okay, okay, I'm coming."

During the descent, we both took the short route across the grassy Giant's chest. Disco skittered, shuttling forward repeatedly before returning to my side. I leant my tools against the door, and Disco urged me inside. She yipped her way in, brushing past my leg, straight to the side furthest from the window. She pawed and barked a dog-speak pattern at the floor as if it was a lid over her food bowl.

Her agitation was so specific, I peered at the floor between her paws. Close to a tile's edge, I spied a keyhole set into a round recess. It was imperceptible to the casual eye, the grey metal of the lock sitting shadowed and inset in the grey rubber tile. Interesting. What could be stored under there?

I tried the shed key, but its chunkiness had no hope of fitting this slender lock. Maybe the key lay hidden somewhere here, inside the shed. That would make sense. Or perhaps it dangled unnoticed on another keyring at our house or with another of my mother's pals who helped with the maintenance work at the Giant. I paced around the shed, scouring the shelves and lifting every implement. The shed was so utilitarian and underpopulated that hiding places were minimal—even something as small as a key should be obvious.

What about the electrical panel? It was the only enclosed compartment in the room. I popped it open, expecting to see a key dangling from a hook, but found only disappointment. But wait! There was something unusual here. I noticed that a cable reached the panel from the incoming power line fixed to the roof. One conduit ran to the light switch; a second conduit with a second switch led out to the array of spotlights that would light up the Giant at night. But a third conduit took wiring from the panel downward, disappearing straight down through a notch in the rubber floor tile. Where would that power lead?

Desperate to find the key, I wondered who else knew of it. I had exhausted the possible hiding spots in the shed, and my ability to detect things out of place was ideal for this kind of search. Obsession has its perks. But nothing seemed remotely out of place.

Well, nothing was out of place *now*.

I realised that something had been out of place when I arrived. I leapt to the nighttime portrait of the Giant and lifted the frame from its supporting nail. Bingo! In a pocket on the back of the frame was a key dangling from a circular ring large enough to accommodate my wrist. Though I shook with anticipation of lifting the tile, I still took a few moments to re-hang and straighten the photograph, returning everything to an unruffled state.

Disco edged back as I slotted the key into the lock and turned it. I could see why the keyring was so large—it offered leverage to lift the heavy tile, backed by a metal plate and hinged at one side. It revealed not only a hidden storage space, as I expected, but the top of a ladder that descended into darkness.

CHAPTER 17 -   CACHE

Faraday

But it wasn't darkness for long. I flicked a light switch set just below floor level beside the ladder's top rung and took a curious look. A well-finished room lurked below the shed! A frisson of nervousness shook me at this discovery, but nowhere near powerful enough to stop me from exploring. I started down the ladder, but Disco came to the hatch and barked at me. She wanted to stay close, so I cradled her in one arm, and we made an awkward descent.

The room was fitted out like a high-tech war bunker. Three folding metal tables supported an array of fine tools and machines that would be unfamiliar to most people. But not to a Redferne—we had all spent time in our mother's laboratory at the Feynman Centre, and I recognised similar nanotech construction equipment here. Blueprints hung from the wood-panelled walls, and a computer with three high-resolution monitors was flanked by its keyboard and mouse on a stand-up desk. There wasn't the typical array of flashing LED lights found in a fully operating lab, and there was no hum of equipment. Everything slept, other than the overhead lights.

A hardback notebook drew my attention to a long desk. A cup, holding a spray of pens and pencils, nestled against its leathery spine. Among the writing utensils, 3 USB drives jostled for space in the cup. Treasure! I scooped them up without a second thought.

My hand hovered over the notebook for a moment before gingerly lifting it. Would I enjoy or regret seeing what was written there? Would it be in familiar handwriting? Disco nosed around the room while I contemplated the notebook's cover, then dared to crack it open to a random page. Sure enough, I immediately recognised my mother's work. Her finely crafted diagrams bristled with side notes and equations that I couldn't begin to comprehend. A date headed each page, and flicking through, I saw her note-taking spanned three years, with the most recent entry days before her death.

A few pages from the end of the notes, a hand-drawn picture of Higgs's face peered back at me. I wouldn't call it artistic, but my mother's illustrations were technically detailed, and this was unmistakeably my sister. Ruler-drawn lines pointed out anatomical highlights, with parts of the eye labelled with terms foreign to me. The bottom edge of the portrait morphed into a bed of thick-veined leaves.

I felt both outraged and privileged. My mother had been coming up to the Giant not only to help maintain it, but to work on a secret side project, concealing it from us and who knew who else. But I also had a comforting feeling that she was still with me, now that I shared this secret with her. A jumble of good memories flooded my consciousness as I stood holding the notebook.

Disco jarred me from my reverie with a flurry of activity across the room, and the notebook slipped open to a page near its end. The book's last third was empty, but the final pages contained a few notes as an appendix. Lines divided the appendix into multiple sections per page. Each section had a letter and a short description. I recognised that some descriptions referred to pieces of nanotechnology, so I figured each was a different nanotech component that Mum had been developing.

The descriptions were vague, but I scanned a few before capitulating to Disco's frenzied leaping in the corner. Beside the letter W was the word 'Whips'. There was S+ which was 'Seeker (Genus)', F for 'Flyers', and S referred to Solar. Each had an associated doodled drawing, like a sunrise icon beside the 'Solar' item.

Disco's insistence made me pocket the book to investigate her fretting. I resolved to keep the notebook close—and the lab a secret—to preserve the warm feeling of being watched over by my mother. Disco ran tight circles and performed half-jumps in front of a rack of unusual, industrial-looking tubes. Each tube resembled a case that might hold an architect's rolled-up drawings, but they were black metal, fully sealed with an unusual cap at one end. The recess in each tube's cap was contoured to accept a specific shaped device – probably an electronic key fob, judging by the metal contact points. An aluminium rack held tubes in slots resembling an oversized wine rack, with the tubes held at a slight angle, requiring a yank to slide them up and out.

I noticed my mother's orderly methods here. The end of each tube was marked with a precise combination of letters, likely taken from the notes in her book. There was a tube marked F-S-W-S^E and another with F-W-S^C. I took photos, focussing on the tubes, blueprints, and a few pages from the notebook so I would have an electronic copy of the most important-seeming material. It seemed sensible to continue investigating the details when I returned home. I took several tubes with me to see if I could figure out what they contained, based on my mother's notes, or how to open them since that was not immediately obvious. There were 36 tubes in the rack, and its lower section held another set of tubes that were open-ended and unfilled. I could see a storage bin containing tube ends on a table.

I had the notebook safely pocketed, so I grabbed 12 tubes, which was all I could carry without fumbling them. One was empty, and I took a spare tube cap to see if I could analyze how to lock and unlock them. Disco calmed as I bundled the tubes in my arms. Why was she so interested in them? Was there a perfume that my human nose failed to discern?

Tubes, notebook, dog, and I awkwardly ascended the ladder in a couple of trips. I put the tubes on the floor as I turned off the light, lowered the secret hatch, and locked it. I wanted to keep access to the lab, so I didn't return the key to its hiding place and instead slipped it into my pocket alongside the Jeep keys. An arc of its oversized ring peeked out.

Disco approached each tube, seemingly more interested in some than others.

Disco

My hearing impressed me. The scritching sound was very faint, but I heard it from outside the hut, although it was coming from the room underground. It was still faint. Too quiet for Faraday. But I heard it in the tubes. Not all, just a few.

We went into the sunshine. Faraday faced the hut, fumbling with the door. I saw a flash from the roof of Angelina's home. Someone stood there, above and facing us. A flash of sunlight off glass as he held something to his face. Faraday turned to head downhill from the hut. His head jerked toward the reflected light and remained angled in that direction for a time. Did he see it? The man, the sunlight, the thing he now lowered from his face? The man ducked so I could barely see him.

CHAPTER 18 - CORKSCREW

Faraday

My mother's lab at the Ides Giant was a secret I kept to myself, though I knew I was being selfish. Clinging to this knowledge wouldn't bring her back. Sharing it might ignite a spark to help us figure out what really happened to her, but I wasn't sure I could share it with Newton or Higgs. Not yet, anyway. I wasn't up to that discussion.

I puzzled through the notebook in my bedroom for 3 weeks, alone, not making much progress. The tubes remained a conundrum. I scoured the house for signs of a key fob to open them and searched the internet to find similar equipment without a hint of success. Disco continued to worry at the tubes. If only she could speak. It seemed her instincts outshone mine.

Figuring I might have overlooked the key fobs at the bunker, I returned and let myself into the secret room, half-expecting to catch a whiff of ghostly perfume. Nothing. No keys, no revelations, no ghost of nanotechnology past. I checked every drawer, nook, and surface, and found nothing enlightening.

Why was I too stubborn to ask for help? There was someone who would help me, who wouldn't let the secret spread. Iain Vanderkamp had expressed misgivings about the UPDA cover-up, and he had worked more closely with my mother than anyone. Reaching a point where I had to accept my own failures, I found his mobile number in the address book we always kept near the home phone and called him from my mobile.

"Iain, hi, it's Faraday Redferne. Listen, I came across a book of my mother's research that I should talk to you about. Could I come see you this afternoon?"

"For sure," he replied, "I'm very interested. But maybe not here at the Feynman Centre. How about I meet you at the motorway services just west of the link road? Is two o'clock good?"

The time agreed, I needed to burn off my nervous energy. I took Disco out for a walk, from our house down to the canal and across the footbridge to Nether Ides. It was humid but not hot, with low clouds only letting the sunshine through at intervals as if Disco and I didn't deserve to be illuminated full-time.

Disco

I became more and more suspicious of that boy each time he walked home from school with Higgs. He never came in the house, but I watched him study the house and the cars in our driveway as if he was trying somehow to analyze them. He also took pictures of our house with his phone. That's not normal.

Faraday took me for a walk. Close to the boy's house but not close enough. When we got back home, I stayed next to him. Followed him around the house. Maybe he would take me out again, and I could get a closer look at that boy.

Faraday

I planned to show Iain my mother's notebook from the secret lab, and the photographed blueprints. I wasn't sure if I would show him the sealed tubes, but I would bring them in case it felt right to me. I retrieved an armful of the smooth black tubes from my bedroom closet, carrying them out to the Jeep and strapping them under the tarp in the trailer with a pair of bungee cords. They were incongruous, secured beside the chunks of tree trunk we had hauled for use as firewood from a fallen tree behind Alan Ryder's mansion.

Disco was following me around looking forlorn, her snaggletooth sticking out prominently, only amplifying the expectant look in her eyes. I might as well take her with me. She could wait in the car if they wouldn't let me take her inside. Maybe I could call her a support animal and dare them to bar her so she wouldn't be hot and anxious. Plus, she liked the fast driving, her eyes squinting almost shut but her nose fully opening to the rushing scents all around her.

I hopped into the driver's seat and patted the bench next to me. "Come on, Disco!" She was waiting for the invitation, leapt through the open door hole, and assumed her navigator's position, nestling next to me on the passenger seat.

I re-traced the route almost by reflex. Down our road, zig-zag into the town centre, use the main bridge to cross the canal, out through Nether Ides to the motorway link road, and south to the motorway itself. This was the route that Newt and I had taken to get to the helicopter crash, and how we sped to Dad's accident. We travelled this way with Dad countless times to visit Mum at the Feynman Centre. And I sometimes pulled on to the link road's western verge and took Disco for a run along the many paths of Nicholson's Woods.

Although it was already past lunchtime, there was a line blossoming from the bakery's doorway. The parsnip muffins' insane popularity had only grown over the past weeks. I still hadn't tried one, having trouble believing they could taste that good. Could they be spiked with something addictive?

I saw a produce van parked at the kerb, and it was from a dedicated parsnip farm. A logo of an earth-encrusted parsnip ran the length of the van's side, the farm's name written in gold lettering that suggested both luxury and purity. If there was a whole van-load of parsnips arriving, those muffins must be popular. I heard they had also branched out into parsnip cakes—similar in format to carrot cakes, but with green-coloured icing.

Once we had cleared the canal, passed Lars' mother's Trove of Wonders shop, and navigated the town centre's more downtrodden section on the Nether Ides side, we surged onto the motorway link road. With very little traffic, I sped up to gift Disco powerful lungfuls of rushing spring air. We eased around the slow curve that swept the road's dual carriageway along the flank of Nicholson's Woods and came to the straight section leading south to the motorway junction. I slapped the Jeep's accelerator down for a little burst of speed before we had to slow for the westbound turn onto the motorway. That's when it all went to hell.

Disco

I loved it. All the smells. I closed my eyes and splayed my legs in front of me in case we changed direction. The woods had their own complex stew of scents. They mixed with the hot engine nuances and the pollen drifting on the humid air. I smelled the deer resting in their daytime hides. And rabbits. Lots of rabbits. The stripe of the freshly painted line separating the black roadway from the grassy verge. I flattened my ears to reduce the wind noise.

The next moment I was airborne.

Faraday

If you have ever seen a jackknifed lorry, either in person or in a video, you know that it looks like the trailer is staging a sudden rebellion against the dictator that has been dragging it around for its entire life, violently whipping and popping the cab and its driver in every unnatural direction.

The same thing happens if another vehicle nudges the trailer from behind. I felt that nudge as the rear of the Jeep's trailer suddenly jostled to the right. But there weren't any other vehicles near me to do the nudging. I drove along the inside lane with nobody behind me. But even with no other cars near me, the rear of the trailer took a sudden swerve to the right.

And although Newton wasn't with me, it was Newtonian physics that kicked in. Every action has an equal and opposite reaction. The trailer's front end slipped left as the rear moved right. And because the trailer was hitched to the Jeep, the Jeep's back end also slipped left. Completing the chain, the front end took a sharp right. And carried on moving right. Now at right angles to each other, the Jeep and trailer engaged in a titanic disagreement. Our momentum forced them almost side to side, like the blades of a folding paper fan, before the trailer hitch broke under the strain.

As I helplessly wrestled the steering wheel, the Jeep pointed directly at the roadside, but still travelled forward along the road's black ribbon. So close beside me I could have touched it, the trailer too faced the roadside but sped forward in our original direction. It was like two souped-up Japanese sports cars drifting around a corner in some neon-lit nightscape. Except it was a spring day. In Middle Ides. And it was happening to us. Slowly, it seemed.

Even if you are not an expert in physics, you know that wheels don't work when they are not rolling in the direction you are travelling. Rubber that excels at keeping your spinning wheels stuck onto the road turns against you—still sticking, but now aiming to stop you dead. This happened to both the Jeep and the recently separated trailer at the same moment. The two wheels on the vehicle's left side bit the tarmac, forcing the Jeep into a roll. It sprung from the road surface like a pole vaulter, building up intention and finishing with a kinetic burst of energy.

Airborne, the Jeep spun counterclockwise. I took a moment to recall that the ancient word for counterclockwise—before they had clocks—was 'widdershins'. It was a spectacularly unhelpful thought. The seat belt pressed like a garrotte into my shoulder and hips as momentum tried to fling me from my seat. We were upside down. The Jeep's metal roof landed squarely on the road surface, my vision a disoriented blur, and my ears filled with the unbearable rasp of metal on asphalt. Then the Jeep bounced on its roof and leapt into the air again, continuing to rotate.

Well, not the whole Jeep. If father was around, he would have attached the nuts that held the Jeep roof onto the bolts that stuck up from the body to connect the roof's corners. But not us. We were still just kids, playing at being proper grown-ups. We expended the bare minimum effort, and lowered the roof onto the bolts without screwing on the nuts. The bolts were long enough that the roof would never shift off them, would it? Well, it would if you were upside down.

Bounce. Airborne once again, I corkscrewed around as the Jeep roof stayed on the road surface and slid forward, sparks erupting like fireworks in all directions. The roof was the only thing in focus for me now, as I continued to rotate. Because if you are a dog resting on a car bench, and that car inverts in an instant, you don't stay in your seat. You get flung out the open door. Or you get tossed into the back seat. Or, as in this case, you get pinned to the car's ceiling. And when that ceiling becomes the floor between you and the road, you spread your legs to make your base as wide as possible and hug the floor like a magnet.

There was Disco, wild-eyed and spread-eagled on the upturned Jeep roof, sliding away from me at high speed down the roadway, worshipped by a spray of multicoloured sparks.

And still, I rotated. A half rotation had dislodged the roof and sent Disco sliding away from me. Another half rotation and I felt my hair whipping straight up to the sky now visible overhead. I wondered how many times I would flip over before I died, determined to count my way through my final moments. I counted another half rotation as I noted 2 more interesting things about my momentum. Now that I was upside down, I noticed that this bounce had taken me pretty much straight upwards, and I was also rotating back toward the proper direction of travel for a car. The retreating spectacle of Disco glued to the Jeep roof, spinning like a malfunctioning turntable, was visible through the front windshield, not off to the side. The other interesting thing was that the trailer was also corkscrewing through the air, and its edge passed so close beneath me it sliced an inch off my flailing hair.

And then it was over. I finished my counting at exactly 2 rotations. The Jeep landed once again on its wheels, miraculously facing the proper way down the link road and rolling forward at less than walking pace. The trailer cartwheeled ahead, jettisoning its contents as it flipped. A gas can arced a good 20 metres into the air. An array of long-handled gardening tools seemed to hang suspended in the air like the skeleton of some primitive robot. The firewood shot in all directions. And my mother's black metal tubes squirted out like cannon rounds from a pirate ship with justice closing in from all directions.

The trailer came to a stop on the grass, bits of debris raining like hailstones in the vicinity. I sensed cars slowing behind me as I braked to a full stop. Disco continued her rotations on the roof for 5 ever-slowing cycles, and then ground to a halt, still on the road surface but a long way in front of me. She stayed frozen in place for a moment, her ears flat back in panic and her head juddering agitated looks in all directions. Then she leapt out, sneezed 3 times, and bolted into the woods.

CHAPTER 19 -   RUNAWAY

Disco

Dogs don't handle these situations well. My instincts left me. Terrified, I spun, shrouded in a cloud of sparks. Don't tell the other dogs, but I was so scared I peed all over the Jeep's detached roof. It seemed like ages before the spinning stopped. Faraday and the Jeep were way up the road. My paws and stomach were scorched. The Jeep roof had heated terribly during its sledge ride. I straightened my legs and bounded onto the cool grass.

Beside me lay one of the black tubes I discovered for Faraday at Alison's hut. It had crinkled and bent in the middle like a stubbed-out cigarette. I sniffed the crack in the tube. Wow! It was a smell combined with another, unfamiliar feeling. Strong, like horseradish. And something separate, like bicycle chains and burning plastic that I felt more than smelt. I sneezed a few times before the dizziness from my unexpected ride subsided.

I was still scared, but my heartbeat was slowing. I remembered my side mission: to protect the pack. What does a whippet do when frightened? What does a whippet do when *not* frightened? I ran. Off into the woods toward Nether Ides.

Faraday

Disco disappeared—hopefully running for home—and I knew I wouldn't catch her. I survived! My limbs were shaking. I grasped at the seat belt, and it took me three attempts to push the button to release the clasp.

That was no ordinary accident. Something had gone wrong with the mechanics. There was a puzzle for me. But I urgently needed to collect my mother's lab tubes and notebook. I slapped at my jacket pocket for the notebook. It was gone! No, wait, it hid in the other pocket. I removed and examined it in the dappled sunlight just to be sure. Yes, the notebook remained safe. I heard car doors opening behind me; people were probably coming to help, but I didn't turn to confirm that. I scanned the road ahead and the verge to locate the tubes.

I spotted all 6 of the ones I brought. The first was a few steps away, with the furthest beside the upturned Jeep roof that had been the shield between Disco and death. I tried to run a zig-zag to pick them up, but my legs moved like a newborn foal's and threatened to buckle, so I settled for walking pace. I picked up 5 of the tubes that lay scattered in a wide radius around the trailer's resting place. Then tube number 6, which lay bent and cracked beside the Jeep roof. Disco's leash was beside it. I had trouble holding them—my hands refused instructions from my brain—but I relied on my reserve of willpower to clutch the tubes. It became my only focus. I hugged them desperately.

As I limped back toward the Jeep, I saw a huddle of other drivers around it, with a phalanx of cars blocking the trailing traffic. Two women broke from the forming crowd at a run and approached me. They offered to carry my tubes, which I politely declined, and they asked me 11 times if I was okay. I told them I was. Ambulance sirens wailed in the distance. No police sirens yet, which have a 'nee naw' sound that contrasts with the ambulance's longer wail.

Accompanied by the two women struggling to figure out how to help me, I arrived back at the Jeep, where a much more authoritative woman glared at me and told me to sit, *immediately*. Something in her voice compelled me to obey, so I plunked myself down, nearly collapsing. I found myself resting with my back up against a rear tire of the Jeep, tubes clutched to my chest like treasure in my arms. I think she asked me things, trying to assess my health, and I may even have answered.

My shoulder hurt. I slumped lower. Was there something unusual attached to the trailer hitch? I wondered about the rhyme 'sticks and stones will break my bones ...' I didn't know anyone whose bone was broken by a stick. Everything got hazy for me then.

Newton

I whipped up the hard shoulder, one wheel on the grass. It was car carnage up ahead. I saw our roofless Jeep, the twisted trailer further ahead, and its contents scattered as if a bomb had detonated. Had a bomb gone off? Was this a follow-up attack to the one at the Ryder mansion? Where was Faraday?

My panic subsided when I pulled even with the Jeep. Faraday rested, sitting against the Jeep's rear wheel, attended by two paramedics. The ambulance, angled with its rear doors ajar, had parked on the Jeep's far side.

I didn't take the time to turn the car's engine off and hurried to crouch at Faraday's side, close enough to speak soothingly, but I failed to achieve any level of calmness. "What happened? Wait, your collarbone is broken. Was there a bomb? Is your head okay? It's bleeding—but not too much. Give me those tubes." If I could have said all six of those things simultaneously, I would have. Confused thoughts fell from my lips in a torrent.

Faraday relinquished his grip on the six tube-shaped metal items he clutched. The paramedics gave me approving nods—I imagined their coaxing voices hadn't found success in getting my brother to co-operate.

"Newt. Finally. Don't let anyone take mother's lab tubes. And look! Look!" Faraday started to gesture with his left hand, but that side drooped below the broken collarbone, and he couldn't lift it. He winced and instead pointed with his right hand at the jeep's trailer hitch, just above his position.

"The hitch. It has something weird attached underneath. While I sat here, I noticed it. It's some sort of high-tech hinge. Not part of the original hitch. Don't let them touch that, or the hitch on the trailer. This was no accident."

Then Faraday thudded his right palm against his forehead—not with enough force to injure himself, but enough to make a staccato slapping sound. I had seen him do this before when he attempted to work through something beyond his reach.

I said, "What is it? Something else I need to investigate, besides the hitch?"

There was a pause while he concentrated. "The skid marks! That's what has been bothering me," he replied. I looked around at the accident scene, but there weren't many skid marks here.

"I don't see any skid marks. What do you mean?"

"No—at Dad's crash. If he was thrown through the windshield, why would the skid marks end right where the car stopped? There was nobody in the car to press the brakes. It would have rolled!"

Faraday fainted. Now that he had solved his own riddle, he could finally succumb to the trauma of the collision. The paramedics bustled him into the back of the ambulance.

Today's accident—that perhaps wasn't an accident—triggered an insight. Was he correct that our father's death had sinister undertones? Strange forces were at work here, aimed directly at our family.

I was glad the awkward genius of my brother kept us teetering on the brink but always leaning toward enlightenment. He was the one with the insights; I was the one with the procedures. The systems administrator for the Middle Ides police was a classmate of mine from both high school and police college. He agreed to trace my father's mobile phone records from the day of his crash, even though I shouldn't. Another secret to keep in our world of deception. If Dad's crash was sabotage, I wanted to know where he was headed, and maybe his phone calls would reveal something about the reason.

Before I left the scene, I noticed the leash that Faraday had let slither to the pavement as he released himself from consciousness. Where was Disco?

CHAPTER 20 - WATCHER

Disco

Panicked, I ran into Nicholson's Woods, following no existing path. Eventually, I calmed down. But I still had my bearings. I picked my way along a series of intertwining paths. My throat was sore. Finally—an opportunity to investigate on my own! My prey, the boy that Higgs knew—he lived in Nether Ides. That bordered these woods. Higgs walked me over the canal one day, and I marked his house with my pee. That helped me remember.

Autumn and winter's remaining leaf litter cooled my paws as I trotted. It was pleasant in here. Dark in places, but rays of sunlight shone through the canopy, warming me on my journey. I heard and smelled many signs of life, though I didn't notice much movement. Dragonflies skittered above the path ahead. Squirrels chased each other from branch to branch overhead. The sunbeams became more frequent and brighter as I neared the wood's northern edge. Wafts of cut grass and human activity reached me. I breached the treeline at the outskirts of Nether Ides.

This side of Nether Ides was unfamiliar. Emerging from the woods, I found myself not quite where I expected to be, but I knew which direction to head next. I was hungry and approached a noisy trio of young boys who fed me their packed lunch remnants. Carrots. I licked out a half pot of yoghurt. Yummy. I licked their hands and left them giggling.

After orienting myself, I found it: the boy's house. I needed to sniff around, so I squeezed under the side gate and crept into the back garden. This was the right house. I noticed the same scents that stuck to his clothes. Creeping cautiously, I investigated as I went. I crossed some grass, a stretch of flowers and raked earth, and on to patio stones as I rounded the home's rear corner. A small, rectangular window at ground level spilt light across the grass. It tilted open a fraction. I crouched and inched closer.

It was a basement room. And the boy was in there. His smells preceded my view of him. I eased my snout forward until one eye could look in. The boy was close! He had his back to me and watched a large computer screen. I saw most of the screen; the rest was obscured by his thick hair.

Several small pictures of human faces came into focus on the screen. Most remained still, but a few moved lazily across the background—a collection of mysterious lines and shapes. There was Higgs's girl friend in the screen's upper right corner. And there was her boy friend that ran around everywhere. And there was Higgs! I saw her face drifting in the upper left quarter. I watched her picture move for a minute before it faded out.

When Higgs's picture disappeared from the screen, the boy became agitated. He threw his hands up in the air. He rocked back in his office chair and talked to himself for a while. Maybe I stared at him too long. He spun the chair and glared at my window. I pulled back, but not quickly enough. He must have seen me.

"Disco? Disco?" He called my name. Like a question at first. Then, "Disco! Come here, Disco!".

His face pressed against the window frame, but I had backed up and stayed tight to the wall. I started feeling my way, reversing around the corner. He couldn't see me now.

"Faraday?" the boy said, then other words I didn't understand. Then he shut the window.

I wanted the comfort of home and my pack. The canal was close. I'd run alongside it, cross at the footbridge and reach home. Well, maybe I wouldn't run. My throat's soreness crept into my lungs, and they burned as I breathed. My legs weren't tired, but my throat ached. I would walk.

CHAPTER 21 -   REVISIT

Newton

When I arrived at the hospital, Faraday lay atop crisp white sheets, tucked away in a side ward. His colour had improved from my last glimpse of him, passed out and ghost-white behind the Jeep. Splodges of mud spackled his face and hair. I gave him a ginger hug.

"Collarbone?" I asked.

"Yeah, broken. They put a padded harness on me, and I have this arm sling to keep my left arm still while it heals. I'll have a lump where the bone cracked, but they don't do any surgery, they let it heal as-is. And they gave me the good painkillers. It was getting stabby. But wait—do you have those tubes safe?"

"Um, yeah. What are they, and why do you have them? You said they were mother's, but I hadn't seen them at the house before—not even when we had a good tidy up of her stuff."

"I'm sorry Newt," Faraday mumbled, looking away. "I should have told you everything when I found them. But I wanted it to be our little secret, Mum and me. They're from a hidden lab."

"Hang on. You mean it was you that cut the fence and lurked around the Feynman Centre? How did you sneak in to inspect her lab?"

"No, no, the lab isn't at the Feynman Centre. It's up at the Ides Giant. I found it a little while ago."

Not for the first time today, the feeling of knowing nothing seared through my consciousness. Absolutely nothing. Things I thought were facts melted away into lies, miscomprehension, and fiction. "Bloody hell, Faraday! I thought we agreed we would figure out all this crap as a family!" It was poor form to punch a hospital patient, but a tempting thought.

I tilted my head down, and covered my eyes with splayed fingers, took a few deep breaths. When I looked up, Faraday appeared crestfallen at his deception but stayed quiet. "Okay," I sighed, "start by telling me about the tubes."

Explaining that he discovered them in the secret lab, he indicated they might contain the results of a side nanotech project our mother had been conducting. But he couldn't figure out how to open the tubes to look inside. He was on his way to discuss things with Iain Vanderkamp when he crashed the Jeep. Really? He'd tell Iain but not me? Then he got distracted by another thought.

"Hang on. My memory is coming back now. Did you check out the device I found on the trailer hitch?"

I reached into the deep pocket of my windbreaker and retrieved a large, clear plastic evidence bag, sealed with a zip lock strip. Inside were two items. "I borrowed the jaws of life from the fire truck that arrived after the ambulance carted you away. Look—I snipped off the trailer hitch from the Jeep and the clasp from the front of the trailer. An electronic device with mechanical parts was affixed to the bottom with industrial strength glue."

Faraday knew better than to break the seal, but he turned the two heavy pieces around inside the bag and inspected them from all angles.

"I can't tell exactly how this thing works without connecting it up to a computer, but I can guess. Look here— there's a piece missing from between these two bits. It must have torn off when the trailer separated from the Jeep. It looks like a powerful clamp activated by the electronics."

I nodded. "Yeah. Maybe I should've left them attached to the Jeep, but I thought you'd want to get your hands on them right away."

"Smart. Thanks." Faraday replied. "So whoever built it used a standard velocimeter component there—this device knew how fast we were going. And there are the remnants of a powered hinge, although its middle is twisted off and missing. My guess is that the device lay dormant until we hit a designated speed. I was accelerating when it went horribly wrong. I suspect that at high speed, the hinge was activated and jackknifed the trailer, forcing it to fold up against the Jeep and causing us to flip. But what powered the hinge? It would take a significant amount of force to swing the trailer away from its natural path when pulled at that speed."

"Maybe another miniature explosive charge? That's what powered the pulse thingy at the club, and of course, caused the explosion at the Ryder mansion."

Faraday looked alarmed. "Wait. We! *We* were travelling at speed. Where's Disco? Did you find her?"

"No, not yet. I came directly here to check on you. She's probably spooked and will resurface. She's so distinctive with her crazy eyeball and everything. Someone will find her."

Faraday fumbled for his phone, first trying to reach for it with his left hand, but realizing that would bring shards of pain, he fished it from his pocket with his right. He made a call and spoke after a short wait for our sister to answer. "Hey. Higgs. Are you at home? Okay. Good. Is Disco there with you?"

There was a pause. Her voice seeped from Faraday's phone as she called in the background for Disco. "No? Okay. I got into a car accident … No, I'm fine … Broken collarbone, but I'm fine. You stay there. Newt is with me. We'll look for her. Maybe she's gone to Granny."

Since there was nothing to do for a broken collarbone beyond the sling, it was easy to check out of the hospital. I took the prescription for painkillers, and Faraday walked cautiously beside me to the car. I only felt a little guilty firing up the flashing blue police light as we set out to find our dog.

* * *

The sunset coloured the clouds as we pulled up at the Orphanage to visit Granny Angelina. Faraday and I greeted the staff at the front desk where Faraday grabbed a banana on offer from the snack tray but avoided the parsnip muffins. When we got to her room, our grandmother hunched in her chair, gazing out the window at the Giant carved into the hillside as it took on an eerie orange outline in the blaze of sunset.

"Ah, my boys!" She seemed both glad to see us and lucid, the old sparkle alive in her eyes. She held her glasses up to her face without bothering to put them on fully and gave us a penetrating inspection before returning them to her side table. "Faraday, you look pale. Are you okay?"

"I'm pretty good. Just a headache and a sprained wrist," he lied. "But we're looking for Disco. She escaped, and I thought maybe she might turn up here since she loves coming to visit you so much."

Granny giggled. Her voice retained a youthful tone—if you spoke to her on the phone, you could easily mistake her for someone much younger. "She likes my dog treats, that's for sure. I'm not so convinced about her loving me in particular, though. But either way, I haven't seen her for a while. Not since I watched you and her up at the Giant a few weeks ago. And you didn't even pop in to say hello! Besides which, I may have fuzzy days, but a headache doesn't come with an arm sling, a shirt half-ripped off, and a hospital wrist band. What's really happening?"

I couldn't believe I tried to gloss over the truth with such a feeble excuse. That wasn't like me.

"Okay, Granny, you got me. There was a little car accident in the Jeep. I broke my collarbone, and Disco ran off in a fright. I last saw her sprinting into Nicholson's Woods. But I'm only a little banged up, and Disco seemed unhurt too."

My phone beeped. It was a text from Higgs, saying that Disco had arrived at the back door.

"Oh, great! Not to worry, Granny, Higgs says that Disco found her way back home. She's safe."

Granny nodded. "That's a relief. Hey, did Higgs tell you about her history project?"

"What, the pond thing?"

"She told you there was a thing in the pond?"

"No, no. A story *about* the pond. Some witches were drowned in there or something?"

Faraday took an interest. "Wait—is there something in the pond too? Is this one of your scary stories? What about the canal? Didn't you say something lived in there?"

She rolled her eyes. "Of course there's something in the canal—we all know that. But yes, Templeton, fear what you might find if you waded into Ashton Pond."

Calling my brother by my father's name was a bad sign. Faraday looked pale, and I felt guilty for dragging him here. I should have taken him home so he could rest.

"Okay, let's get you back home," I said. We made our farewells to Granny and slipped into the dusk.

* * *

Although Faraday flagged, he wanted to show me the secret lab. I couldn't deny that I wanted to see it too. "Quickly, then. Let's check out the shed."

"I don't have the secret key with me, but I'll show you the hidden hatch. We can come back later and have a proper look. I should tell Higgs too, I guess."

We trudged up the hill in silence. I imagined he felt remorseful and maybe foolish for not talking to me earlier, but it was hard to gauge Faraday at the best of times.

When we got to the hut, it was obvious we wouldn't need its key. The wood-panelled door stood ajar. The lock had been removed—sliced off with bolt cutters. But no light emanated from the hut. Whoever had been in there was likely long gone. But I used my police voice and called out, "Who's in there?" The only answer was silence.

I motioned to Faraday to get behind me, and I swung the door open, remaining off to one side in case an unpleasant surprise lurked within. Only darkness greeted us, so after a pause, I crossed the threshold and flicked on the interior light. I heard Faraday mutter a dejected, "Crap!" behind me. The secret lab clearly wasn't so secret anymore; there was a floor panel hinged up and open. My first glimpse of the ladder descending into my mother's private space was yet another twist of the chaos grinder that consumed us bit by bloody bit.

We made sure the lab was uninhabited and descended, Faraday moving cautiously to avoid jostling his sling.

Through clenched teeth, Faraday gave a strangled but furious yell through gritted teeth. "There were a bunch more tubes down here. Gone. And the computers—gone too. God, I'm such an idiot. I *thought* I saw someone watching us through binoculars from the roof of the Orphanage that day, but when I looked again, nobody was there. I figured I imagined it. Stupid, stupid!"

CHAPTER 22 -   BUTTER BOX

Disco

It was a considerable trek from the car crash to that boy's house and then home again. But I wasn't tired. Just hungry, with a sore throat. My stomach rumbled. Pausing at the end of our street, I nibbled at a clump of grass. Then waited. Soon, I vomited under a lilac bush. I was careful not to get any on my front paws. I sniffed it, but it didn't smell that tasty. Slightly oily. I didn't eat any of it and completed my journey home.

At the front door, I could hear Higgs inside somewhere. She was talking to someone whose voice I could barely hear. Sounded like maybe her girl friend. I circled to the back door, barked and jumped, scratching at the door with my front claws. Footsteps. Higgs approached and opened the door.

I hustled to my water bowl and started drinking. I drank the entire bowl of water, and she re-filled it. Then I wolfed down the kibble in the silver bowl beside the water. I devoured every nugget and was still hungry.

Higgs refilled the bowl, and I ate that too. I couldn't believe I was still hungry after that. Higgs chatted to me and ruffled my fur, evicting dust and fluff from my dodge through the woods. She gave me a third bowl. I munched this batch at a more leisurely pace, and finally, my hunger fled. Then sleepiness washed over me. I plodded to my bed. It was an ancient wooden box that smelled like it had held big blocks of butter, but such a long time ago that only whispers of a buttery ghost remained. Blankets lined the box. And my stuffed fabric sea monster toy. I closed my eyes even before I stepped inside, feeling my way to comfort. The last sensation before I fell into a deep sleep was Higgs unscrunching my blanket and covering me.

Faraday

By the time we got home, my collarbone ached with a dull throb at the core of my existence. The front door hadn't fully closed behind us when a motorcycle pulled up to the house. Only one visitor ever arrived in this fashion—of course, it was Chronos.

Our house had a centre hall layout, with a closet, several hooks, and a token bench that allowed a narrow de-robing space when you entered. Chronos filled the whole space himself, so after ushering him in, Newt retreated to let him navigate over the threshold. His feet in their black biker boots seemed to take up every square inch of the welcome mat.

"Faraday," he boomed. "I heard there was a crazy car crash, and that you were in hospital but miraculously escaped with only a broken collarbone!"

"Yeah. And I was at the stage in my training where I knew I could finally defeat you in a wrestle-off." I smiled, feeling the warmth of his concern for me.

"Well, I've broken six different bones during my misspent life, including a snapped collarbone when I was twelve years old. I was trying to impress a girl with a tightrope-walking impression across the top tube of the swings in the Giant Grove school's junior playground. After a week, it'll fade into the background."

Higgs came to the kitchen doorway, just beyond where a visitor could escape from the hallway into either the front room or the dining room, or proceed up the central staircase. The kitchen's brighter illumination cast her in silhouette, slivers of light glinting through her spiked hair. It was a stark contrast to the bulk of Chronos overwhelming the front hallway. "Dude! I remember that. There was literally an outline of your body in the mud when I went to the swings the next morning. Legend!"

Chronos had seen Newton and me earlier this week, but I realised he hadn't seen Higgs since the burning teacher incident at school. "Come here, you little punk. Are you still running things around here?" Newt and I squeezed back as the two of them had a brief ritualistic tussle.

Then she turned to have a penetrating look at my face before hugging me gently, intentionally avoiding my left side. She murmured, "Don't scare us like that, Faraday. We've had enough trauma around here without any trouble from you."

I felt myself welling up, and although no tears rolled down either cheek, I could feel my nose going, and I had to dab it with my sleeve. It was a strange mixture of emotions; I wasn't at all concerned with my close brush with fate, but I was grappling with the feeling that I would have let her down and caused her pain if I'd suffered more than a broken bone.

Then Chronos caught sight of Alan Ryder, who was visiting and hung back in the kitchen. Alan's sons had circulated with Chronos at school, so they were no strangers. "Ah, the butler is in. Where's my cuppa?"

"James, it's been a while. Well met."

It was strange to hear Alan call Chronos by his real name. It was only us that called him Chronos, but almost everyone else called him McCann or, more often, Canny.

Amid the small talk, Alan reflexively prepared a round of tea for everyone. Maybe Chronos had a secret subliminal power to compel people to make tea. As superpowers went, that would rank somewhere between Aquaman—what kind of superpower was conversing with fish? —and Batman, who didn't have any superpowers, just oodles of cash.

As he was brewing, Alan had a favour to ask of Chronos. "Oh, and James, tomorrow evening is the polo club's annual celebration. I could use an extra hand at the club. Low-key security, especially with the unexplained events that have been happening recently. Can you come and do a night's work for me?"

"Of course I will. I can get someone else to cover for me at The Pinnacle. But I'm warning you now, if I'm working, a few snacks are bound to go 'missing'. Text me the deets."

Our kitchen had a narrow and well-worn wooden table. The tabletop was the Redferne Rosetta Stone—it held the impressions of words and handmade drawings where over-zealous homework or shopping lists had been completed with high-pressure pencil work. We jostled into place around that table, instead of moving to the more comfortable front room sofas or the much more spacious dining room table. In our uncertainty, there was something comforting about huddling up.

Once we got into the serious conversation, I realised how much there was to reveal. To repent for concealing this from my siblings, I figured I might as well go full out and include our trusted friends in the confession.

"Listen, everyone," I said. "I have a secret I shouldn't have kept and some theories I've been withholding. I think what happened to me today was no accident, but was triggered by something that happened a couple of weeks ago. And pinning every strange event that's happened in town recently on Mr Shinoto seems like a real stretch to me."

Higgs' face had a pinched look. "What secret? I thought we were done with secrets."

It was telling that she was more concerned about me keeping secrets from her than my attempted murder. "I know. I'm really sorry. I thought I had an innocent secret that could be mine and Mum's alone. But I should have told everyone earlier. I showed Newt already. When I went up to tend the Ides Giant, I discovered that Mum had a nanotech lab concealed in the maintenance shed's basement. It seems she was working on something she didn't want them to know about at the Feynman Centre. Disco and I found it, and I took some of her experiments home. I think it's nanotech, but it's in black metal tubes that I can't open."

Newton couldn't stop himself from interrupting. "He was on his way to show them to Iain Vanderkamp this afternoon when the Jeep crashed. We returned to the lab just now—it's been ransacked. Someone's watching us."

I continued. "And that leads me to my suspicions. My crash today was definitely not an accident. We found a device attached to the Jeep that caused the crash. Whoever planted it probably expected it to be destroyed in the crash, but we found it mostly intact. It was powered by a small explosion, I think, that probably should have also destroyed the evidence."

"Nothing wakes you up like a near-fatal experience," Chronos said. "Let's hear the suspicions."

"Right. Someone was watching me the day I discovered Mum's secret lab. Maybe we're on the verge of uncovering something big, and they want me out of the picture. So they sabotaged the Jeep. That's suspicion number 1. I also had an epiphany about Dad's death. I think it may have been like my crash—sabotage, not an accident. That's 2.

"And the anti-terrorist swarm that pinned everything on Mr Shinoto? The lorry crash, the EMP burst, the Feynman break-in, and the explosion at your place, Alan? That seems too tidy to me. There was never any satisfying explanation for the tree-growth incident at the Feynman Centre, and the person spotted leaving the explosion was described as a hoodie-wearing teen, not a middle-aged Japanese man. Suspicion number 3—Mr Shinoto is a scapegoat. He set fire to his classroom but was not responsible for the other incidents. His arrest is a cover-up."

There was a moment of stunned silence. Newt broke it. "I'm feeling it. Think about the results from the explosive material analysis. They reported that your gate, Alan, was blown up using dynamite, not any kind of military explosive. We're still checking the quarries in case there was any dynamite stolen. But sophisticated explosives powered the EMP—it used C4. That suggests two different attackers."

Higgs chimed in. "And Dot has been vocal in doubting Mr S. could have engineered those attacks. She was there in the burning classroom, and she reckons it was a mental breakdown, not a calculated campaign of terrorist attacks."

"That's all disturbing news," Alan said. "Maybe one or two were pranks, although the weird drawing on the mailbox still suggests a connection to the other events. I convinced myself this was wrapped up, but now I feel very uneasy again. I should get back to the house—Jane is back from Edinburgh now, so maybe it's best not to leave her alone. What do you think, Newt? Is it safe for us to stay there still?"

Newt nodded. "For now, it's okay. There have been no new incidents in the last couple of weeks, so it feels like you'll be perfectly safe. Just be extra vigilant and call the police, or me, right away if you notice anything suspicious."

Higgs grabbed my tense hand, which was pressed on the table. "But wait. I mean, someone really tried to kill you? And Dad too? Who?"

"That's the problem. I don't have any idea who would want to kill me. Maybe it's something to do with those tubes."

"Can we see them—the nanotech tubes?" Chronos asked. "Seems like they might be the key to this whole misadventure."

I asked Newton to fetch the tubes. It wasn't a good idea to leave them unsecured if they were the root of this mystery. Newt laid out the 5 intact tubes and the cracked 6th one on the table so everyone could have a look.

"What are the letters on the end?" Higgs asked.

"Good question." I glanced at Newt as I replied, since we hadn't made it this far in our discussion yet. "Check out this notebook I took from the secret lab. It's filled with Mum's notes and diagrams. It has a codex for the lettering in the back, but it's infuriatingly vague."

I flicked to the back of the notebook where Mum's handwriting catalogued the lettering scheme. We looked at one intact tube, marked 'W/S^R'. "So that tube contains something to do with whips/seeker, whatever that means. And the one that flew the farthest from the crash and cracked on the road says 'W/S^C/F', so whips/seeker/flyer. But a different variety of seeker."

And then a massive wave of fatigue hit me. The physical, mental, and emotional toll of today's events fell on me like a collapsing wall. I sat in our kitchen, still draped in my jacket with my shirt in tatters where the doctors had partially cut it from my shoulder. "That's enough for now. Hopefully, the solution will come to me in a dream. But Newton, hide those tubes. We haven't got a real clue what's going on yet."

I got up and headed for my bedroom and much-needed sleep, but I had to pause for a moment and lean down to Disco's box, where she snored a faint cadence, to stroke her silky-soft ears. I murmured, "You're the lucky one here, not me. You weren't even wearing a seat belt."

Yes. Seat belts. We hadn't addressed Dad's accident yet. I needed another look at his car, now that I'd had my revelation about his crash. It looked like someone was out to kill me, like they had killed him.

Higgs

I saw Faraday's prescription bottle sitting on the kitchen counter where he had left it upon his return home. I wanted to be useful, so I filled a pint glass with water and took it to his room. He was already asleep when I crept in, the duvet pulled up to his chest, with his sling still on and his left arm cradled above the bedding. He is two years older than me, but I often feel he's my baby brother, and that I should watch out for him. I left the water alongside the painkillers and turned out his bedside lamp.

Alan was leaving as I descended to the hall. "I'll see you at the polo club tomorrow, Higgs. Let's at least try to put this month of troubles to the backs of our minds for a night. It'll be fun, as always."

"Year of troubles, you mean," I said.

He nodded in silence, looking at his shoes. I hugged him and said there was no way I would miss the party.

The smell of cigar smoke led me to the back door, where Chronos and Newton were sitting in deck chairs at the border between patio stones and lawn. "I don't understand how you can smoke those things. They're so obnoxious."

"And I don't understand, young lady, how you fail to appreciate the finer things in life. Sure you don't want to try it? I adore a cigar-smoking girl!"

"Gross. Don't even look at me while you're smoking it. I'll smell it in my hair tomorrow, and I'll be barred from the polo party."

Newton changed the subject. "I can't see how the pieces of the puzzle relate. Has Middle Ides slipped into a warped alternate dimension? It's hard enough pretending to be Mum and Dad here without this frustrating, complicated set of events. I really didn't sign up for this."

That's unfair, I thought. "In case you hadn't noticed, we all have to be Mum and Dad now. Not only you. So keep doing what the crappy situation demands. Fight it, fight everything!"

Chronos was a natural diffuser. "Fighting? Now you have me interested. That's my line of work. Who do I need to fight? And when? And where? Out behind the school bike sheds?"

Consider us diffused. Newton cocked his head as he looked across from his darkened chair, squinting in the light that slanted around me onto the paving stones. "I'm sorry, Higgs. I know we're in this pile of crap together. I'm whingeing at the world, not grasping for sympathy. I'm up for the fighting part too!"

Behind him, I could see a swarm of orange points of light in the night sky. I said nothing in reply, but tried to figure out what they were. Newton and then Chronos turned to gaze in that direction.

"You've got to be kidding me," Newton said, exasperated. "Those kids are launching the sky lanterns again? Look at them all. There must be over a hundred. I can't be bothered to drive to Little Ides only to find there's nobody around at the launch point. Look—they're going up from the hill over the canal tunnel. I'll call this in for the uniformed police to handle."

"They look regal, though," I said, watching them fan out and drift along, illuminating the night sky across Middle Ides like an eerie fleet of burning ships washed on an invisible tide.

I left Newton and Chronos in the darkness under the sky lanterns that winked out one by one, to talk themselves into thinking they were all grown up. I went up to my room to talk myself into thinking I was still a child.

That night I dreamed that faeries landed on the roof of every house in Little, Middle, and Nether Ides, delivering bundles of good luck or bad, but I couldn't figure out what our packet contained.

CHAPTER 23 -   VINE

Higgs

I awoke with a start, a warm hand clutching my forearm and urgent whispers in my ear.

"Higgs! Higgs, wake up." It was Newton, crouched beside my bed, his eyes glancing at me while scanning every direction through the screen of my bedroom window.

"Wha—?"

"Shh. Do you hear them out there?"

Yes. Wings, fluttering. I slithered out the side of the duvet closest to the window and squatted in the protective lee of my brother's bulk.

Newton held my father's bulky wristwatch in his left hand. Its face was a round computer screen, and the time was an afterthought, digits parked in its upper right-hand corner. Most of the space on the screen showed other information: the temperature, air pressure, your heart rate and body temperature when worn properly.

It flashed an alert. Dad had mentioned a few of the unusual things it could detect, like the radiation alert that had startled him when he visited a town in Ukraine near the Chernobyl Exclusion Zone.

The current alert wasn't for radiation, thank goodness, but it was one that he had demonstrated to us before. Somewhere in the basement were a pair of infrared goggles we used to take turns wearing during night time walks in the woods. They let you see infrared light, lending an eerie array of pastel colours to your surroundings, with plants, animals, and people appearing in stark contrast to inanimate objects. More impressive was when you used an infrared flashlight. The beam wasn't visible to the naked eye, but it lit your environment up like daylight if you wore the goggles.

The infrared alert on Dad's watch face was flashing on and off—but mostly on. This meant that a powerful infrared light shone on us. Someone was spying on us.

"I was fiddling with this thing out back after Chronos left, and the alert started to flash," he hissed. "Then I noticed the dragonflies."

Aha! That was the noise picking at the frayed edges of my perception: the haphazard vibration of cellophane wings. I could vaguely discern them now, fluttering above the yard, illuminated only occasionally by the light of a mostly cloud-obscured moon.

"But look at them, Newt. They're flying *wrong*. That's not normal dragonfly behaviour."

They hovered a fraction too long and too steadily. When they darted off on whatever mysterious missions crossed dragonfly minds, they didn't follow an erratic path, nor did they flit far. Their irregularity was too regular.

"They've got to be machines, Higgs. Tiny drones. And when any of them faces this way, the IR alert on the phone goes berserk."

We crept closer to the screen. "I see six of them. No, seven—there's one behind the tree branch there," Newton said.

I added to his tally in the barest whisper. "Two more back there by the garden shed. Nine! Why are they here?"

"Maybe it's those tubes. Maybe it's us. I don't know anything anymore."

In hushed tones, Newton started to theorise that the dragonfly drones were related to the watcher at the secret lab.

Huddled together in semi-darkness, we tracked the dragonflies' ever-changing dalliances, but he stopped short. We both took one synchronized step back as the dragonflies swooped into co-ordinated action.

In a blurred burst, eight of them clustered together, hovering in a tight formation a few metres from the window screen. But the ninth one sped at us, halting dramatically at the screen. It showed its belly and fanned its wings as it flared to a stop. Six insectile feet, like split-ended hairs, latched into the tiny squares of the screen's mesh.

Close up the dragonfly was less like a living creature and more like an automaton. It was bigger than a proper dragonfly. The hum of its wings possessed the whirr of an electric motor, and the eyes were somehow less alien than they should have been. But I had no time for further inspection. Events sped up.

I clutched Newton's hand, my nightdress pressed against the back of his thick cotton shirt. My chin buried itself in the wispy hairs of his neck as I peered in horror through my window. Six points of sparking crimson erupted at the dragonfly's feet before zig-zags of fire crossed the screen. As sections of the screen peeled away, disintegrating, the remaining dragonflies fanned out, all directing their beady-eyed gazes our way.

Were these demonic devices sent by the same people who had spied on Faraday? They weren't from Middle Ides, or they would know if you messed with Faraday Redferne you'd better keep at least one eye peeled for me.

A stuttering hiss of tiny pneumatic exhalations accompanied a stinging rain that splattered Newton and me. The dragonflies were firing at us! Dozens of tiny needles stuck in my exposed arm, stinging sizzles at each entry point making me recoil my arm. They littered my nightdress and protruded from Newton's cheek and the back of the hand that he raised for protection. The slender darts had wispy, feathered fletching, like weaponised dandelion fluff.

All nine of the tiny airborne machines re-arrayed themselves. They seemed almost cocky as if their work here was complete, and they remained only to watch the result of their handiwork. Were the darts poisoned? Was an invading virus or armada of nanotech already setting sail in our bloodstreams? I didn't know, although the thought was making me woozy. But even nine *thousand* flying tin toys wouldn't invade my house unopposed!

My clutching hand welded to Newton's and I uttered a primal bark that would have made my Viking ancestors proud. Enraged, I stepped from behind Newton, raised my free hand in a clenched fist, and thundered it down on the windowsill. I visualised the slender darts forming an unwanted pattern on Newton's cheek and knuckles. We would not be treated like this!

Surging to the tattered screen was only meant to scare off the attackers, but something more occurred. Every tiny dart shot from our clothing and speckled skin, reversing direction and flying in shards of blue fire back at the hovering dragonfly-machines. Each withdrawing dart brought a sense of relief.

The remnants of the screen fluttered outward in the wake of the streaking sparks as they struck their targets. The dragonflies shuddered back with each little impact as they too became limned in indigo energy.

By the time I screamed, "Away, now!" the dragonflies were insect-shaped clouds of smoke that hung motionless in a physical manifestation of surprise before sublimating to nothing in the slight breeze.

Newton stumbled back, looking confused and shaking his hand free of mine with difficulty as if stung. Oddly, a length of leafy vine coiled from his collar, looped around the sleeve of his shirt, and snaked from around my wrist as I released his hand. He flapped his arm in alarm as it slithered free.

"Where the hell did that vine come from? And did those little buggers just try to kill us?"

Tears pattered on the floor as my pent-up rage flooded away, but I could still respond with no hint of a quiver in my voice. "Maybe. But they won't be trying that again, will they?"

"Wait—did you do something?" Newton raised an eyebrow and tried to assess me in the shrouded moonlight.

Did I do something? I wasn't sure. But the sight of the leaves on the vine that lay in a trail like indecipherable cursive writing on the bedroom floor triggered memories of that night so long ago. The night my grandmother's voice told me I was a tree. But I couldn't tell Newton that.

"I was only angry. They must have self-destructed."

CHAPTER 24 - SPECTACLES

Disco

My eyes opened. Wow! It was morning already. I slept straight through. The blanket still covered me. I normally fidgeted out of it during the night. Hungry, but my stomach still bulged from last night's feasting. I arched my back to its fullest height and enjoyed an extended tongue-lolling yawn before stepping out of my box bed. My sore throat and lungs were completely recovered. The oily taste had vanished. I needed action. Who would play with me?

Faraday was asleep. I nosed past his door. He breathed deeply and slowly, so I retreated. I heard someone in the upstairs bathroom, so I ventured in. It was Newton. He was drying his snout and wore his work clothes. I brushed against his leg and received a scratch behind the ears. He said a few friendly sounding words that I didn't understand. I sensed he was going out without me, so Higgs was my only hope.

She was stirring in her room, so I went in to try to persuade her. She ate a croissant with jam on it. How had she made that in the kitchen without waking me? I jumped onto her bed and flounced around, hoping she would understand it was time to do something together.

"Okay, okay, Disco. Get your leash!"

Higgs

I was combining a visit with my grandmother and the opportunity to make progress on my school project. The mornings were still cool, although the afternoons were increasingly balmy as we meandered toward summer.

Lars had agreed to meet me at the gate of the Orphanage, and he jogged up shortly after Disco and I arrived. He was breathing deeply after his run from the centre of town, but he wasn't sweat-drenched. He greeted Disco with a ruffling of her ears as she stretched her front paws up Lars' side, and he looked at me quizzically. "Did you get a haircut? You're looking even cooler than usual today." His Swedish lilt made his pronunciation of 'cool' verge on the comical, but I took it as a compliment.

"Uh, no. But I actually washed it for a change." I smirked in return. "Anyway, let's go in. You can meet my grandmother, Angelina."

"What's she like? Super-old?"

"Well, yeah, she's pretty old. I don't know her age, come to think of it," I replied. "And she's weirdly senile. She drifts in and out of the state where she can have a practical conversation. But she's ever so nice. I'm sure she'll like you."

"Excellent. And hey, do you want some candied parsnip? I picked it up at the bakery on the way over here. It's delicious." Lars produced some golden, caramelized sticks of what I assumed were parsnips, wrapped in a clear cellophane pouch tied at the top with a flourish of thin red ribbon.

"Ugh. No thanks," I replied. "But Granny would probably appreciate some. She likes weird stuff, as long as her teeth can take the strain. And don't tell me you have gone gung ho for parsnips now too. What is it with everyone?"

Lars considered the question as we strolled up to the impressive double doors of the Orphanage, Disco in tow. "Oh,

I *love* parsnips now. It's possible that it was an uncommon thing to eat before, but once a few people start cooking with it, you realise how tasty it is. Come on, try one!"

I begrudgingly pulled one of the sugary sticks out of the packet and took a tentative bite. It was okay, I guess. Sugary, and I'm not sure I tasted the parsnip flavour. But it wasn't anything to swoon over. "Out of four stars, I rate it as *meh.*"

We swung open the carved front door of the Orphanage. It always surprised me how little effort opening the doors required, given how substantial they were. There must have been a well-designed hinge system at work.

Once inside, we paused at the reception desk, which was an extended oak-panelled bureau. It was attended by one of the house staff who I recognised from prior visits, a vaguely attractive woman in her twenties dressed in the starched standard light orange uniform. We paused there for Disco, who knew about the not-so-secret cache of dog biscuits in a drawer behind the desk, and she had her desire for a crumbly bone-shaped treat fulfilled by the attendant with remarkable dexterity. The attendant smiled with restrained amusement as she reached into the drawer and flicked the biscuit behind her back, over her shoulder and into her outstretched palm before a ceremonial offering that lost its glamour when dog drool drizzled onto her hand. There were a few plated slices of carrot cake on the desk, and as the woman wiped her hand, she said they had a few extra slices from last night. Would we like some?

Lars was never one to refuse carbohydrates, so he said, "Ooh, yes, I love carrot cake!"

"Actually, it's parsnip cake, but I can see why you'd think that. They look similar," said the woman. "Look at the little 'carrots'—they're drawn using white icing instead of orange."

What was going on? How could parsnips have moved from the vegetable league's lower divisions, where they had lingered for years with the likes of okra and fiddleheads, to vault into the realm of potatoes and carrots? I didn't get it.

We started up the stairs to my grandmother's room. Fork and plate in hand, Lars motioned a gesture of thanks to the woman at reception and called back something that might have been, "Thank you!" if his mouth hadn't been crammed so full of cake.

Atop the staircase, I let Disco off her leash, and she bounced along the corridor to Angelina's room. She always navigated there without prompting. We could hear a little excited yipping and my grandmother reacting with a joyful chorus of, "Disco, my girl! Good girl!"

My grandmother had been there the day that Disco found us. That was about seven years ago, when Disco was a lost puppy wandering the canal path in Little Ides. Granny and Faraday were piloting our family's narrowboat when Disco came by, and my brother used every ounce of his eleven-year-old boy charms to persuade our parents to adopt this abandoned and comical-looking whippet. I'm sure both my pleading whines and Angelina's positive premonitions about the puppy helped swing the decision. Disco had been part of the family ever since.

When we arrived at Granny's room, Disco was already in my grandmother's lap. They snuggled in the armchair, bathed by the soft light from the rear window. After a few more introductory cuddles, Disco settled into a comfortable position lying in the heavy purple fabric of Angelina's pleated skirt. Then my grandmother turned her head slightly and looked at the dog in a sceptical, appraising way as if she had noticed something new and intriguing. She reached for her glasses, had another good look at Disco's face, then removed them and made a quiet 'hmm' noise to herself. It was like she was trying to diagnose a canine illness, but all she detected was a patch of ear mange and a mild case of kibble breath.

I fluttered in an exaggerated pirouette into her room. "Hey Granny, this is my friend Lars. He's going to do homework here with me for a while."

"Hello, Lars. Nice to meet you. I think Higgs has told me about you. Did you move here from Sweden?"

Lars nodded. "Yes. My mother and I moved here a while ago. It's nice to finally meet you, Mrs Redferne. Would you like a piece of candied parsnip?"

A sparkle in her eye greeted Lars's earnest enthusiasm. "Thank you, no. I seem to be immune to the charms of that particular vegetable. And they look like they would snarl up my dentures something fierce." She donned her glasses again and had a closer look at Lars. "Hey! You must know Higgs's friend Dot too, right?"

"Of course. But I guess she's not as far behind in her schoolwork as us, so she doesn't have to do homework on a Saturday morning." He rolled his eyes. "And I know Higgs has questions for you about her project, but maybe you can help me too. I chose to write a report on the local geography, which is way different than what I'm used to in Sweden. It's on the composition of the hills heading northeast from Middle Ides. You must have explored this region much more than I have. Do you know anything I can add to my report?"

Angelina thought for a moment, still stroking the peak of Disco's bony, pointy head. "Maybe I can help you both at the same time. Are you still writing about the Pendle Hill witches, Higgs?"

I nodded.

"Well, you kids may not have heard this because people stopped telling this story long ago. But my mother told it to me, and I couldn't resist investigating it for myself." Angelina leaned back in her chair, giving Disco more purple lap fabric on which to build herself a temporary home.

Granny gestured out of her window. "A little way beyond the Ides Giant, over the brow of the hill there, is a big pond. I have heard it called Ashton Pond, but I'm not sure if that's its official name, or maybe the name of the farmer who owns the land. If you go up Peaks Road and take the second dirt lane on the left after the hilltop, you can follow as it skirts the brow.

There are nice sections where the tree branches reach out and intertwine overhead—it's like a tunnel, it gets so dark. Eventually, you will see the pond on your right, and you can hop over the old drystone to reach it. I'm sure you could find a place where the wall has collapsed almost to the ground and step over, unless they have fixed it up to keep the sheep in since I was there last.

"The council planned to drain the pond ten years ago; a quarry business wanted to use the site for producing gravel. But your father stopped them, Higgs. He used some influence from his job, and they cancelled the quarry. Which was fortunate because I don't want to think about what might have happened if they had drained that pond. That might help you, Lars—there is obviously good rock for producing gravel up there, and you can see what looks like limestone and chalk in our friend the Giant here. You two should walk up and look at the carving.

"Anyway, when I was a girl, we called it the Pond of the Pendletoad because of the story. And you know the other story about the pond, Higgs—I mentioned it last time. As I told you, there were witches hanged in York, and then their bodies were carted here and sunk into that pond. After the priest who did that horrible act left, the witches hereabouts wanted to ensure the dead bodies would be left in peace, as is only proper.

"There is good local magic here, especially atop the ancient hill rock, amplified by the presence of the Giant carved below. So what they did, those witches, is they magnified the natural elements around the pond. Arranged the rocks. Planted the right reeds. They foraged and captured a particular breed of toad and brought them to the pond's bank. I don't know exactly which ritual they performed, but the toads were part of the spell to deter anyone who might threaten to disturb the waterlogged corpses.

"The spell altered the toads' normal behaviour. Normally, you hear toads making their rough croaking sounds in the distance, but as you get closer, they sense your presence and go silent. And they make more ruckus overnight than in the daytime heat. But not the toads up there; after the spell, they get *noisier* if people approach, and they croak out their warnings all day long.

"You may not consciously notice this unusual behaviour, but whether or not you identify what's happening, you get a primal feeling of fear when you walk into that crescendo of toad calls. It's creepier on a misty morning or evening, which seems to happen up at the pond more than you'd expect. You two should go up there and experience the dread in the atmosphere like I used to.

"But that wasn't the only effect of their spell. One toad must have been at the magic's centre. After the spell took effect, he was another voice in the overwhelming toad chorus. But he slowly grew larger than his warty friends. His croaking lowered in pitch as he grew."

I felt myself being drawn in, imagining the scene up at the pond, with a large toad croaking plaintively through the mist. My arm hairs were standing up as my imagination amped up the tension. Lars leant forward too, hardly daring to take a breath.

She lowered her voice to a gravelly whisper. "But that toad eventually found that his entire family and every other toad had died of old age, and he was still at the pond, still growing and croaking gruesomely among the younger toads that had inherited the spell. Ten generations of toads passed, and still the giant toad grew and croaked, croaked and grew. He submerged himself in the pond so that only an eyeball or two was above the surface. And still he grew. He lives there still today, like a grotesque elephant, submerged in the dark pond waters, fulfilling his duty to protect the long-decayed bodies below.

"He is the Pendletoad, and on a still night, you can open my window and hear the distant rumble of his croaking." She closed her eyes, casting her mind back to unknowable memories.

The story was clearly fantastical, but the way she told it and the conviction in her voice had both Lars and me conflicted, struggling to figure out how we could disbelieve it. Lars and I sat in silence for a while, considering how to fit this into our school projects. Angelina seemed to doze off, and Disco settled, enjoying the quiet.

We spread our books and papers out on the round table and added to our reports while dog and grandmother snoozed in the morning sun's warmth. Her head drifted to the side, her grey-swirled hair flattening asymmetrically as it nestled up against the wing of the armchair's back. Forty minutes later, she stirred and shimmied her way to a full sitting position. Yawning, she said, "You may not believe the story of the Pendletoad, but you should visit the pond someday. Or at least listen for it at night. I'm sure it would carry to your house too, Higgs. And I want to give you something." She beckoned me over to her. "Think of it as an early inheritance." She took her gold-rimmed spectacles from the side table and handed them to me. "They have always been passed down the line, and with all the bad blood between the original families popping up, I thought it would be nice for you to have them. You might need them."

I'm not sure whether she thought I needed glasses or was just giving me these because they were finely-crafted antiques, but I accepted them graciously. "Oh, thank you, Granny!" I gave her a hug that made Disco squirm out of her lap.

I inspected the glasses now that they were in my hands. Although the circular lenses were small, the frames were heavy; I guess a sign that they had a high gold content. The rims around the lenses were no wider than the rim of a pottery tea mug, but fine details of workmanship covered them and the arms. It was not apparent when I saw Angelina wearing them, but there were patterns engraved across the frame's width. I guess they qualified as a Redferne family heirloom. I felt a flush of warmth at being given such an item from my grandmother.

"What were you saying about bad blood? And wait, Granny, don't you need these to see properly?"

"No, no. I don't need them to see. I have another pair of glasses over by the bed for reading." She blessed me with a reassuring smile, and gestured for me to keep them as if she feared I would return them.

As we left the Orphanage, with the mid-morning sun angling in from the east, Lars asked, "Did your grandmother's story help you with your project? I put a side note in my report mentioning Ashton Pond, but should I call the Pendletoad story a *legend*, or something else? To me it's like Norwegians and trolls—you are never sure whether to mention trolls as if they are a fact of life or something completely invented."

"It's weird. I can't decide. The way she tells it, you completely believe it at the time, but after the storytelling is finished, you reconsider, and it doesn't seem possible."

"How about we call it a true legend then?" Lars smiled, checking out my hair again. "Hey, let's see the treasure she gave you. It's always cool to get something that's old, sentimental, and valuable at the same time."

I pulled the pair of glasses out of my backpack and handed them over. He felt the weight immediately and said, "Wow, they are a treasure!" After closer examination, concentrating on the engraving work, he pursed his lips and widened his eyes at me. "Let's go to my mother's shop and get lunch. I'm sure she has a bracelet that matches these engravings."

CHAPTER 25 - WONDERS

Disco

I trotted beside Lars while Higgs rode her bicycle. It was an easy run. Downhill toward the town centre. The bakery and the restaurants cooking lunch made my nose twitch.

I had seen Lars and Higgs on the screen at that boy's house. I wanted to show her. But how could I guide her there? I was getting hungry again.

Higgs

The Trove of Wonders, Lars's mother's shop, lurked just over the canal bridge. Everything below the canal is technically Nether Ides and features the less upmarket stretch of the High Street. The shop was an arrangement of bargain goods. I shouldn't use the term 'arrangement' because it wasn't arranged in any normal sense of the word. It would be better described as a chaotic selection of wares, ranging from cheap Chinese knick-knacks through to vintage clothing and a hoard of estate jewellery. We arrived there right after opening, before any customers. Lars's mother liked dogs, so I leant my bike against the wall in the side alley, and we brought Disco in with us.

She greeted us with enthusiasm, dancing along an aisle to us and smothering her son in a flurry of kisses and hair tousling that made him—at least when it happened in front of me—wriggle to escape. "Oh, Higgs. Who cuts your hair? Do you think they can do something with this?" She rolled her eyes as she pointed to her curly mix of red and blonde hair that resembled a violent jailbreak from her headscarf.

I swear she felt obligated to demonstrate as many 'wonders' of the shop as she could by wearing them. She jingled with dangly bracelets, and her multiply-pierced ears showed off a series of hooped earrings that looked like a challenging section of a dog show course. She had a sturdy stature at odds with Lars's wiry frame, and the haphazard layers of shirt, cardigan, and scarves she normally wore magnified the effect.

"I know it's only eleven o'clock, Morsa," Lars used the Swedish word for mother with her, "but have you made lunch yet?"

"Of course! Of course! Come on back, I made us sandwiches, and we can share them with Higgs. And maybe a dog treat too, Disco?" I found it amazing that her accent was like a caricature of Scandinavian, but Lars already spoke like a local, except for an occasional word that came out all bouncy.

Lars's mother wasn't hungry yet, but she hovered in the doorway and chatted with us in the cramped back room while monitoring the front. "And have a parsnip muffin," she called back to us. "I got them fresh from the bakery, and they are lovely."

After finishing his sandwich and three muffins, Lars motioned for me to show his mother the glasses from my grandmother. "Oh yeah. Mrs Janssen, have an eyeball at these. Lars said you might have something with similar engraving here."

She took the pair of glasses from me and recognised something about the engravings. "Ooh, yes. Come take a look, over here."

She squeezed behind a jewellery display case, opened it from the back, and fished out a bracelet. Covered with the same style of elaborate squiggles as Granny's specs, it was a bracelet in the Wonder Woman style. A slender wrist could slip through an opening in the wide cuff. Once it gleamed on a wrist, the urge to deflect imaginary bullets would come naturally.

I held the glasses up next to the bracelet, and they looked like they had been sisters in a former life. "You should take it, Higgs," she said. "They threw it in with some of the finer rings and broaches at a recent estate sale."

"No, no, I couldn't," I protested, not wanting to seem a charity case.

"I won't hear that," she said. "It's not a Cartier masterpiece. It's only gold plate. Treat it as an early birthday present—or a late one!"

"It's fine, Higgs," Lars said in a persuading tone of voice. "Here, I'll wear it for a while and then give it to you once we get to your place." He slipped it onto his wrist, where it looked silly and didn't make him Wonder Womanly at all.

"Geez. It feels quite cold on your wrist. I don't really get how you girls wear these pieces of jewellery. It seems annoying. Well, not you, obviously, since you avoid anything more glamourous than those little earrings." He turned to his mother as Disco and I weaved our way to the front. "Have you got a bottle of water? Those muffins leave a bad taste in your mouth."

His mother handed him a bottle produced with a flourish from somewhere under the cash register. "Especially after three of them," she scolded, but with affection wrinkling the corners of her eyes.

I walked my bicycle back over the bridge, where we turned west and headed toward my house. Lars walked beside me, leading Disco, who strode along between us with her springy whippet strides.

"Look at that delivery van." I pointed to where a large van ahead of us was dropping off goods at the bakery. It had a large parsnip logo along its side, and the company name emblazoned above the picture. Pendlethwaite Parsnips. "I wonder if that farmer is related to Dot?"

"Well, whoever it is, he's doing a good bit of business around here," Lars replied. "And I know I said I would wear this bracelet until we got to your place, but it's already aggravating me. Here, you wear it."

"Embarrassed to be seen wearing it around town?" I giggled. "Give it here, you Amazon wannabe."

I slipped it onto my wrist, but it wasn't as cold as Lars had reported. It felt warm to me—maybe it had absorbed his warmth. I figured I'd complete the look, pulled out the golden glasses and popped them on too. The arms were loose; I would either need to have them tightened or convince my head to grow a few sizes bigger. I was expecting them to be highly magnifying, but surprisingly they had no magnification. It seemed they were decorative, for someone who enjoyed wearing fancy glasses but had perfect eyesight.

That didn't make much sense. Granny slipped them on and off almost unconsciously. Why would she do that if they didn't help her vision? I swivelled my head to survey the street. Perfectly plain glass, they didn't change my close or distance vision. I lowered and raised them twice, trying to detect even a trace of optical power. Nothing! Well, when I looked at Lars, he looked smudgy with a faint rainbow aura. Maybe the lens needed wiping. But he didn't look magnified.

"I don't believe it," Lars muttered, bringing me out of my contemplation. "I've just washed the last of those muffins out of my mouth, and suddenly I want more. Wait here while I grab some from the bakery. And for old lady glasses, they go well with your hair." He handed me Disco's leash and promised to return momentarily with a fresh crop of muffins.

CHAPTER 26 -   TUBES

Faraday

My collarbone was an anchor tugging at my shoulder, waking me from a long sleep that I hoped had energised the healing process. I eased myself upright and noticed that someone had left the hospital bottle of painkillers and a pint glass of water on the painted side table I inherited from Granny's former house. Mother's research tubes stood on end beside the table—Newton must have smuggled them in while I lay dreamless. The broken-open one rested at the feet of the others, too unbalanced to stand on end. Adjusting my sitting position, I reached over with my good arm and dispensed two tablets.

I drifted with my eyes closed, replaying the events of yesterday and the recent frantic weirdness. It occurred to me that I had stood up Iain Vanderkamp yesterday, not contacting him from the hospital, although I guess I had a good excuse. My mobile battery was drained, so I plugged it into its charging cable beside the bed. I closed my eyes and breathed deeply for 98 seconds before I heard it chime, indicating it had enough charge to come back to life. I retrieved it to call Iain with an apology, and a barrage of missed text messages confronted me.

There were a smattering from people asking if I was okay— Higgs, Chronos, Alan Ryder. A few from Iain, wondering why

I hadn't shown up to meet him. I picked one of those texts and responded by calling him.

"Iain, I'm sorry about yesterday. I had a spot of bother on my way to meet you."

"I heard! Traffic was stopped on the link road as I drove home, and saw your dad's jeep off to the side with police inspecting it. Is everyone okay?"

"It was only me and our dog in the Jeep. Miraculously, we are both intact. It was a double corkscrew, but I landed back on the wheels if you can imagine that. I broke my collarbone, and my dog flew clear from the Jeep but landed safely. It could have been a *lot* worse for both of us. Easily fatal, although I'll try not to think about that."

"Oh my goodness! I'm glad to hear your voice then. I know our meeting seemed crucial to you. Is there anything I can do, or do you want to park this for now and catch up later?"

I adjusted my position to get more comfortable, which proved awkward while my only working arm wielded the phone. "It seems even more critical today than yesterday. I found a bunch of my mother's research that she conducted away from the Feynman Centre. I figured you might look at it and tell me what it's all about. You'll understand what she was working on better than I ever could."

Iain sounded excited. "I worked for years with Alison so I should know whether it was something she was pursuing at the Feynman Centre or not. What kind of stuff do you have?"

"I have her notes in a notebook. And a USB drive with a bunch of files on it I can't really understand. And I grabbed several black metal tubes marked with a categorization code, but I can't open them because they have these weird cap locks."

"Are the tubes long? Like a metre or so?"

"Yeah."

"Send me a photo of the cap. I might have seen something similar."

I told him to hold on for a minute while I pivoted my legs over the bedside and used the phone to photograph the standing tubes' round ends. I sent the photo.

"Oh, boy. Those are Fūjikome tubes. We use them to hold experimental nano-material. When you build nanotech that is still at the experimental stage, you often build it right inside the tube so you know exactly where it is. The tubes have sensors built in, so you can connect the tube to specialized equipment and analyze the success of your build without risking exposing it to an uncontrolled environment."

"So the tubes are there to protect the contents from outside contamination?"

"Sort of. But often it's also protecting the outside world from your experiment. Whatever you do, be very gentle with the tubes. The sensors are easily damaged. That indented spot on the tube end is both for connecting the analysis computer, and there's a place to insert a crypto key if you need to open the tube. Let me turn on my camera and show you something."

Iain switched to a video call. I saw he stood behind a house—presumably his house—while talking. "Hey. Can you see me now?"

He fished something out of his jacket pocket. It was a keyring, with two sets of keys but also 6 small items, each tethered to the main keyring with its own smaller ring. They looked like a cross between an electrical fuse and a poker chip. Each was a square that looked like plastic, but could have been metal. Marked with different colour patterns, each had a gold-plated connector that would fit into the space on a tube cap like the ones beside my bed.

"These are crypto keys that work to unlock my own Fūjikome tubes at the Feynman Centre. So your mother must have set aside some keys like this somewhere. It might only be one key—normally we use the same key for every Fūjikome tube in one experimental run. And whatever you do, if you find the key, don't open the tubes until I have analysed what's inside. It's possible they're empty, but we don't want to take any chances. Sometimes the nanotech can be harmful if released."

"Um, okay." I checked the photo I had sent him and breathed a silent sigh of relief that the ruptured tube was not visible in the frame. "Listen, are you going to the polo club party tonight? I'm still planning to go, so maybe I could show you the tubes there."

"Amazing. Yes. I'm on the guest list, so I'll see you there. I'll grab my laptop and my connector cables so we can have a peek at what's in the tubes if you want. Bring them along."

"Perfect, Iain, perfect. And I want to talk more about my mother's death again too."

As soon as I hung up the call, I panicked. Should I have been regurgitating that detail over a mobile phone? If someone was watching me in the shed up at the Ides Giant, couldn't they be monitoring my calls? Could I trust Iain? *Calm down, you can trust him.*

I took 9 deep breaths. But I had another mission, so I struggled to a standing position and got into my jeans using a sequence of awkward tugging steps and generous cursing. I grabbed the keys and headed out.

I couldn't raise my left arm, so when I encountered Higgs and Lars as I left the house, they were both surprised and amused to see me wearing the only button-up shirt I owned. It was a short-sleeved Hawaiian shirt with a wild toucan and palm tree pattern. I was so eager to investigate Dad's crash that I hadn't bothered to wash or comb my hair. It must have looked somewhere between Einstein and a punk rocker.

Disco sped toward me as soon as she saw me emerge from the door. The leash jerked out of Lars's grip, and she yipped and circled me three full times before jumping up at my waist. I realised that I had seen her the night before, but she hadn't been awake in my presence since the accident. I leant over to pat her head and neck, but I didn't bend too far because gravity reminded my collarbone it was broken the more I strayed from an upright position. Mother had always called out, "Shoulders back and down!" as I hunched my way out of the house, so she would have been proud of my newfound desire to stay in perfect posture. "Disco! Good girl! I can't believe you're uninjured after flying out of the Jeep! But I guess you were just sliding along on the roof the whole time. You're superdog! Or super-lucky at the very least."

I looked at the Jeep keys dangling from my right hand and shook my head. "Argh! I'm such an idiot."

Higgs and Lars looked at me as if I was an alien that had plopped in from planet Zarg. On reflection, I was alien, even in my normal state of mind. "I planned to drive to the police impound and look at Dad's old car, but I somehow forgot that the Jeep isn't really available right now. Apparently, somebody crashed it yesterday. Oh yeah—that was me!"

Higgs looked concerned. "You could call Newt and get him to come back for you. He's gone to the station. Or it's not that far from here. We can walk there with you if you want—right, Lars? It will only take half an hour."

Lars nodded. "Of course we can. Come on, Disco, more walkies!"

As we wound our way through the streets, heading west, I gave a more detailed accident recap to Higgs and Lars. I think I was as incredulous as they were as I described what happened. It was almost like I had watched it happen to someone else, or seen it in a movie. Describing it made me realise how close I had come to ending my life as a trail of unidentifiable gore along the road. The chances of landing right back on the wheels after the double flip seemed less than zero.

Higgs remained quiet for several paces, then glanced at me sideways and said, "BACKYARD LUST."

I understood what she was playing at and imagined the letters in my mind. Lars looked puzzled as I worked on the anagram, but he said nothing. His intuition must have indicated the missing sibling context.

It didn't take me too long. I chuckled. "Yeah, I am a 'LUCKY BASTARD'."

After another silence, I continued. "And you know what else is lucky? It's kind of lucky that I had the accident because it knocked something loose in my mind that has been troubling me since Dad's death. It wasn't an accident, his crash, I think someone killed him. I know it's painful to mention this Higgs, but it's important. I'm sorry." I cast a glance at her face, and she stared straight ahead, with a fixed facial expression that looked like a struggle to maintain.

"I still don't know why he wasn't wearing his seat belt, but the accident threw Dad from the car, right through the windshield. That would have happened as soon as he stomped on the brakes and started to skid. But after he was ejected, the car wouldn't have come to a complete stop yet. It would have rolled forward with nobody to hold the brake pedal down and finish the job of stopping the car. But I saw the accident scene. The car hadn't rolled an inch from the skid endpoint. The brakes were either locked up, or there was somebody or something else pressing the brake pedal."

"So that's why you need to inspect the car now after leaving it uncollected in the police impound all these months?" Higgs's voice wavered. I noticed Lars pat her on the back sympathetically, and gave silent thanks he was there because I didn't feel capable of offering Higgs any comfort. I always tried to shield her and keep her away from more sadness, but I was useless at addressing her existing grief.

Higgs's nostrils flared as she took a deep, audible breath. When she spoke, it was quiet but firm. "When you tell me who did this to him, I'll kill them myself."

CHAPTER 27 -   Q'S WITHOUT A'S

Newton

Although I was the last to bed, I was the first awake, and headed out early to get the questions spinning in my head answered. I hated the direction we were headed. There had been enough crap to organise in our lives when we thought our parents had died of nothing more sinister than misfortune. Now that both our parents' deaths looked like they had much more to them than we thought, it brought out a horde of uneasy feelings in me. I felt my clothes didn't fit, that my watch strap was chafing my wrist, that I wasn't a real police officer, and that I had forgotten every single thing I had ever learned.

My hands trembled as I drove, but I somehow made it to the station in Mum's red and black electric BMW. Parked, I straightened my arms against the steering wheel, pushing myself back into the seat as hard as I could. Then I let my arms dangle and breathed out hard, emptying my lungs completely. I stayed this way, airless, for as long as I could stand it, then took a series of deep breaths to recover. I can't say I felt better, but I felt composed enough to talk to my colleagues. I would see if I could return a modicum of control to my life.

Typical investigations dragged on, with abundant paperwork. This was different—things had progressed overnight. When there were open cases that involved a personal connection with a police officer or a police family, forensic experts worked overtime and requests for information accelerated. Two items of interest awaited me.

The first report was not that surprising, since Faraday had already discovered the device attached to the hitch. Its purpose was clear: when the vehicle got up to a high speed, the powerful hinge would spring into action and force the trailer to jackknife, causing a rollover. It had fulfilled its intended purpose, but whoever planted it could not have contemplated Faraday's luck—ending back on his wheels instead of cartwheeling off the road at high speed.

The techs ran queries against the logic circuit remnants in the device and confirmed that the hinge became active at 70 miles per hour. My first reaction was that I should have a word with Faraday about travelling that fast on the motorway link road, especially with the doors off the Jeep. But that seemed harsh.

The police techs couldn't find much other evidence to latch onto. The device had been attached recently, but we knew that because we had only attached the trailer ourselves within the last week. The hitch was entirely new, so someone had replaced our well worn original with the sabotaged version, and they had been careful not to leave any fingerprints or DNA traces. A small explosive charge powered the hinge, and its maker was a mystery. It seemed engineered for this specific purpose, as opposed to being assembled from commercially available parts.

The real questions still swirled in my mind. Who was the device intended for? Faraday? Me? Any of us? And why? I had my suspicions—that we had got too close to uncovering something, and unseen hands were moving against us to keep their activities concealed. I knew we were within touching distance of *something*, but I wasn't sure what. It was like a giant magnet, unseen on the other side of a wall, tugging at our coins, our watches, our keys.

I had also asked around about the UPDA acronym, to see if anyone in the police force knew what it meant. It wasn't the

Urban Planning and Development Authority, which was in Qatar. And I eliminated the Universal Property Development and Acquisition Corporation, which was a Florida-based oil and gas company. My Detective Chief Inspector thought the 'A' might stand for Agency. There was no known British agency called the UPDA, but he implied that there were secretive agencies, shielded from the public eye. He would surreptitiously chat to a friend in the Intelligence Services to see if he could discover anything helpful.

So nothing of particular interest on the UPDA yet, but my phone record requisition had arrived. The speed of obtaining this report shocked me—I only called in the order last night. I'd have to figure out who to thank for those results appearing so quickly!

The call list from my father's mobile phone had no notable numbers on it. There were a few scattered calls to numbers I recognised—mine, Higgs's, the pizza place that had been our last dinner together. The intriguing part was *not* on the list. The final outgoing call appeared on the report, and they triangulated its position to our house, confirming my father made his final call while at home. He dialled only a few minutes before the time of his accident, so it seemed he made the call immediately before departing in the Jaguar. But what wasn't in that report was the identity of the receiving end. The phone number showed as a series of Q's: QQQQ QQQQ QQQQ.

I paid attention in my basic training session on obtaining telephone records, and this was definitely not possible. The telephone companies couldn't connect a call without the full number being known, and their systems were obligated to track caller and receiver numbers, not only for billing, but for forensic cases like this. It was another example of how civilian privacy bleeds away silently until little remains.

I called my DCI and mentioned this discrepancy. He agreed it was an oddity and would talk to his contact in Intelligence about this too. I heard the urgency in my own voice, and he said he would try to get back to me that afternoon.

I rubbed my eyes, thinking. I needed things back under control. Faraday had nearly been killed and I've seen him flip from intense investigation mode to a wreck as pressure mounts. Higgs knew less than half of the story; she'd erupt with rage if we got any evidence of malice in Father's death. And there was still the unsettling cover-up at the Feynman Centre surrounding the death of our mother and the mysterious UPDA visitors. All of that without even considering the dragonfly attack from last night.

I had slept poorly, worried about possible ill effects from the tiny darts the dragonflies sprayed at us. Had we been poisoned? I felt fine. Was the attack a warning of some sort? And what was the deal with that vine? Did it have some connection to the mutant tree growth at the Feynman Centre?

I called Higgs. When she answered a bit groggily, I asked, "Are you feeling okay, after last night?"

"A bit tired, and I have these uninvited acupuncture prick marks up my left arm, but otherwise, I'm good. Why? Are you *not* okay?"

"No, no. All good here. Just a bit worried about the darts. I thought we were being poisoned or something, but they shot back out of us before they seemed to do anything. I still don't understand what saved us there."

"Hmm. Me neither, really. But no, I'm as healthy as ever. Probably even healthier after some breakfast. Where are you?"

"I'm at the office, catching up on a bit of work. We need to tell Faraday what happened too. But wait until this afternoon, and maybe we can figure it out. Together. See you soon, Higgs."

I considered my possible next steps. I hoped my Chief Inspector could uncover some clues from his friend about the phone records, so I decided to focus on what had happened with my mother. That wasn't a police investigation—at least not yet. More of a personal side job. It was time to finish what Faraday had set out to do yesterday and talk to Mum's assistant,

Iain. I left the police station before dialling his number on my mobile.

CHAPTER 28 - JAGUAR

Faraday

Lars chatted continuously as we trudged, mostly to Higgs but also to Disco and occasionally to me. I think I answered, but used a part of my brain that wasn't busy developing a list of the mechanical inspections I planned to revisit on my father's car.

We reached the vehicle impound, a patch of uneven gravelly dirt on the west edge of town, surrounded by a chain-link fence topped with barbed wire. 28 vehicles roosted haphazardly within as though parked with intentional randomness as part of an art installation. They existed in various states of distress, ranging from gnarls of metal barely recognisable as cars to pristine and expensive-looking ones that screamed 'big city drug lord'. A single-storey brick hut slouched beside the gated driveway. No sign identified the compound's purpose, but Dad used to take us up here as kids to see what kind of cars the police had confiscated.

We approached the gate, and a uniformed police officer strode from the hut to greet us. I recognised him, and maybe Higgs did too, but I couldn't remember his name. Despite my exacting memory, somehow matching a name to a face almost always eludes me without multiple introductions. This frustrated me further because this man knew us by name. He unlocked the gate and swung it open, removing his hat as he spoke. "Hey, Faraday, Higgs. Finally coming to pick up your father's car? I kept it ready for you. I start it up and run it for a few minutes every week. And as you can see, Detective Redferne—I mean, your brother—sent someone out to replace the windshield."

I hadn't considered taking the car away from here. I had only thought to inspect it further, using the full set of tools I had spied in the hut on previous visits with my father. "Beauty! Thanks, John, brilliant" Higgs replied before I could formulate my thoughts enough to respond. She was clearly better at remembering names.

"Can you drive now? I mean, are you old enough already?" he asked.

Higgs and Lars laughed, both used to people underestimating her age. "She's 16," I replied. "So she's getting there, but no licence yet. I'll be the designated driver today."

He smiled at Higgs. "Well, for a sixteen-year-old your hair looks really good." That was a weird thing to blurt out, and he turned a combination of scarlet and simultaneously three shades whiter, as his eyes widened. He tried to correct it by hastily adding, "and yours could use a bit of work, Faraday." That didn't seem appropriate either. He doubled down on the losing conversation by looking at Lars and trying to come up with something to neutralise his previous two errors. "And yours looks … normal?" His hesitancy and up-talking was well-timed, and everyone chortled.

"Nice recovery," Lars said.

He fished the key to the Jaguar from a wall of hooks inside the hut and handed it to me. "Normally there's a form to print out and sign, but I'm having a quarrel with my computer today, so I'll get Detective Redferne to do the paperwork when I see him next. She's all yours."

The three of us and Disco surrounded the old Jaguar, while Officer John held the gate open. My father repainted it a lustrous British racing green less than a year ago, so although this Jaguar S-Type was from the 1960s, its paintwork urged onlookers to doubt its age. The graceful curves of the leaping jaguar hood ornament cast a slender shadow across the oval grille between the four headlights.

"Cool," said Lars. "I haven't been in a fancy car like this before."

"It's a first for me too," I added. "I've never driven it."

"You can ride up front, since it's your first time," Higgs said to Lars, as she and Disco slipped through the passenger side door onto the bench seat in the back. Lars joined me in the ageing but well-maintained leather bucket seats. The eight-ball black gearstick knob, the leather-clad transmission tunnel, and the handbrake separated us. The design and materials of a 1960s car were markedly different from a modern car; my mother's BMW was all high-tech and efficiency, whereas this car had a human touch and a more rugged, magical quality. But if you wanted to play your own music, this car was definitely not for you. It was either the radio or listen to the engine roar.

For this trip, it was the engine, which brought back a flood of comforting but melancholy memories. Disco barked three times with excitement as the engine sputtered then thundered into life. She too had spent many happy journeys standing with her chin resting on my father's left shoulder as he drove. I slotted the seat belt into its buckle. It slithered out. I tried again, but it didn't click. After a few tries, I gave up.

"The driver's seat belt isn't working. I guess that explains why Dad wasn't wearing it." The buckle would face the full force of my investigation at home, but I raged privately as I adjusted the rear-view mirror. What a trivial problem to cause a death!

I was cautious as the car crept forward. My skills at driving a 1960s stick shift were shaky, I wasn't wearing a seat belt, and this was the first time I had been in my dad's car since he died in it. I couldn't suppress the reflex to check the seals on the replaced windscreen—had it been fitted properly? There was also the critical matter at hand. I had convinced myself that I would find something rigged in the car that had caused the brakes to lock up. Was it safe to drive? Evidence pointed to the positive, as our man John had driven it inside the compound after the accident, and the police mechanics checked the car for any problems and found none. Nor did I.

After the first three turns, I relaxed. The 35-minute walk over translated into a 4minute drive home, but that didn't prevent me from getting a double Disco drool streak down my left sleeve. Nor did it allow time for Lars's running stream of enthusiastic comments about the car to fizzle out.

Higgs gave me a serious look. "I know you're going to get your tools out and inspect the car right away, aren't you, Faraday? We'll carry on with our homework, but give me a shout as soon as you find anything interesting."

She was right. I was already making a mental list of tools needed to inspect the brakes and the seat belt buckle.

CHAPTER 29 -   WRENCH

Disco

Driving in Templeton's car again was pleasant. It had been a long time. I wondered when he would come back. The kids forgot to leash me or escort me inside. After the car ride, I was free to roam around the garden. Or further. The driveway gate stood open. I didn't leave, though. Not without Higgs, because I had something to show her.

I wasn't the only one off-leash. That French bulldog from along the street waltzed past the gate. She was almost always off her leash and roamed the neighbourhood whenever she wanted. She paused mid-step when she noticed me and made a hard turn through the gate.

Mandatory sniffing. We bowed to each other as a brief signal that we didn't plan to be aggressive. As if that would ever happen between us!

"Hey, I saw baby badgers this morning!" She looked excited about it. So was I. I hadn't seen a badger before, but I had smelled them in the forest a few times. "One of them was eating a hedgehog."

I felt the need to outdo her. "That's barking!" I replied and filled time while I thought of something interesting to say by flicking some larger pieces of gravel around the driveway with my front paws. "But did you see those flaming lights in the sky the other night?"

"Amazing! You heard them burn up and fall from the sky, right?"

I yipped agreement. "Hey, you're cleverer than I am at getting humans to do things. Could you stay a while and help me get Higgs and her friend to walk me over to Nether Ides?"

"Of course I can. Let's go sniff around behind your house first and try to track the badger family."

"Or some hedgies," I agreed.

Faraday

While I raided the cellar, selecting the tools I would need to re-inspect the Jaguar, I looked through the filing cabinet for service receipts. Had a mechanic looked at it recently? I trusted the garage that Dad used for the car. It was a classic sports car specialist in Frome, up in the hills. As I expected, they had done the last work on the car, and not too recently—five months before the accident.

I balanced a car jack, a mat to lie on while I examined the brakes, and a selection of tools between my good hand and pockets. By the time I had carried this clumsily clutched paraphernalia to the car, a hand cramp threatened, and my collarbone ached. I let everything drop to the ground. From the corner of my eye, I noticed Disco and that dog from up the street frolicking around beside the house. They were having fun, so I didn't call her. I set to work jacking up the Jag's rear end. I figured that I could see the skid marks leading to the rear tires after the accident, so I knew that the rear brakes had fully engaged at that point.

Even under close inspection, the brakes seemed in perfect working order. I had thoroughly examined them right after the accident, but I needed to satisfy my inner compulsive demon to be confident I hadn't overlooked anything.

There was a long-handled wrench in my hand and a flashlight beside me when I heard footsteps on the gravel, and a pair of black men's work boots came into view between the Jag's removed wheel and my position. A massive gloved hand descended into view and picked up the tire iron from where I left it. The booted man spat—a productive effort that splatted to the gravel somewhere nearby.

A broad northern accent erupted from the boots' owner. "Keep your bloody nose out of other people's business!"

I didn't recognise the voice, and I amused myself at his combination of metaphor and mild swearing. I imagined myself with a nose bleed, gossiping with the neighbours— sticking my bloody nose in. But I realised this was no time for wordplay when I saw the boots' stance widen and the tire iron hook the car jack right beside me. The boots skidded on the gravel, and the jack began to slide and topple. Above me, the Jaguar, missing its rear wheels, shifted to one side as the jack lost traction. I had started to squirm out of harm's way, but the car collapsed with a whump, my head and torso still beneath.

Receding footsteps on the gravel, walking, not running. I couldn't feel my legs. My hand shook where it still clutched the giant wrench. My rapid breathing rasped out in slower and slower bursts.

Birdsong echoed somewhere above me. Wait, I *could* feel my legs. They wriggled and kicked.

"Higgs! Help me! Get me out! Get me out! Where did that guy go?"

No reply. I tried to move myself. If only my feet could find purchase, I could slither along the mat. My fingers still encircled the wrench. I noticed this from the corner of my eye as if it was someone else's hand. The wrench handle was embedded in the earth beneath the gravel, and the other end forked around the axle overhead. My reflex must have been to turn the wrench to halt the collapse of the car when the mystery visitor so rudely dropped it on me. It was all that separated me from a crushed skull. I surrendered my quivering grasp, worrying as if my hand strength was contributing to its support.

I dug in my heels and pulled. Progress was slow, but I inched my way toward daylight. I slid on the mat and turned my head to the side to give myself enough clearance to emerge from beneath the car. A smudge of road dirt from the sill of the rear door accompanied a slight graze on my cheek as I popped free.

I sprinted as best I could to the pavement outside our fence and glared both directions. No sign of my attacker.

I'm not going to make it to adulthood. That's the second time in two days someone has tried to kill me.

The man wore gloves, so there would be no fingerprints. But I looked around the discarded tire iron for a clod of spittle.

I knelt on all threes, cradling my left arm to reduce the throbbing, as I searched for my attacker's phlegm. There it was! I gingerly pinched a large shard of gravel encrusted with the man's DNA. I carried it with care to the house, calling for Higgs and Lars as I entered. They must have left while I was under the car. Snatching a ziplock bag, I deposited the gravel nugget complete with its DNA-filled drizzle.

"Gotcha, you evil git!"

I'd best get Newton analysing that spit sample. But there must be something I was missing about the car—better keep looking.

I jacked the car up again and replaced the wheels. After I lowered it, I examined the driver controls to check for anything unusual.

I slid my torso in through the passenger door, resting on my stomach and right elbow on the seat while my legs dangled out onto the driveway. I kept my left arm clutched to my chest to dull the pain, and the throbbing fled my mind as I attended to the investigation at hand. First, I looked at the seat belt clasp using the beam from my phone. Annoyingly, it turned on in flashing mode instead of the steady beam. I wondered why this was a primary function of the phone's torch. Did the miniscule chance of needing a flashing phone light when lost on a snow-capped mountain really justify it? I switched it back to its normal beam and peered into the slot in the seat belt clasp where the buckle would normally dock.

When I was younger, I disassembled and reassembled everything we owned that my parents would allow me to fiddle with. A spring-loaded pin should be visible. It gets displaced as the seat belt buckle slides in, or when someone presses the button to release the belt. The pin wasn't visible as I peered through the slot. I wearied of having one eye screwed closed, trying to discern the interior workings, so I put my set of small screwdrivers to use and opened the clasp's body.

The scene inside the housing was decidedly abnormal. It was scorched, as if a small fire had broken out, but not enough to damage anything outside the clasp. It was invisible unless you dissected it, as I had. Fragments of the pin that should hold the belt buckle properly clasped fell onto the leather seat as I opened it further. The spring that normally held the pin in place through the rectangular hole in the buckle was only discernable as shards of curly metal debris. Clearly, a small explosion had occurred inside. It was enough to ruin any chance of the seat belt being used to restrain the driver while creating no obvious signs of sabotage.

This confirmed that my father's crash was no accident either. Someone intended it to look like one, but they had used sophisticated technology to take control away from the driver.

Positioning the proper torch from the toolbox for my next phase of investigation, I texted Newton. "Got Dad's Jag from impound. Seat belt sabotaged with tiny explosive. Looking again at brakes now. Come home ASAP." I put the phone on the dashboard but then sent a second text. "Oh, and a guy just tried to kill me. No idea what he looks like, but I snagged his DNA. And I'm okay."

I traced the path from the brake pedal back to the brakes. My subconscious registered the pinging sound of incoming texts above me as I worked with my hips on the seat and my head in the driver's footwell. The torch needed adjustment, but I still ignored the phone. The noise registered as little as a mosquito's whine during an absorbing conversation.

Eventually, I found it. Another small electronic control box spliced into the brake actuator controls, like the remains of the control added to the Jeep's trailer hitch. Someone had planted this pair of devices in my father's car so that the brakes would slam on and release the seat belt simultaneously. Likely, as with the Jeep, they were set to trigger only at a certain speed, high enough to produce a fatal crash.

I experienced more than heard a thundering sound as if I was crouched behind a waterfall, but I knew it wasn't real. I squeezed my eyes shut. My father had been murdered! The sound gave way to ragged breathing. It took me a moment to realise it was my own. I squeezed my eyes shut and slowed my breathing until I felt not calm, but not in a full-on jittery panic.

Mustering the energy, I wriggled from the footwell, which elevated the dull ache in my collarbone to a knifing half-way between my neck and shoulder's wingtip. I ignored it.

There was the whir of an electric car motor as Newton pulled into the driveway, window already rolled down. "I've been texting and calling, but you didn't answer. What good is the technology if you don't use it? What happened?"

CHAPTER 30 -   ANTOINETTE

Higgs

Lars and I sat at the kitchen table. We cleared dirty cups and a crumb-strewn plate away before getting organised to work on our school projects. Faraday clanked about in the basement as we searched for a pencil sharpener, eventually finding one on the windowsill next to the vitamin bottles and three potted cacti. These were the only remaining live plants in the house, the last survivors from the menagerie of flowers, herbs, and ferns that wilted in a series of extinctions after Mum died and my father couldn't find the willpower to tend them.

The clanking travelled to the driveway, culminating in the ratcheting clicks of a car jack as we settled down to write. A light breeze blew the springtime through the back door, riffling our notebook pages while we concentrated. But the peacefulness was cut short. An invasion of dogs burst through the back door and engulfed us in a cacophony of clicking claws, yipping, and scratching sounds, as they leapt and frolicked beside the table where we tried to work. It was a small invasion, consisting only of Disco and Antoinette, the little French bulldog from the Averys' house. Antoinette was a known free roamer of the neighbourhood, but she was friendly and had enough common sense to stay away from the road.

I tried to ignore them, knowing I had to make headway on my project, and that the evening would be a write-off because of the polo club party. I attempted to shoo them away but with only fleeting successes. Lars wasn't helping one little bit. He laughed at their antics. "Look at them, Higgs! They want to play with us. Let's take them for a wee run around."

"Ugh! Well, we're not going to make much progress with them gallivanting around like this." I was sure that Lars had no idea what gallivanting meant, but it's one of those words that sounds like what it means, so he didn't question it. I sighed. "Disco, get your leash."

Disco

"Haha, I don't believe it. It's working!" A little frolic, suck up to the boy, and Higgs agreed to walk us. I heard her say "Disco" and "leash", so I sprinted across and picked up my leash from where it lay abandoned inside the front door. First lesson of being a dog: always know where your leash is.

I signalled with a few head flicks to my bulldog friend. "Get them over the footbridge to Nether Ides, and I can point the way to that boy's house."

She shot out the back door. I dragged Higgs's friend along by the leash. Higgs was still putting on her shoes, but she would catch up. We set off across the back garden and exited through the side gate.

I pulled on the leash hard enough to restrict my breathing, but it was worth it. Higgs's friend broke into a trot behind me. That eased the pressure. Higgs ran to catch up.

Higgs and the boy talked. My friend and I were communicating too, but we didn't have to use our voices. We used primary dog language, positioning our heads in certain ways, getting closer together, touching, adjusting the pattern of our paws striking the pavement, and watching where each other's eyes were roaming. I found the eye communication difficult because one of my eyes didn't follow instructions properly. But I could live with that, though the bulldog found it amusing. That eye often settled its gaze on things I would not have noticed otherwise.

We walked almost to the school, where the path cut off to the canal footbridge. Higgs said something to the boy, and she motioned me to turn around and head back home. I pulled at the leash, but I wasn't strong enough or clever enough to make the boy start down the path. He tugged in the other direction, and I found myself steered home.

My mission! Ruined! How would I ever get Higgs to look at my discovery in that basement?

But like I told you, my friend is smart. She barked twice and raced along the pathway. Higgs came back to see where she went. She stood there, majestic atop the arched footbridge. She gave the three of us a good hard stare and growled in a low voice that I didn't know she had. She inched backwards over the bridge hump until all that we could see were her ear tips. A compelling performance. I willed it to work.

Higgs

Oh, that Antoinette was a pain sometimes. Just as we turned around, she took off barking. Next thing I knew, she was astride the canal footbridge and backing over the brow, growling. She had street smarts, but I thought she might pursue something across the canal and get lost.

"Jeez, Antoinette. For real?"

I reluctantly started along the path to the bridge and motioned for Lars to follow with Disco. When we got mid-bridge, Antoinette reversed, still growling, then turned and disappeared from view around the corner of the hedge that lined the pathway. We jogged over to see where she had gone, but she stopped as soon as she turned onto Canal Street in Nether Ides. She had a quick look at Disco then crossed the street with Disco alongside, straining at her leash.

Lars got into the mystery. "Maybe she smells something? Could it be a skunk? I've never seen a skunk."

"Uh, Sweden boy, there aren't any skunks in England. You've been watching too many American videos." I said this in a deadpan voice, but his boyish enthusiasm amused me. We continued walking at pace, chasing some invisible lure as if we were a school of mindless fish following a fisherman's bait.

And then I was embarrassed to find we had stopped right in front of Gregor Radzinski's house. If he looked out and saw me here, he'd probably think I was stalking him. He likely pegged me as weird already, without this to add fuel to the fire. "Come on, people—people and dogs. This is far enough. Let's go home."

I turned away from Gregor's house, and heard Lars behind me, chiding, "Come on Disco, you heard her."

But I looked back, and Disco was frantic, standing right up on her hind legs at the extreme range of her leash, trying to get onto Gregor's lawn. Antoinette gracefully hopped over the small shrub border as Disco made a powerful lunge and the leash twanged tight in Lars's hand before he lost his grip. It was an amazing leap; Disco cleared the hedge with an impressive amount of room to spare. I don't think I had ever seen her jump that high before. Both dogs vanished from sight, making gentle yips from somewhere behind Gregor's house.

"I tried to hang on, I really did," Lars said. "But she's much stronger than I thought."

"Well, you let her go, you can go get her. I'm not going to get caught prowling around Gregor's house." I was exasperated, and it showed in my voice.

"Wait, this is Gregor's house? I'm not going to get caught in there either. At least he likes you. If you get caught, he'll easily forgive you. You'll probably get tea and a plate of biscuits out of it. How about we go in together?"

It made sense. I reluctantly nodded in agreement. "Okay, okay. But let's not get caught."

We cautiously sidled through the gate, then stooped and hurried across the lawn at the side of the house, following the arc where the dogs had scampered off. As we peeked around the corner, we saw them, and they were in a very curious pose. They both sat stock still, perched on their haunches, in front of a small window that looked into the house at ground level. They didn't turn to us as we crept closer, trying to keep our breathing silent but knowing that we wouldn't evade the dogs' sharp senses.

We slinked right up, the final approach taken at a crawl. Eight eyes peered through the window. Or maybe seven; I noticed that one of Disco's eyes was tracking a butterfly that drifted lazily above the grass to our side.

I didn't immediately clue in to what the dogs fixated on. It was unusual for dogs to pay attention to video screens, so it wasn't my first instinct to look at the computer screen. Instead, I scanned the basement room for signs of a cat or something else dog-attracting moving around. But then Lars inhaled sharply, and he pointed a pinky finger at the high resolution computer screen on the desk below.

That screen had a street map of Middle Ides in precise detail. Superimposed on the map, we recognised the faces of several schoolmates from the West Ides school. Each face appeared in an oval hovering over the map, with an arrowhead indicating a specific location. Lars and I both appeared there, with hastily-taken photos. Our images sat side by side in the map's lower-left corner, and our two arrows pointed to the same spot on the map. My eyes were binoculars, zeroing in on the our location on the map, and it became clear they indicated Gregor's street, here at the back of his house.

Lars and I simultaneously lifted our heads and scanned the area. We were being tracked, and it was natural to look for cameras. I snapped two swift photos with my phone's camera, but Lars looked spooked by the whole thing. His voice came in an urgent whisper. "Let's get out of here. Something bad is happening."

The alarm in his tone made me bristle. It's frightening enough to have someone staring at you, but this was a whole other level of unwanted attention. The hairs on my arms and the back of my neck rose in alarm. I think Disco sensed this too. A ridge of fur rose along her spine, like when she got territorial at an unexpected knock on the door.

Two or three rapid reverse crawling steps, then twenty running paces and all four of us were back at the roadside, Disco dragging her leash behind her. Lars shot along the road at a sprint, but then realised he was abandoning us and turned to wait until we caught up.

"What in the Underworld was that?" he said once we had crossed the canal and slowed from a run to a brisk walk.

"I don't know. Some kind of tracking system? The map extended as far east as Little Ides. I saw Dot's picture in the top-right corner, where the Pendlethwaite estate is. He's tracking all of us!" I would never get my homework done at this rate.

CHAPTER 31 - INTERFERENCE

Newton

Faraday summarised what he had found in Dad's car and recounted the fracas with the black-booted attacker. Since his epiphany at the Jeep accident site, I had been preparing myself to accept that our father hadn't just died—he was murdered. The phone record quirk persuaded me a step closer, and this discovery in the Jaguar confirmed it.

I made myself step back and consider how this appeared from a policing perspective. "The forensic team combed through the vehicle and didn't find either the seat belt problem or the device in the brake controls. They'll think we fabricated this if we reopen the investigation now."

"Yeah, I feel you. It looks suspicious that the car sat in the pound for months with nothing wrong discovered, and then on the day I retrieve it these signs of sabotage appear like a miracle. But you believe me, don't you? The forensic team wouldn't have looked for any computerised devices in a vehicle of this age, and it's tiny and well-hidden. I also doubt anyone wore the seat belt between the accident and today. They towed the Jag from the scene to the pound, and maybe nobody bothered to put the belt on to drive it around on the lot."

"Of course I believe you! And there's more." I told him about the phone record discrepancies.

"Newt, come on! This is enough. Ask them to open a full case. They attacked me twice. Cops should be swarming all over this investigation now! Dad was murdered, and nobody but us is investigating?"

"I can't, Faraday. It really isn't enough. If I go to them now, they'll think we're unhinged, trying to imagine a crime as we search for a way out of our loss. We need more."

We were both quiet for a moment. Faraday would see the logic in what I said. It was always logic that worked with him, even when he got fired up.

"How about this? I'll report the attack on you and take in the spit sample so they can run it against our DNA database. But I won't say anything about the car tampering."

Faraday paused. "Well, let's find something else. I found the car servicing records, and there was nothing abnormal. But we could look at the phone bill. Dad was such a Luddite he kept getting the paper bills despite pressure to accept online billing."

That was a great idea. Maybe someone tampered with the online records recently and expunged a number that would be on the paper copy. We hurried to the basement and pulled open the same filing cabinet drawer that Faraday had checked earlier. The phone bills were in a separate file alongside the car servicing history.

Faraday pulled out the file, laid it atop the filing cabinet, and flicked to the last bill. Then he had to page back a few months because we weren't organised enough to end the cell phone service for Dad's phone right away, and several bills had no call time logged. We spotted the right bill—the columns of detailed call information contrasted against the previous, sparsely annotated pages.

"Damn! Same thing here. Look how the last number he called is blanked out. And more blank ones down here. Bloody hell!" I swept the whole folder aside, and the pages of several years' worth of phone records scattered in an arc around me. I shouted in wordless frustration while Faraday stepped back, looking helpless.

"Wait, Newt, wait! There's one thing that nobody could tamper with. You know how Dad always had his journal with him and took notes about everything? Maybe there's something written there. Where did we put it?"

Faraday started opening filing cabinet drawers and frantically hunted around the basement shelves, nooks, and crannies. He wasn't looking thoroughly, as if he expected Dad's leather-bound notebook to eject itself into his hands, if only he could make his gaze fall on the right spot. For once, I was the calmer sibling. I remembered that we had filed it somewhere, but I struggled to recall where.

Faraday aborted his search, cradling his left arm. He had tried to move something on an upper shelf and jarred his injury. I looked away from the tears of pain and frustration welling up in his eyes, and a memory flashed into my mind. I strode to Dad's desk, which was still strewn with much of the clutter of his work and side projects. "It's in the little desk drawer."

My memory proved correct. I fished the small notebook from the shallow central drawer in the oak desk. "Come on, let's sit you down before you pass out on me. We can look through this on the sofa upstairs."

Faraday

Newton was right. I needed to sit. I asked him to get me a cup of tea and another round of my painkillers. Desperate to pore through Dad's notebook, I realised the price of my tea was that I wouldn't start without him. Skimming my fingers over the cover's texture—worn leather softened by 100,000 casual touches—consoled me, knowing it had conspired with Dad's jacket pocket countless times.

With a mug of tea each, we opened the notebook. The first few pages were names and address details of various people, organised tidily in black ink and his familiar, precise printing. We looked at the first few names. Some people we knew, others were names he had mentioned, but many were unknown to us or added using only initials. I let the notebook fall open to the final written pages to see what he had been jotting just before he died.

The last notes were about unusual activity in Haiti. He had been to Haiti several times for work—whatever his work actually entailed—but not within the last year of his life. Most notes were cryptic. They seemed intended only to record details for his own recollection. They weren't coherent enough for anyone else to make sense of. Dates appeared at the top of each section of notes, so at least we had a smidgeon of context for piecing together the mostly impenetrable musings.

Reading backwards from those final notations, there were a few sections that meant little to us. Something about Romanian gypsies, a train derailment in Mongolia, and a reference to a Pendletoad, whatever that was. Both Newt and I pointed at the same time to the same section of dense acronym-laced text as we turned the next page.

"Hidden folder in UPDAweb. Thrúd was investigating nAno???"

UPDA. There it was again.

Newt said, "Why doesn't anyone know what UPDA stands for? I asked at the police station. My boss hadn't heard of it, but he's asking quiet questions of his contacts in London."

My brain stem fizzed. "But Dad obviously knew about the UPDA. He had access to their systems and found something. I can't imagine him hacking into anything—he could barely operate his smartphone—so it seems like he had legitimate access and uncovered something unexpected."

"Let's keep looking. Now we have something to scan for. UPDA."

This was a perfect job for me. With something precise to scan for, I could do it at high speed. I turned page after page, not reading, but waiting for that pattern of letters to leap out at me. There it was again, in notes from 2 months before his death.

"UPDA re-org. My new director is HPL."

And a month before that:

"New headlights. UPDA anti-tracking. All 3 cars."

I flicked backwards, turning each page faster than the last, but certain I wouldn't miss another instance of UPDA if it appeared on any page. It was like I was a fashion photographer, shooting frame after frame with the intuition to intervene when the right shot was in the can, without going back to find the perfect image. But then I stopped flipping pages, troubled by something that I couldn't quite identify somewhere in the mad jumble of processed text.

"Help me here, Newt. I saw something jarring on one of these last pages, but I'm not sure what. Take a look."

I turned back a page, and we both scanned it. There was nothing decipherable. Back another page, then another. I spotted it. A small item printed in the margin.

"nAno and Higgs – manicures."

Both Newton and I came to the same set of conclusions at the same time, and we ping-ponged the logic between us.

"'nAno' is Dad's shorthand for Mum. I remember her and Higgs going for a manicure together a few months ago," Newton began.

"The capital A is for Alison, and nano is her specialty. I thought it was only a strange way of printing earlier."

"So he suspected UPDA was investigating her."

"And he worked for the UPDA. The mention of the re-org suggests he was getting a new boss."

"And they gave him some special high-tech car headlights."

"But close to his accident, he found a secret file that made him believe his own organisation had been investigating Mum for some reason."

"It sounds like the person he figured led the investigation is … *Thrúd?*"

I felt my eyes widen and pulse race and realised I was clutching a handful of my hair in my right hand. "This will sound like a *Scoobie Doo* episode, but there are 2 things to look at immediately, and we should split up to get them done quickly. I'm going to check out the headlights, you look at Dad's contact list and see if you can figure out who Thrúd is."

My collarbone still throbbed, but there was no way I was waiting for the painkillers to kick in. I adjusted my arm in the padded sling and pushed myself off the sofa with my other arm. The tools were still out front, so I left to inspect the cars. Newton had already turned to the journal's beginning and was looking at the finely printed list of contacts.

I started with the Jaguar. It turned out that the most sophisticated tool I needed to make the initial investigation was the torch app on my phone. I knelt, finding myself eye to paw with the leaping jaguar hood ornament. The car had four headlights—two owl eye main lights above the closer-set pair of smaller fog lights—framing the bloated-top oval of the front grill.

When I directed the torch beam into the smaller pair of lights, I saw something foreign inside the clear glass of the bulb. A white device hugged its lower contour. It blended well with the colour of the bulb, but a tiny red LED glowing on the device revealed it as an anomaly.

I detected the same device with ease in both Mum's electric BMW and the Jeep, now that I knew what to look for. There wasn't much more to investigate without breaking the bulbs. I desperately wanted a closer look, but I remembered that we were trying to gather enough evidence to get the police involved without making us seem like nutters. I would leave the forensics to the police this time.

I didn't understand what Dad implied when he scrawled 'anti-tracking', but the predicted device existed in 6 headlights of our 3 cars. That was proof that Templeton Redferne was involved with or worked for the UPDA. Whatever that was.

Newton

I analysed the list of names written in the first few notebook pages. Although the pages were small, it amazed me how many contacts squeezed into the available space in Dad's precise, condensed print.

My concentration was broken for a moment as two text messages arrived. One was from Iain Vanderkamp, returning the voicemail I left earlier and saying he would see us at the polo party. The other was a terse message from my Detective Chief Inspector. He had been unable to make contact with his Intelligence officer pal, but he would try again on Monday. I was optimistic that Iain could furnish us with more information, but disappointed about the defunct line of inquiry through my police channels.

Thrúd was a strange name. I wasn't sure if it was a first or a last name, so I made an internet search for it on my phone while I surveyed the fine print of the contact list. Faraday could have done this task ten times quicker, but it sidetracked me pondering 'Thrúd' at the same time as I considered each printed name in the journal. I had an inkling of who it might be before I found the name and phone number, helpfully placed in a section—mostly of initials—under a heading of 'UPDA'. It would have made my job easier if I had spotted it earlier.

I put the digits into my mobile phone and went to the front step where Faraday uncoiled stiffly from behind the BMW's grille, rising into the afternoon glare. "There are definitely miniature devices inside the headlights of all three cars, although I can't tell what they do without breaking a headlight and checking it more intimately," he said. "But we both knew there would be, didn't we?"

"Yes. Not surprised." I nodded. "But let's talk to Thrúd." I pressed the call button and turned on my phone's speaker. The call connected.

Faraday looked panicked. "Don't let him see your phone number!"

A thin smile tightened my lips. "Come on, I'm actually a police officer, not some teenager angry after a breakup. I added 141 before dialling to hide my number. Oh, and if my internet searching is correct, Thrúd is a 'she', not a 'he'. Let's find out."

Two more rings emerged from the phone before the clatter of the call being answered. The sound of a female voice. With a single word, we heard the hint of a foreign accent. "Hello?"

We remained silent. I held my breath as if the sound of exhaling might reveal my identity to the woman on the phone. There was a short pause, then another, "Hello?"

I spoke deliberately and neutrally, lowering and slowing my voice in an impromptu attempt to disguise it. "I know what happened at the Feynman Centre." Then I hung up.

Faraday's mouth was half-open as his eyes flicked away from mine and then back again. "Wait. Wasn't that—?"

I cut him off. "Yes. Almost definitely."

CHAPTER 32 -   'SNIPS

Higgs

So much for our homework! The afternoon's revelation about Gregor had Lars and me befuddled. The first half of the way home from Gregor's place was a blind sprint. Plenty of thinking and discussion occupied the second half, once we caught our breath.

"There's a lot to figure out here," Lars started. "He's actually monitoring everyone at school, and a few adults too that I noticed—but *why* is he doing it?"

I was quick to add to the list of unanswered questions. "And *how* is he doing it? We don't know that either. Is he tracking our mobile phones?"

"Well, my phone is charging back at your house, so it's definitely not that."

"And what about Disco and Antoinette? They practically dragged us here. How did that happen? It's like they knew Gregor was spying on us. It doesn't make sense."

"Yes, that is weird. I hadn't thought that far. You are so smart!"

My fists clenched involuntarily. "Maybe we should run right back there and ask him. Then we'd find out."

But Lars was, as usual, the voice of reason. "Well, it's true that we caught him with his beard in the letterbox. But what if he's dangerous? And why would he tell us anything? What are you going to do, threaten to set Antoinette on him? He would just laugh."

I laughed too. "Lars, around here we don't get our beards in letterboxes, we get caught with our hands in cookie jars."

He nodded. "That sounds a lot tastier."

"And less sexist too. Or wait, do most Swedish girls have beards?"

We chatted more on the way back home, but no sensible answers surfaced. Disco paused at the doorway as if saying a voiceless goodbye to Antoinette before the bulldog trotted toward her house. I unlocked the door and called a tentative "hello" into the house, but there was no answer. Mum's car was gone, so I guessed that the boys were both out together. Maybe they wanted to help Alan with last-minute set up for the polo club party.

My brain pulsed with the desire to decipher Gregor's scheme. "I'd say the only thing we figured out was that we *can't* figure anything out."

Lars thought for a moment. "Well, if a smarty trousers like you—"

"Smarty *pants*."

"Okay, if a smarty pants like you can't figure it out, we need help. Where are your brothers?"

"Not here. I could call them, I guess."

"Or what about Dot? She knows Gregor too. Let's call her."

I called Dot, but I wanted to speak face to face, so I told her there was something important that Lars and I needed to talk to her about. She appealed to me for more details but eventually agreed to get dolled up early for the polo club dinner and come to my house to pick us up.

"Okay, Lars, she's going to give us a ride to the polo club. I have to get ready, so make yourself a snack or something. Help yourself to whatever you can find in the fridge or the cupboards. But check the best before dates—some stuff may be ready to slither off on its own."

I dashed upstairs. There wasn't time for a shower, so I slapped on a fresh layer of deodorant and a black velvet Alice band to push my hair back and hopefully distract anyone from examining it up close. I slipped out of my jeans and trainers and picked out a mid-length orange floral dress. I wasn't a dress-wearing kind of girl, but I was now the same dress size as my mother had been, so there were several to choose from. It felt both saddening and comforting to put on her clothes. I could never decide if I enjoyed doing it or not.

It felt respectful to wear the bracelet that Lars's mother had given to me. Does a gold bracelet match an orange dress? Who knows? I went with it. I slotted the matching spectacles into my handbag. I could show my new 'treasure' to the boys later.

Taking a long gaze in the mirror, I looked more womanly than I felt, but I wasn't sure if that was only me seeing Mother in the reflection or if I really looked more than a girl. And although I wasn't a dress aficionado, my shoe selection was enviable. The closetful were all mine.

I picked out a pair of shiny black leather pumps. They were both scuffed at the toe, so I carried them downstairs and started the hunt for shoe polish. Lars had finished snacking, or possibly had found nothing edible, and he turned from gazing out the back window when my stockinged feet slid in.

"Wow! Fancy! And surprisingly, your hair looks even better. Let me take a photo for my mother. She'll love that you are wearing the bracelet."

I could tell he was only giving me an honest compliment, as a friend, and it wasn't awkward for either of us. I still puzzled about the hair thing, though. All I'd done was pull it into a more spiked up position with the Alice band. But, whatever.

I opened three or four drawers in the kitchen before finding the black polish and a brush. I set to work re-introducing shine to the shoes, angling some elbow behind the strokes. The soft rasping of bristles on leather soothed me into a brief trance.

"Could he have cameras all around town?"

Lars considered it, then discounted the idea. "That's too many cameras. And he had Dot on the map—do you really think he has cameras inside the Pendlethwaite estate? It's making me feel uncomfortable to think about it, but maybe he planted tracking devices on us."

"On everybody? But we'd notice, wouldn't we? Feel a lump in our clothes or wherever he might attach a device?"

A car horn sounded outside. I judged the polish job sufficient, grabbed my phone and slipped on the shoes. "Don't forget your phone, Lars. It's still hanging from the charging cable there."

I scrawled a short note to the boys, saying that I was at the polo club early with Dot. Lars was already out the front door, ogling the shining black Mercedes waiting for us in the driveway. It came with a driver, of course—a perk of being a Pendlethwaite. Dot waved from the back window and opened the door for Lars.

"This is amazing. I get to ride in a Jaguar and a car with its own driver on the same day. What's the driver called again? A chuffer?"

I left the front door open a crack, and walked over to the car where Lars had already slid in beside Dot. She was *really* dressed up. She had on a tailor-fitted black jacket over a frilly white blouse, and what looked like a real ruby pendant on a gold chain around her neck, a dramatic contrast to her pale skin. She clearly had more prep time than I did, and had washed her hair. "This is like the three bears in Goldilocks," she said. "One of us is underdressed, one overdressed, and you are the baby bear, Higgs: just right."

"Ha, yeah. Well, baby bear didn't have enough time to do a proper job of dressing herself. And I hate to get dog hairs all over your car—and us—but can Disco come too? She loves the polo ponies, so we can leave her at the stables while we are inside at the party."

I knew Dot would agree, but asked out of politeness. I glanced sidelong at the driver whose job doubtless included removing every tiny whippet hair from the car.

"Of course! Bring her out."

Lars volunteered to take Disco in his lap since he wasn't invited to the party anyway, and he could shed any clinging dog hairs as he jogged home after our pow-wow. The drive was short, and we spent the time on inconsequential chit chat. I motioned that we should hold off on the real conversation until we were beyond the driver's earshot. Dot looked worried, still not knowing what we were so desperate to talk about, but she restrained herself for the entire trip.

The driver released us to the pavement outside the polo club gate, and the three of us (plus Disco) huddled up close to the peeling white paint of the concrete wall surrounding the club. The green expanse of the polo field lay beyond the car park, with the clubhouse a hive of preparation activity on our left.

I couldn't quite blurt out the news, so I said the first other thing that popped into my mind. "So ... we saw a Pendlethwaite Parsnips lorry outside the bakery. Is that your father's company?"

Dot looked at me wide-eyed, and burst into tears. "I *knew* you'd figure it out. I'm so sorry. I didn't mean it."

This took me aback, but I did what any good friend would do and held her in a tight hug, saying in neutral but reassuring tones, "It's okay, Dot, it's okay."

Lars stood helpless behind Dot. He shrugged, opening his palms to me and giving me quizzical eyebrows. I tried to communicate with only my eyes, flashing the universal signal for, "I'm confused too!"

"I should never have helped them cast the spell!" Dot wailed, still clasping me apologetically.

"Wait, what spell?"

She released me, but stayed close, dabbing her eyes and nose with the lining of her jacket sleeve, trying to avoid leaving any exposed smears. "I helped them cast the anti-science spell, and I was supposed to think purely about that. But my dad made me throw in an extra thought—how good parsnips taste. And then ... well ... I accidentally thought the third thing. And now look what happened to poor Mr Shinoto!" A muted wail accompanied more tears.

I looked her in the eye reassuringly and gripped her shoulder. "Okay, slow down. It's all going to be fine, just tell us what happened."

Lars was looking impressed and amazed. You could hear it in his voice as he followed on with, "You cast a spell? Really? That's so cool. And it worked amazing! Look at everybody eating parsnips!"

"I know you might not believe me, but it's true. They come around to our house for secret meetings, and then they brought me along to be the 'pure thinker' needed for this particular spell. They get everything set up, and I'm in the circle's centre. You know how focused I get when I'm really concentrating, so they got me to focus on one pure thought. The spell takes that thought, and it came out in my breath in a form that lets the idea take hold in others. But only if the breath gets lit on fire. Then it can affect people near to the flame. So they got me to breathe into a series of paper bags. I guess they took the bags and burnt them somewhere so the spell could affect the people they wanted to fall under its influence."

This would have been unbelievable if I heard it from anyone else, but with Dot, I knew in my core that she spoke the truth. "So they wanted you to think about making people act against science?"

"Yes, they hate science. They are followers of magic, so of course they don't like science. They think it's interfering with nature, and they are always saying that nature is the foundation of magic. I focused on this drawing that I made to keep me thinking about only one thing. It was an atomic drawing of a carbon atom that I copied from our school textbook. I added a frowning face in the middle as a reminder that I should put negative feelings into the thought. I held it in front of me in my left hand while they chanted, and then I closed my eyes and thought of only that idea. Well, not only about that. I kept my right hand in the pocket of my hoodie, where I was holding a freshly-picked parsnip that my father gave me. My dad isn't one of *them*. He doesn't know any magic, but he lets them meet at our house."

"And you said you thought a third thing too?" I prompted.

She looked down at the tips of her silver boots. "It's embarrassing."

Lars stepped forward and put his arm around her shoulders. "Come on Dot, it's us. We won't tell anybody. It can't be that bad." Disco leant against her leg in a show of emotional support.

"It's Higgs's haircut. My mind wandered, and I started thinking about how on point it looks."

I chuckled, then laughed out loud, doubling over. That explained a lot about the last little while, with so many people admiring my perfectly average hair.

Dot murmured, "It's not that funny." But she was smiling again.

Lars was laughing too, then stopped. "Wait! Parsnips, Higgs's hair … you put the spell on me too!" He looked at his hands as if somehow he might detect a magical residue on them.

"I didn't put the spell on you directly. Lord only knows what they did with the magic-filled paper bags, but they must have burned one somewhere near you."

"Nobody was burning any paper bags near me. Not that I saw anyway, and that's something you'd notice. But I deffo have the spell on me because I can't stop eating parsnips. Neither can my mother, so she must have it on her too."

I wanted to get to the problem's root, but I still reeled at the thought of my best friend casting a magic spell that had affected most of Middle Ides. "So who are these magicians, anyway? Are you one of them?"

"Well, I have a knack for magic, apparently. They started to train me, but I can't do anything on my own yet. And I don't know who they are. A couple of them have familiar voices, though they try to obscure them, but I never get to see any faces because they dress in hooded robes and wear frightening masks the whole time. Their masks all have different designs— metal, leather, and feathers formed into exaggerated animal faces. There's a long-beaked bird, a lion, a wolf, and a few others. Six or seven altogether. And although they call themselves witches, two are men. I definitely recognize one voice, and I'm sure I'll figure out who it is eventually. And I get the feeling that they are local, although they often refer to themselves as the Pendle Hill cabal. I think they have some history there. It's up north somewhere, isn't it?"

"That's what …" Lars began.

But I finished, "… My grandmother was talking to us about! Some priest dragged over the bodies of a group of witches from Pendle Hill. They were hanged at York. He sunk them in the pond up there in the hills somewhere. This group must be linked to the original Pendle Hill witches' cabal somehow."

Lars smirked. "They're the Knights of the Drowned Cabal."

We all smiled at that line. The name would stick. "But why didn't you keep to the one pure thought? Why did your father make you mix in the parsnip stuff? I thought you guys were rich. It's not like Lord Pendlethwaite needs to pump up his parsnip business using magic, does he?"

She shook her head. "My dad isn't doing as well as you might think. Yes, we had a lot of money, but some of his businesses are struggling. He thought this would be a harmless and easy way to improve things for us. I don't think Dad wanted me to get involved, but you know how he had liver cancer a couple of years ago? He told me the cabal used another spell to infuse ginger root with an anti-cancer spell that kept it at bay. They threatened to stop producing it for him when he refused to get me involved initially. I wish I'd never got mixed up in this mess."

Then I remembered why we met early with Dot. "I'm glad you confessed all of this, Dot, I really am. But you aren't going to like this next part. We had no idea about your spell. We wanted to talk to you about something Gregor did."

"Jeez," she started. "I guess you would have found out eventually, anyway. Just don't tell *anyone*. My dad would kill me if he knew I even told you two." She laughed, a little bitterly. "So what did Gregor do?"

CHAPTER 33 -   PONIES

Disco

Higgs and her friends were talking. They huddled together in their pack. I was on my leash still, but nobody held it. And I could smell the horses. I loved the horses here. And most of them liked me, except for that shaggy one. She was cranky with me for some reason. My rogue eye swivelled to look at the stable building. I slunk off through the gate and trotted the length of the fence to the stables skirting the polo field.

I could understand a few things that horses said, and they could understand some parts of dog language too. There were fourteen horses in the stable, so I popped from one stall to the next saying hello—even to the shaggy one. My leash dragged behind, looking more and more like an exotic caterpillar as it picked up pieces of straw.

I had another friend here too. He entered the stable as I finished greeting my horse friends. He was a boy named something like 'Rover', but that was a dog name, not a people name. Maybe I got it wrong. He probably loved me more than the horses and shouted, "Disco!" in a loud but surprisingly high-pitched voice when he saw me.

He limped towards me, favouring his good leg. The other one was twisted to the side and always had been. I sped over to him. I thought I was getting faster these days. All the walks must be making me healthier. I jumped up and tried to lick his face. He tumbled backwards but landed softly on the stable floor. We had a minor tussle. He was always cheerful. Eventually, we both calmed down, and he got to his feet. The boy unclipped my leash and slung it over a stall door.

He grabbed a brush, and I went with him into each stall. He brushed the horses lovingly. They bent their knees and lifted their hooves without him asking. He picked out the little pieces of stone or mud that stuck around the horseshoes' contours. He re-braided one horse's mane while I paced circles around and underneath, brushing up against the horse's legs.

To explain horse ideas to a dog is a challenge. But this boy spent so much time with the polo ponies, and with me, that he managed it. He talked the whole time. I didn't understand the words, but he signalled and coaxed the horse to tell me the secrets of jumping over hedges and fences. The horse showed how to move your legs during the approach; how you lean back for a moment, then push mostly up, not forward. And the landing is important if you jump high. I took a few practice leaps in slow motion. The three of us pranced around the stall, laughing, until I got the hang of it.

CHAPTER 34 -   BROKEN

Higgs

"Now that we made you accidentally reveal you're a witch," I gave Dot a reassuring smile at this point to signal I was only being cheeky, "let's talk about something else. Gregor is tracking and spying on everyone at school."

Dot asked four questions that all meant the same thing. "What? Gregor? Really? What do you mean?"

Lars explained what we had seen, with plenty of interruptions and additions from me. I showed her the photos of the tracking map on my phone. They weren't great quality, but her brow furrowed as she brought my phone screen close to her eyes.

Dot wrinkled her nose for a moment, formulating her first questions, but Lars asked one first. "Could Disco and Antoinette be magic too? Is that how they led us there?"

He was full swing into the spirit of this magic stuff. I guess that reflected his implicit belief in Dot. She laughed and said, "I've never heard of magic used on or by dogs, but I'm hardly an expert in this stuff. I'm more like Robin than Batman when it comes to magic. But I'm reassessing Gregor's behaviour at school," she continued. "He sure moves between all the cliques, so I'm guessing he plants tracking devices on people individually. If he was tracking their phones or somehow hacking their social media accounts to get their location check-ins, he would need to install something on their phones, and he wouldn't need to interact with them at all. Could he be hacking them from his computer?"

"I left my phone at Higgs's house, but I saw myself on his tracking map, so it's not a phone tracker," Lars said.

"But he's always flitting from group to group, from person to person, so maybe he attaches some kind of device to them. Or I guess I should say, *to us.*"

I considered this. "Hmm. He is touchy-feely, isn't he? I always figured that was his way of being friendly, but now it's giving me the creeps."

Lars had his own experience. "Yeah! Even in the boys' change room, he's like that. Remember I told you that his signature prank is to spray his deodorant down your back while you are changing shirts?"

Dot smiled at the changing room reference. "Get away, Lars. He's not tracking you by smell. He'd need to plant a device on you, not just a spritz of 'Girl Magnet' behind your ears."

I blurted out a response before I considered its implications. "If my mother was here, she'd tell you that even a puff of mist could be a fleet of tiny machines, built to do something miraculous."

CHAPTER 35 -   POLO

Faraday

Newton looked dapper in his suit, complete with a textured black waistcoat. I still wore my only shirt with a collar, the same Hawaiian pattern I had worn all day. It likely had gravel dust and car grease in places, but people darted strange looks my way no matter what I wore, so I hadn't bothered changing. I wore nicer shoes than earlier—a pair of black Chelsea boots. I crammed my pockets with the usual assortment of potentially useful items, and I loaded the nanotubes into the back of the car to show Iain when he arrived at the party.

Higgs and Lars hadn't returned with Disco yet, but their homework lay arrayed on the dining table, so we knew they'd be back at some point. Dot would likely pick them up on her way to the party, so we'd catch up with her there.

We rolled up early and had our choice of spots in the parking lot of the polo club. Chronos' motorbike crouched on the paving stones alongside the stables. He ambled to the car as we closed its doors.

"Boys, good to see some of you are looking sharp!"

Chronos was dressed in modern bouncer attire: steel-toed boots, black slacks, and a black suit jacket unbuttoned over a crisp white shirt. No tie, removing any chance of being choked with it in a scuffle.

Newton said, "Hey, brother. Anything we can help with since we are here early?"

"I've been asking Alan the same question for the last hour, and he insists everything is just so. I've been sampling the catering, and I agree with him so far. You could help by trying a range of drinks, which I'm avoiding because I'm technically on duty."

"We'll go for a wander around the polo field until more people arrive. I haven't been over to the far side since they put up those new risers for the spectators. Tell Alan we're here, and that you can text us if he needs any help."

"I'll mention there's a one-armed Hawaiian character out here willing to help. Maybe his ukulele player called in sick, and he needs an urgent replacement."

"Don't be jealous of my threads," I said. "Oh, and do you know Iain Vanderkamp, who worked with Mum? If you spot him, tell him I'm here, and I'll catch up with him soon. He can text or call when he arrives."

"Will do. Quiet drink at the end of the party?"

We both agreed, then strolled in the lea of the stables toward the green expanse of the playing field.

I wanted to run through our evidence, to make sure that Newton agreed with my conclusions and had nothing else to add. We talked as we walked, staying close and keeping our voices low.

"Two car sabotages, a near crushing by a mystery person who I can only identify by spit and boots, and redacted phone records. Those are the key unsolved elements."

Newton nodded. "Agreed. And further cover-up in the Feynman Centre at the time of Mum's death. The diary points to the UPDA, which Dad was working for, being involved." A twitch rippled across Newton's features that involved eye-widening, an eyebrow wave and subtle nostril dilation. "Damn, brother—I haven't even told you about the attack on Higgs and me last night!"

"Wait. Somebody tried to kill you too? And you forgot to mention it?"

"Not really somebody—some *things*. There were some tiny drones disguised as dragonflies in our yard. They sizzled the screen in Higgs's bedroom then fired a load of tiny darts at us. I thought maybe they were poisoned, but we're both feeling okay today. And there was a thing with a vine. All very hard to describe and impossible to explain. Higgs and I can tell you the whole story after the party."

There's a mental technique called 'parking'. It's a way of handling information or emotion that threatens to overwhelm you, placing it to one side so you don't need to process it immediately. You can come back to it later, more rationally than in the heat of the moment. An attack on my siblings by dart-wielding mechanical dragonflies in the middle of the night triggered something deep within me that I wrestled down and parked.

"Okay, I want to hear about that. Later. What about the phone call to Thrúd? It re-opens a whole raft of earlier mysteries, doesn't it? And by the way, how did you figure out who Thrúd was?"

As we rounded the end of the stables, a high-pitched voice greeted us. "Hi, guys. Is Disco with you?"

It was Grover, the stable boy. The polo club employed him, but even if they didn't, it would be hard to keep him away from the place. He adored the horses and had done since he was a toddler. He started here as a weekend job when he was 13, and because school never really worked for him, his parents negotiated for him to work here full-time from his 15th birthday.

I sympathised with him, although he was at the other end of the spectrum from me. He was in my year, but he had trouble learning anything at school, whereas I learned too much for school to be very useful. It suited neither of us. But despite his learning difficulties, he had an incredible empathy with the horses. With little instruction, he kept every polo pony in top condition, figuring out their niggling injuries as if he felt them himself.

"Grover! Hey, my man. We didn't bring Disco with us this time."

"Can you let her come with you next time?"

"Yes, of course," Newton said. "I can drop her off with you tomorrow, then go see my Granny up the road while you play with her. She'd love that."

"Okay. Thank you. What's your name again? I'm going back to the horses now. The Spanish guys aren't riding them tonight."

I wanted to correct him that the star polo players weren't Spanish, they were Argentinian, but realised the distinction would be lost on him, and I'd end up in a conversation leading nowhere fast.

"I'm Faraday. You can remember it by thinking of me bringing Disco to visit you. That means it's a *furry day*."

"See you tomorrow, Furry-Day."

Newton was smiling as we walked onto the field. "He's met you two hundred times. But you might be in with a chance of getting him to remember your name this time."

"I'd tell him to envision a newt when he looks at you. But I'm not sure he knows what a newt is. Let's save that for another day."

"Anyway, back to Thrúd. While you were looking at the devices planted in the headlights, I did some internet searching. Know who Thrúd is, in Norse mythology? It's Thor's daughter."

"Trust Dad to come up with that. Thorisdottir! Of course he'd call her Thrúd."

"So if she's involved, Scarlett's tidy pinning of the first crop of weird incidents onto Mr Shinoto is a cover-up. Could there be a wider conspiracy involved in the lorry attack, the explosion just up the road, and the EMP at the club?"

I massaged my shoulder, avoiding the collarbone itself. "The UPDA has both hands in the mix, twisting things. I still don't know what their remit is, but I'm sceptical of everything in that investigation now. And I *never* believed that Shinoto was responsible for what we experienced that night behind the Feynman Centre. He's a science teacher, not a magic tree charmer."

"That's another excellent reason not to report our suspicions about everything in a formal police case yet. Whatever UPDA does, we don't have any leverage to fight against it. We may not be able to keep anything we report a secret from them, judging by how effectively their clamps worked earlier."

I scuffed at the grass. We had arrived at the far side of the polo field from the clubhouse. "You're right. But what's the way out of this? We can't decipher everything without asking for help, and we can't ask for help because the UPDA has their filthy tentacles everywhere."

My phone beeped as I said this. It was Iain, texting his arrival. "Wait. There are still people who can help us. Let's see what Iain has to say regarding the nanotubes."

We picked up the pace for our return walk. What would Iain be able to tell me when he inspected the nanotubes? Tell *us*, I should say. No more secrets.

"Do you think we're all in danger? I've escaped death twice already."

"Probably. The Jeep attack could've got either of us. You were the unlucky driver, but it could just as easily have been me. Or all three of us. The second attack targeted you specifically, but perhaps that's because you were the first one of us that Mr Boots encountered."

"Agreed. And to me, the two incidents feel unrelated. The Jeep attack was impersonal and remote, using technology to hide the intention and to make it appear like any other car accident. Same with sabotaging the Jaguar. But this afternoon, that was different. That's a person appearing at our house with ill intentions. And delivering a message first. With the omnipresent CCTV coverage these days, that's a reckless way to approach whatever problem we represent."

Newton squinted with an expression like he had swallowed and regurgitated a spoonful of fish oil. "We'd better figure this out fast. We're back to square zero, with everything unexplained, very few avenues to ask for help, and the UPDA interfering at every step. Let's hope Iain can give us some clues."

"Faraday, over here!" I spotted Iain's scraggly profile moving toward us through the filling car park. I waved him toward our car.

"Wow, look at you, Faraday!"

"It's my only collared shirt."

"No, no—the shirt looks good. But you're a bit of a wreck if you don't mind me saying so. It sounds like you were lucky to walk away from that car accident."

"Phew, yes. It's not like in the movies where the hero just strides away from a flaming wreck with not a hair out of place. But let's ignore all that for now. I really want to hear what you can tell us about the nanotubes."

"I've been waiting for this show and tell! And hi, Newton. I didn't mean to leave you out, but you look like a proper party-goer, not a co-conspirator."

We reached our car, and Newton popped the boot open. Iain leaned in and peered at the tubes, picking up and inspecting one. "Yep. These are the same style of Fūjikome tubes we use in our experiments at the lab. Same kind of crypto key, too. Like this one."

Iain fished a keyring from his trouser pocket and showed us the array of plastic slivers with exposed metal contact points that I recognised from our video call earlier. The gold contacts were the teeth for the key to interact with the locks on the tube caps. He tried each of them on the tube and scowled when none of them produced any results.

"I wasn't optimistic, but it can't hurt to try."

He inspected the ruptured tube and shone the light from his phone inside. "This one sure looks like it held experimental nanotech. I see what look like traces of the residue that we often use to suspend the nanodevices during storage. I'll need to check with a microscope to know more."

I held out my hand. "There are a couple more things that might help. Take these USB drives that I found in Mum's secret lab. I couldn't interpret anything on there, but you'll have more luck, I'm sure. I also created a folder on one called 'Notebook'. It's got photos of the pages in Mum's notebook that I took from the site."

Iain took the USBs and slipped them into an inside pocket of his suit jacket. "Seems like I might leave the party early. I'm not patient enough not to dig straight into this. I feel like a proper intelligence officer on a top-secret project."

Newton locked eyes with Iain. "It needs to stay a secret, right? We're not sure what's going on here, but this isn't just a side hobby of Mum's. Both our parents are dead, under suspicious circumstances, and we know we're being watched too."

Iain glanced around, shuffling his weight from one foot to the other. "Okay, I won't connect these tubes to my laptop right here. And you'd better keep them for now—it's better if we keep the USB data and the tubes separate. That way if one gets compromised, we can still work with the other."

Newt put a hand on the car's hatch to close it. "Wait a second. Take a quick peek at the notation on the tubes and try to decipher it. Here are Mum's notes on the labelling."

Iain looked at the photo on my phone of the notebook page with the annotated list of letters that appeared on the tube ends. He inspected the tubes, referring to the photo as he progressed through each one. He paused at the broken tube. "You say this one broke open near your dog?"

"Yeah. It flew the farthest from the Jeep and landed on the road right beside Disco."

"Is she okay? Like, she's healthy still?"

"She walked with us this morning, she seems perfectly fine. Even perkier than normal. Why?"

"Well, you see the annotation on the tube, $W/S^C/F$? I'm sure the F is what we had been working on at the Feynman Centre. It's nanotech capable of flying. Well, self-directed floating is a better description. We only managed to get them to re-direct themselves slightly while drifting on air currents. And the S^C could well mean 'canis seeker'—something that targets dogs. My initial guess is that she was working on nanotech that would drift around and seek specific targets. But the C is cryptic. It could also mean bats—chiroptera—or several other families or genera of animals."

"And what does 'whips' mean?"

"That part I'm unsure of. We started working on how groups of nanomachines could bond and work together, like Lego pieces forming a structure that can do something more useful than individual nodes can on their own. So maybe she was building nanotech that would combine on or in a dog, or other animal, to perform some sort of whip action. That's vague, but I'm really speculating now. I'd need to look at the schematics to give a proper answer. It's possibly something like a nano dog groomer that you spray onto your dog, and it automatically straightens and aligns strands of fur."

I chuckled. "If that's what she was designing, I'd say it's a failure. Disco looks the same as ever. Although I can't say whippets need much grooming, so maybe you're right."

Iain glanced around furtively. Newton closed the car boot. "Will you call me as soon as you get any insight into what she was doing? Seriously, call me even if it's the middle of the night, especially if you spot something that's puzzling to you. I want to know as soon as you find *anything*."

"I will, guys, I will. And I feel bad about not telling you sooner about those happenings when Alison died. I'd like to talk more about that. But not here. Not now. I can't shake the feeling we're being watched."

CHAPTER 36 -   PENDLE HILL

Faraday

The guests arrived, a trickle at first, then a horde. I monitored Iain as he mingled, noticing his instinctive palming of his chest, checking the USB drives remained safely stowed in his inner pocket. He avoided contact with Newton and me as if men in black glasses and earpieces might descend on us at any moment.

At events like this, I tended to shadow Newton or Higgs, so they could rescue me if I ran out of conversation topics or nudge me if I started off on a tangent and eyes glazed over. The polo party was a particular social whirl for us. There were many of our parents' friends circulating who we rarely encountered and took this prime opportunity to repeat their condolences and ask after our well-being.

I noticed Dot and Higgs arrive, both dressed several rungs higher on the swankiness ladder than I was. They were intercepted on their way into the room by an older gentleman with a missing ear who I recognised from Higgs's earlier description. He beamed at them and broke into animated conversation. I wanted to slip over and meet him, to figure out how he knew Granny so well, but Newt and I were accosted by three of the visiting polo players. They were conspicuous in the crowd, being the only ones wearing polo jerseys. Their short sleeves distinguished them from those in more formal dress. This was intentional—Alan insisted on it to identify them as the guests of honour.

"*Hola*, Mr Redferne," one of them said to Newton. "Do you remember me? Your father helped me with my work visa when Mr Ryder brought me over from Buenos Aires to play for the team."

"I remember you, but I hate to admit I have forgotten your name."

"I am Gabriel. Gabriel Diaz. And my fellow players here are Faustino and Marco Antonio."

I offered my unslung arm, and a round of handshakes ensued. "We used to come to the matches often, with our parents, but we haven't come at all since last year. My favourite part is when you have to change ponies mid-match, and you gallop off to the stables for a quick switch."

"Ha. We hope for that to not happen, but sometimes it is not to be avoided."

I knew the basics of polo handicapping, but probably not enough to sound educated. Each player was rated between -2 and 10, where the difference in the teams' total handicap was added to the lower-rated team's score at the end of the match. The last British player to achieve the exceedingly rare 10 handicap died in 1957. The current 10 handicapper list was all Argentinian.

"And what's your handicap? Is the team looking good this year?"

Gabriel answered while his countrymen nodded in harmony. "We play in the 20-22 handicap tournaments. Faustino and I are both playing at 6, but look at Marco Antonio there. He was an ugly child, so he practised more than us. He's fantastic. An 8!"

Their laughter echoed above the susurration of the conversation in the room. Both Gabriel and Faustino slung their arms over Marco Antonio's broad shoulders and shook him.

"Our number four is here somewhere too. He's our secret weapon—for a 2 handicap, he's a great defender."

Most polo players have ratings of 2 or less—about 90 percent—so being a talented 2 still puts one in the top 10 per cent worldwide.

"Let's go for the question Alan likely asks you every week. Will we beat Manchester Polo this year? That's the important thing, isn't it?"

Marco Antonio, just as handsome as his teammates despite their ribbing, answered. "We plan to show them our horseshoes."

I laughed at the expression, imagining these three darting past their opponents, clods of turf flying into the faces of Idesians' bitterest enemies. "I hope so! Newton, we should go to some matches."

The players made their excuses and circulated. We weaved our way over to Dot and Higgs.

Higgs

The clubhouse was filling with guests by the time we entered. I affected nonchalance in my passing fist bump to Chronos as Dot and I smiled our way across the threshold where he loitered. I spotted several familiar faces bobbing on the sea of jostling shoulders. Newton and Faraday were talking to the club's polo players. Alan Ryder waved as we entered from near the window-laden far wall.

Our newfound acquaintance, Beauregarde Device, was nearby when we strolled in, and he approached with a wry grin. "Let's hope there aren't any detonations after we meet again this time, eh?"

"Agreed! One explosion is enough for any lifetime, in my opinion. Plus, Dot had to extinguish her flaming science teacher shortly after that incident at Alan's house. Too much action around here for my liking."

"I heard about the science teacher. I'm a nature lover than a scientist myself, but what the reports say he did is so extreme. It's hard to understand what would make a person behave like that."

Dot, if it was possible, seemed to turn paler at the comment. "It was horrible. I don't want to remember."

"Well, despite that horror, let's hope science can find a way to protect the natural environment. I'm glad to see that's a primary goal for your generation."

I nodded. "Exactly. We'll all be amazed at what happens when today's youth doubles down on our priorities. There's enough wisdom out there to accomplish the changes we so desperately need."

"Good for you, Higgs. Look, I've been meaning to ask you something. Angelina was always into the natural practices hereabouts. Maybe you'd consider following in her footsteps? I help to organise some people who take a keen interest in keeping nature's balance. It might not make sense to everyone, but I think we've gone too far with all this science and technology. Your mother would have had a different opinion, but it just seems like we're trampling the spirit of the natural world. Want to come along and participate some time?"

He produced a business card from his suit jacket pocket with a practised flourish and proffered it. "Sounds interesting. I'll give you a call next week, and you can tell me more details."

He smiled and gave a half nod. "Excellent, just excellent. I think Dot is already involved. It's good to have some youth members so we can pass the torch."

Beauregarde sauntered off, waving at a woman in a purple hat who beckoned to him.

I looked sideways at Dot. She eased into an increasingly vigorous series of nods. "Yes, yes! He's one of them. I think he's tiger mask, but I deffo recognise the voice now."

Faraday's shirt flapped around his sling-cradled arm as he deked his way through the crowd toward us. I almost laughed out loud at his sorry state. "Aloha," I said.

Newton arrived in his wake. "Hey, girls. You're refreshingly young-looking. What do you guess the average age of the crowd is?"

Dot smiled, a touch of colour returning after the previous conversation. "You're right. I don't see too many little kids around here, but I seem to remember Higgs and I spent most of our time outside or lurking under draped tablecloths in previous years. So it's possible they're here, hiding."

"Was that guy who just left your new one-eared friend from Granny's?" Faraday asked.

I rolled my eyes. "Did you see any other one-eared old men here? That's him. Beauregarde Device. He's trying to convince Dot and I to come out to some meetings he's organising. A nature preservation thing. But he's a little odd."

Faraday stared at the back of Beauregarde's receding head as he picked his way through the crowd. His eyes narrowed as if he could see one layer deeper than anyone else. "Something looks familiar about him. I should remember seeing him before, with that unusual ear stub, but I can't quite place where I've bumped into him."

"Yeah. *Eerie*, isn't he?" Oh, how we laughed.

"Anyway, boys, I have more Middle Ides weirdness to tell you. But it's a long story, so later, after the party." I gave the slightest glance in Dot's direction, and she responded with a hint of a resigned shrug.

Newton tugged at Faraday's shirt collar, then smoothed it down. "Hey, leave the ladies alone now, puppy dog. Higgs, we'll catch you near the end, and we can all have a quiet conflab once Chronos is off duty. I'll snag a bottle of Champagne now and get him to hold it for us."

Faraday gave us a facetious half-bow as he backed away. Dot recognised an older woman, a friend of her father's, so I gave her a playful push on the shoulder and circulated alone.

After a complete circuit of the room and far too many looks and conversations of condolence, I encountered a man that used to help Mum maintain the Ides Giant. He was a former history professor at Leeds University and looked the part in a sports jacket complete with leather patches at the elbows. He was old enough to deserve grey hair but had a thick head of glossy black locks that fell in waves to his shoulders.

"Good evening, Higgs. You look so much like your mother, now that you're growing up. It's great to see you again."

"Professor Alwyn! And you're looking remarkably unchanged."

"I'll take that as a compliment. Do you ever do any maintenance of the Giant these days, or is that a bit behind you now?"

I shrugged and glanced down and to one side momentarily. "Nah. I rarely go up there. Faraday still does. But hey, I do have some history questions if you're game."

"Of course. Normally I just bore people with it, but there's a glimmer of hope I might not put you to sleep if you've got something specific in mind."

I outlined Granny's tales of the witches and the pond, omitting the parts where the Pendletoad crept in. If anyone might know more, it would be a local history buff.

"That's interesting. I should go up and see Angelina. She might know more than I do. But there are several things to relate. There are old hand-written diaries that mention your man, the priest, bringing the supposed witches from Pendle Hill—hanged at York—here to Middle Ides. So yes, your grandmother's story of them being sunk into Ashton Pond could very well be true.

"And that was an unusual witch trial. Many of those accused truly believed they had magical powers and didn't deny the charges. The normal state of witch trials was for the accused to plead innocence. But not in this case. There were twelve charged in total, in 1612. I can't remember every name, but it started when they accused Alizon Device of putting a curse on a local shopkeeper in Pendle Hill, who subsequently fell ill. Her grandmother Elizabeth Southerns was a rumoured and renowned witch, and both were ultimately found guilty and hanged. But maybe Angelina didn't tell you about one of the families mixed up in the affair. A family embroiled in a longstanding feud with Elizabeth Southerns and her family?"

"Um, no. What family is that?"

"Ha. That was a cheeky omission. It was the Redferne family, dragged into the mess along with the Southerns and the Devices. Yes, there were Redfernes on trial too. If I recall correctly, there must have been one or two hanged, because the only person found not guilty was Alice Grey."

"Whoa. Run that back. Granny was going off into fuzzy land, but she said a while back, 'the Redfernes all know. Always watching grey devices. It's still happening.' Now you're mentioning the Greys, the Devices, and the Redfernes—all tied up in these witch trials?"

I nodded in Beauregarde's direction. "And there's a Device there, right? Alan's neighbour?"

"Of course, that's Beau Device. Yeah, I guess he might come from the Lancashire Device family. I hadn't really considered that before."

I felt as if scorching water filled me from the chest up to my ears. "There's too much going on in this town."

The professor smiled. "That's the brilliant thing about history. It surrounds you, even if you rarely stop to consider it. I wonder if we could get a grant to investigate Ashton Pond. Imagine if the remains linger down there. Your ancestors, even!"

I imagined Lars standing beside me. His eyes would be bulging from his skull and his lips trembling with the urge to mention the Pendletoad.

"And look at your bangle—that must have a history too!" I held out my wrist to offer him a closer inspection. "For sure. Celtic engraving work there. Possibly Scottish. Is it old?"

"I don't know really. I got these old inscribed glasses from Granny, then found this matching bracelet at the Trove of Wonders."

I produced the glasses from my handbag. He pushed his own glasses up the bridge of his nose and inspected them closely, turning them as he peered. "That's quite the heirloom. Exquisite workmanship. Did she tell you their history?"

"No. She only inferred I might need them, for some reason."

I put them on to model them properly. As my gaze swept the room, I noticed that most of the guests had the same rainbow aura around them that I had seen around Lars when I wore them previously. Professor Alwyn glowed pleasantly, as did many of my parents' old friends, but Dot, my brothers, and Beauregarde looked the same with the specs on or off.

Dot scooted in and bumped hips with me. "Hey, there you are!"

The bubbling cauldron in my mind was coming to a boil, but I didn't recognise the potion. It was time to delve into Dot's magical escapades.

CHAPTER 37 -   NARROWBOAT

Higgs

The polo club party was pleasant, but recent revelations distracted me too much to enjoy it. "Let's exit stage left, Dot. Are you up for a stroll outside?"

Dot nodded, so we figured we should say a final thank you to Alan Ryder, who lingered at the entrance to the principal room. We made our way over, slaloming through the crowd with an occasional wave and murmured greeting as we recognised people.

"I can remember one party here when you two were only about four or five years old." Alan chuckled. "You disappeared under a table over there in the corner where we arranged the desserts, and you pulled the tablecloth down so you were barely visible. Your mother was frantically trying to find you, Higgs, and when she flicked up the tablecloth, both of you had thick masks of cupcake icing on your faces. If I remember correctly, you were blue-faced, Dot, and you were orange, Higgs."

A wide smile transformed my face. "I can vaguely remember that—Mum was really mad but laughed at us too."

It was Dot's turn to chime in. "And then she hurried us through those doors over there, onto the grass to clean us up. And you had those enormous dogs. They came and licked our faces clean."

Alan roared. "Stunning memory, yes! Those were our Russian wolfhounds, Doris and Judy. They were so tall they had to lower their snouts to do the licking. It's amazing that you spent your first party here covered in icing, and look at you both now! All grown up. I'm so glad you still show up, even though it must be a bore for you."

Honestly, this was the most interesting polo club event I had ever been to, but not for reasons of social entertainment. "I'm so grateful to you for having me. And my brothers. Attending events like this prove we still exist."

He gave me a fatherly hug and offered Dot an exaggerated kiss on the hand before moving off to talk to some of his other guests.

I nodded at the exit. "Come on Dot, let's find a quieter place to discuss your status as Little Ides's youngest witch."

We strolled arm-in-arm onto the lawn between the entrance to the clubhouse and the parking area. The night was warm, and clusters of party-goers decorated the lawn. Cars negotiated the car park, with a few latecomers still arriving. It didn't seem private enough to discuss sinister powers. "Let's go to our narrowboat. It's tethered around the next bend in the canal at the other edge of the polo field. We'll grab Disco on the way back."

The gibbous moon reflected from the canal's gentle arc in a series of silver-threaded ripples glimmering on the polo ground's opposite margin. Dot and I walked slowly but purposefully toward it, skirting the playing field as we talked about Gregor.

I was still uncertain about how to feel. "He's a lot nicer than most guys at school. Why would he want to do something like this?"

"I don't get it either. He gives me the creeps a bit, but most boys give me the creeps, so I guess that's nothing unusual. And at least he talks with us. That's more mature of him than the other losers. But could he really have planted trackers on us that are too small to detect?"

"You should see the stuff that my mother studied. There are substances and tiny machines that can do crazy stuff, but you need a microscope to get a hint of their existence. So yeah, I can easily believe that something sprayed like a mist can track a person. But he can't make that kind of stuff from spare parts in his garage; it takes a mass of specialised equipment to create anything like that. Somebody must be backing him."

"But that still doesn't make sense. If he has some high-tech helpers, why would they want to track school kids? In Middle Ides? Wouldn't they want to track criminals or endangered species or something more interesting?" Dot shrugged and shook her head slightly.

"It's possibly a trial run," I said. "And if it works here, they can use it for real on something more important."

"Hey, should we see if Lars wants to join us? We sort of ditched him because he wasn't invited to the party, but it will save re-explaining everything to him later."

I figured that was an excellent idea, so I texted him and he replied that he was locking up his mother's shop, and would run up to the narrowboat.

We arrived at the canal's towpath and turned east, heading to my family's narrowboat mooring a short distance away. Narrowboats are well-named—they must be less than seven feet wide so that two can pass each other in normal parts of the canals webbed across England, Scotland, and Wales. There are sections where only one narrowboat can proceed at a time, and there were two such circumstances just east of our mooring. The first was the Ides Aqueduct, built in the 1790s, that allowed the canal to cross the Ides river valley. Its seven stone arches carried the canal in a metal-lined trough, across to meet the steep and rocky hillside of Little Ides Rise. From there it continued into the Little Ides tunnel, emerging on the other side to views of the Pendlethwaite estate.

Narrowboat navigation protocol demands one to turn on their bow light when entering the tunnel in a first-to-enter right of way tradition. Sometimes a narrowboat crossing the aqueduct would encounter another already in the tunnel and must bide its time at the widening beside the tunnel entrance. Two narrowboats can wait there, one on either side of the tunnel entrance, allowing a third narrowboat venturing through the tunnel from Little Ides to emerge and pass onto the aqueduct. We could see all of these picturesque elements as we turned to follow the canal.

The Redferne narrowboat was like most others that still travelled the canals. Narrow, like its name, it was still fifty feet long, with an almost indestructible metal hull and painted what would have been called fire engine red in its heyday but should now be named 'fading embers red with a lot of chipping'. Its name was The Red Fern, and it rested among a set of six permanent moorings, with neighbouring vessels Slow Hand and Falling Star.

The towpath was cement here, and the narrowboats were tied off to the T-shaped cleats fixed into the towpath. Some narrowboats had one line at each end tied off, and longer ones had a third line reaching out from the middle. Because there are no tides or waves in a canal, we fasten the lines without slack, the narrowboats hugging the towpath walls with protective foam fenders squeezed between wall and hull.

Although the boats that originally plied the canals were working boats, teeming with cargo and drawn by a canal horse, almost all modern narrowboats had been converted for comfort. Typically, this meant one or two beds, a galley kitchen and dining area near the rear, and a bathroom, often complete with a cramped shower. A well-outfitted narrowboat might have limited headroom, but would make a comfortable and charming home if one was prepared to live in its confined space.

The Red Fern was well-appointed enough to work as a permanent home, but it was only ever used for family canal trips and these days rarely left its mooring. It was more like a hidden getaway for us; a place to stretch out with a book on the roof for a sunny afternoon, or a secluded spot to meet with friends on a rainy morning or starlit evening. It was the perfect place to have a quiet chat with Dot to help me handle her earlier revelations. Did she want me to help her escape from the Knights of the Drowned Cabal? Or, now that she had exercised her fledgeling powers, did she need me to support her in exploring them in a more positive way?

As we approached the line of moored boats, a voice called out from the next boat along from The Red Fern. A man stood in the stern of Falling Star, his form no more than a black outline in the single overhead streetlight's meagre glow.

"Higgs, Dot. I'm glad you are out here. We can talk freely now."

Dot whispered harsh words in my ear. "That's Beauregarde again."

I swivelled around to whisper back. "Okay, let's be cautious. He's a bit intimidating, but I want to talk to him now that there aren't all the eavesdroppers at the club. Stay close."

I gave him a half-wave as we approached, still keeping a healthy distance. "Hello again. Listen, I think you were trying to suggest back at the polo club that my family was involved in some concealed magic. What exactly were you getting at?"

He half-leapt, half-stepped from the stern onto the towpath, still several paces in front of us. He appraised Dot for a moment, then asked her, "Does she know about you? What you can do?"

Dot nodded and mumbled, "Yes. She knows."

He returned the nod and smiled. It was a crooked, unfriendly smile that he may have believed was encouraging but bordered on scary. "Good. That makes it easier. And yes, Higgs, I was trying to tip you off that I know that your grandmother and Templeton are like us. Practitioners. Magic runs through the Redferne family, just as it does through mine and several others in Middle Ides."

I interrupted him. "I'm not convinced. How do I know you aren't making this up to scare me?"

The one-eared man looked genuinely surprised. "Oh. You didn't know your own history," he said.

"But think carefully. You can't remember any times when he or Angelina managed to do something inexplicable? You might have seen something as a child and suppressed it, or put it down to an overactive imagination?"

I cast my mind back. My father was a definite believer in the supernatural, but I couldn't remember anything concrete. It wasn't in his nature to don one of the masks that Dot had described, or to perform ritualistic spells. My grandmother, sure. She had an aura of mystery that whispered of magic powers, and there was her urging voice in our back garden that night that seemed like a lifetime ago.

My father had always been interested in esoteric topics. I remembered several conversations at the dinner table about whether the Icelandic belief in elves had a root in reality, or whether the voodoo healers in Haiti could perform medically useful interventions. My mother always poured cold, scientific water on these ideas, but she still engaged in the discussions and I could tell that she didn't trivialise or fully disbelieve the propositions. Maybe Dad knew about the magic that Dot had described to Lars and me earlier, but he had wanted to shelter us from it.

"Let's assume I accept that my father and grandmother have insider knowledge of magic. I never saw any evidence of it, so really, what does it have to do with me? Why are you trying to tell me this stuff that's only semi-believable?"

"Okay, if you don't remember anything about your family's magic, what about Dot? Do you believe her? Do you think she has some magic in her?"

My voice flared. "Of course I believe her. She's my best friend. But it seems like she's only a pawn for you and your cabal to work through! It's like you're using her for her innocence. I'm not sure she wants to be involved in your petty magic."

I glanced at Dot, but she didn't leap in to agree. This would have been the perfect time for a, "Hell no!" but I would stand with her, regardless.

Beauregarde took a step closer to us, and I felt Dot's grip tighten around my arm. "There's nothing to fear, Higgs. Magic is part of the natural world, but it's well hidden, like the untapped water that runs beneath the ground, or the pollen that floats, invisible, on warm spring air. And it is a talent that not everyone possesses. It courses through you, Higgs. We can all tell. Even your grandmother knows it, although I have never been able to coax her into encouraging you directly. We can train you. You and Dot both. Come for a few sessions with us and see what you are capable of. Your family is intertwined with us, so all I'm trying to convince you of is to use some of your natural ability."

My instinct was to fight. "Piss off! Wait until I tell my brothers and Mr Ryder what you have dragged Dot into, and what you are suggesting to me. Let's see your poxy magic get you out of that!"

"Now, now, Higgs. It's not like that at all. I'm simply offering you lessons to build your talents into something better, something you can use however you want. You're painting the picture that magic is somehow evil or corrupting, but that attitude is so 1600s. Magic was never about destroying things or bringing power to yourself. Its goal is enhancing the natural world around us. Give it a chance."

"Forget it. Mr Shinoto wouldn't agree with your rosy story, and neither do I. It doesn't matter what you believe my father or grandmother were involved in. You and your friends are finished! Come on Dot, this has gone far enough. We're going back to find Newt right now."

I swivelled on one heel, spinning Dot in a tight arc around me as she gripped my arm like a vise. I felt her tremble with nervousness at the confrontation, but I wasn't scared at all. Angry, yes, but not frightened.

But that changed almost immediately.

CHAPTER 38 -   SHARPIE

Higgs

When we turned together, Dot and I came face-to-chest with a large, black-jacketed man who had made a stealthy approach while we spoke to Beauregarde. Another man, wiry and shaven-headed, advanced from the shadows of the trees flanking the towpath as the first man grabbed Dot and I by our linked arms. Each of his meaty hands encircled a forearm as if we were dolls about to be cast aside.

Dot let out a truncated scream as he ensnared us, but I wasted no time and sprang into silent action. I stamped on our attacker's toe with my full weight. He cursed and released his grip, but quickly grabbed Dot again while I stumbled back a stride.

"Get them both onto the boat. Don't hurt them, though!" hissed Beauregarde. "If she calms down, I'm sure I can persuade her, but if not, we'll have to make sure she stays quiet." The first attacker leant in and, with his free hand, encircled Dot's thin waist with one arm, lifting her bodily. She went limp, softly repeating, "No … no … no …"

The other man approached me at speed, lowering himself into a balanced fighting stance, but he still hadn't closed the full distance between us as I backpedalled along the canal. Aligned with the back end of The Red Fern, I swivelled and sprang to the small, bench-lined navigator's well, avoiding the tiller.

My fingers knew the four-digit code to open the door between the narrowboat's dining room and the open-air rear deck where I stood. Four rapid beeps were followed by the snick of the lock opening, but the entire time I kept my eyes fixed on the second attacker's harsh features. He crossed the towpath and raised a foot to the narrowboat's edge, but he didn't have quite enough momentum to vault himself up. He stumbled back to the towpath, unbalanced.

Then he took a two-footed leap onto the deck. But not before the door shut behind me and the lock turned into place. His tense face was framed by straining neck muscles, and he glared from inches away through the glass door pane as he tried unsuccessfully to turn its handle. He assaulted the door, but it was as solid as the steel hull and refused to budge. I scrambled for my phone in my handbag. My handbag! There it lay on the floor beside my pursuer. I must have dropped it in my hurry through the doorway.

There was only one other way to enter without breaking a thick windowpane or defeating the metal bars that sealed the trap door, amidships in the roof. The stunted hatch from the front deck opens to a set of three stairs from the front lounging deck into the bedroom section. Was it locked? I made a scrambling run through the interior, dodging my way through the galley kitchen, past the bathroom and bedroom to the hatch. Booming, heavy-booted footfalls paced me overhead along the steel roof.

Thankfully, the hatch lock was engaged. It rattled as the man outside tried to force it open. The lock was sturdy, but I had less confidence in the wooden hatch itself. It shuddered and began to crack under the impact of furious booting.

Through the panel, my bald-headed adversary called out, "Get over here! We can smash this in, nay problem."

I dodged back to the kitchen. Was there a way to get a message out? How could I defend myself against two thugs, each twice my size? My prospects looked dismal, and I heard the first signs of wood panels splitting behind me.

I grabbed a Sharpie pen tethered to a small whiteboard beside the galley kitchen sink and ripped it from its string. Anagram. Anagram. Come on, don't fail me now! How could I tell the boys where to find me if I didn't know where these beasts would drag me? It needed to be something these buffoons wouldn't suspect was a message.

Wait! There was a way they *could* find me, wherever I ended up. I wrote directly on the countertop in thick black letters: DISOWN SOCK

I pulled the red cylindrical fire extinguisher from the bracket beside the stove and held it up in front of me, feeling its weight. I wasn't surrendering without a fight. A quick glance over my shoulder showed the one-eared silhouette knocking on a window. The sound of splintering wood from the bow accompanied the hatch tumbling in fragments to the interior of the boat. I glimpsed the moon through the new opening before it was eclipsed by the shadow of an adversary entering the cabin.

I coiled myself, ready to fight, holding the fire extinguisher extended behind me for maximum wind-up. In the distance, I heard a series of three loud but low-frequency grumbling noises. It sounded like the aggressive warning croaks of an enormous toad. Seriously?

CHAPTER 39 -   GREY

Newton

"Hi, Emeline." Come on, Newton, was that the most interesting greeting you could come up with? I had been thinking about this encounter in the lead up to the party and expected awkwardness. And it would have been *really* awkward if she had been my teacher at West Ides, but she was only two years older than I, so thankfully she had taught only Higgs, not Faraday or me.

She smiled and locked eyes with me. Should I glance away? Did my returned smile look artificial? "Newton, I thought you'd be here. It's my first opportunity to see you outside your role as Higgs's guardian."

This wasn't a disaster yet. I needed to dream up something impressive or clever in reply. But the contours of her lips distracted me. "Um, yeah." I needed to focus. "Higgs mentioned the project she's doing in your class. Something about Pendle Hill?"

Those lips parted, and a brief laugh escaped. It was half-amused, but with a somewhat serious undertone. She cleared a sheaf of her striking hair behind her ear with the hand that wasn't cradling the champagne flute. "Yes. We are investigating local historical events from the 1600s, but she settled on that topic herself. An interesting coincidence, given your family. I sent her to talk to your grandmother about it, but it's always hard to guess if you'll get a sensible conversation from Angelina or not, these days."

The undercurrent of this answer puzzled me. There was a lot to unpack. Why would it be a coincidence that Higgs chose that topic? Coincidence with what? Higgs mentioned that Granny Angelina knew extra information about the Pendle Hill events, but it was a surprise that Emeline knew my grandmother, and must have known her since before she got mired in her 'foggy days'. Emeline also implied that Granny would push Higgs's project in a direction that had relevance to our family history. I thought, in a small town, that everyone was supposed to know everything about each other. It seemed I wasn't in the correct gossip circles.

"You know my grandmother? How?" Oh no! This was veering off into police interrogation territory, instead of the hoped-for chance to break the ice. Fortunately, it didn't seem to deter her. She still smiled and didn't withdraw.

"Oh, you don't know either? The Greys and your father's family have a colourful shared history. Well, your grandmother's family, to be precise. It's like we are traditional allies, fighting off anyone that threatens our tiny kingdom. Angelina was a Templeton, and any Templeton will always be a welcome face to a Grey, like me."

A physical flinch passed over me at her use of the name 'Templeton'. It must have been noticeable, because she touched my forearm and said, "I'm so sorry. I wasn't thinking. Of course, that was your father's first name, and I should have avoided it. I got lost in the genealogy."

I knew that my father got his first name from Angelina's maiden name, so it wasn't a surprise. "No, no, it's fine. I don't want everyone to walk on eggshells around us. So many things might trigger those memories, and nobody will know them all. Not even us."

She withdrew her hand, but gradually, casually, not like she recoiled from some horror. "What a relief. It seems you are coping okay, under the circumstances."

"So, what did you expect my grandmother to tell Higgs about Pendle Hill?"

"What Angelina might say on any subject is a riddle I haven't yet solved. I wasn't sure how much Higgs—or you, for that matter—knew about those events already. But it seemed a marvellous opportunity for Angelina to talk to Higgs about … *stuff.* It would be a shame for her knowledge of local history and her special skills to not be passed down to you three."

I remained unsure about the history Emeline referred to, and the skills that might be passed on was a subject that begged exploration. But those topics could wait.

I opened my mouth, preparing to move the conversation to something more neutral, hoping to salvage this chance to chat with Emeline without it devolving into some deep family examination. I secretly hoped for an inspiring idea to rescue me from my open but wordless mouth, but it didn't arrive on cue. Instead, a different form of intervention arrived, and it had every likelihood of ending in a train wreck. It was Faraday.

My brother leapt to our side, coming to a two-foot stop almost touching me, his Hawaiian shirt flapping as he steadied himself. He let out an audible, "Ouch!" and adjusted his arm sling. Surely he would now spew some statistics about car tire density or from how high you needed to drop a bowling ball to break a one-inch thick plate of glass. Any chance of making a wonderful impression on Emeline would evaporate.

What he actually said was an even bigger disaster than anticipated. "Hi, Miss Grey. He won't have said it, but Newt likes you. I mean, *really* likes you. You should go for dinner with him sometime."

To my surprise, Emeline laughed, and glanced back and forth between Faraday and me twice. "Seriously?"

This was a prime opportunity for tongue malfunction, but it somehow produced a confident answer. "Well … yes, actually. And feel free to leave now, Faraday."

He smiled and thumped me in encouragement on the shoulder, wincing again, then sauntered off, looking proud of himself.

"So, yeah. If you agree to come to dinner, I promise I won't bring him."

"I didn't expect this, but yes, of course I will. How's Wednesday?" She pulled her mobile phone from her handbag and started fiddling with the calendar. "I already have your number in here, so how about I call you around seven on Wednesday evening and we can figure out where to go?"

This was unbelievable. Faraday was king where facts ruled, but a court jester in the realm of social interaction. Friendly fire saved me, for once. "I can't wait. I'll talk to you then!" If not sooner, I thought.

This had worked out perfectly. I didn't want to spoil it, so I made an excuse to leave. "Well, I need to round everyone up and head home. It's been an interminable day. See you Wednesday." I gave her a long look before turning away, trying to discern if she had simply felt pressured to accept the offer, or if she truly desired it.

CHAPTER 40 -   TRACE

Newton

I spotted Faraday at the grand room's outer reaches, probably terrorising Alan Ryder and two of his guests who I didn't recognise with his off-kilter ideas. I made my way over, a spring in my step after the success with Emeline.

"Alan, thank you so, so much for continuing to invite us. I'm going to steal Faraday away from you, find Higgs, and head out."

Alan pulled me in for a powerful hug. "It's early, but it's been a busy week for you. I saw Higgs and Dot strolling on the lawn a while back."

"Thanks, we can go look for her. And I'll update you if I get any more word from the station concerning the lorry and wall incidents. Come along, Faraday."

We stepped out and scanned the lawn loiterers, looking for Higgs and Dot. Faraday raised an eyebrow at me. "It worked, didn't it? With Emeline."

I could hear the smile in my voice. "Unbelievably, yes! After I recovered from my heart attack. We're meeting for dinner on Wednesday. But she said some interesting things, about Higgs, Granny, and that Pendle Hill stuff. It's like she knows something concerning our family that's still hidden from us, and she's afraid to say it out loud. That's the actual reason I wanted to leave now. I want to find out what Higgs discovered.

I feel like we haven't seen her for a month, even though we talked an hour ago."

She wasn't visible in the vicinity, so I called her mobile phone. No answer. I flicked through my contacts, found Dot, and called her. No answer there either. I sent Higgs a text, asking her to message me back, then called Lars.

He was breathing heavily when he answered. "Yes, I know where she is. I'm almost there now. She's up at your longboat."

"It's called a *narrowboat*, Lars. You'll find that a longboat is what your ancestors used to invade us, you scrawny little Viking." We both laughed. So did Faraday, who leaned close in a professional eavesdropper's pose.

"But why are you calling me instead of her? Dot's there too, you could call her. And did you hear the Pendletoad making his noise?"

"Huh? What's a Pendletoad? What noise?"

"Your grandmother told us the story of the Pendletoad."

"Oh yeah, she used to frighten us with it when we were little. And so did our father. But it's just a scary story. What does that have to do with Higgs and Dot?"

"It sounded like a story to me too, but I heard a giant toad voice—like a very, very giant toad—a few minutes ago. Is it real?"

"Okay, whatever. I'll tell you what. I'll call Higgs again, and then Faraday and I can walk over to the canal. We'll see you there soon."

I called Higgs and Dot again but got no reply from either. They both rang, but neither girl answered. Faraday had already started walking more briskly, so I hustled to keep pace with him as we passed the polo field and headed to the canal.

A running figure sped toward then past us as we stepped from the fringe of trees onto the dimly lit towpath. The person scrambled to a stop, turned, and sprinted back to us. Once he faced us, we realised it was Lars. He clutched a handbag, which decidedly didn't go with his casual outfit. I recognised it as Higgs's bag.

Breathing hard, he leaned over and pointed back the way he had come, to where The Red Fern was moored. "They're gone … found her bag … door smashed in … come on!" Without waiting for us, he sprinted back the way he had come.

My feet moved without instruction. We ran, nearly keeping up with the fleet Swede. Lars headed to the bow, but Faraday and I chose The Red Fern's stern and leapt at the same time as Lars sprung over the gap at the prow. Even as I keyed the door's unlock code, I saw that there had been mayhem inside.

A side window informed us of a struggle with its spider web of radiating cracks. There was foam sprayed liberally in spurts from the dining table forward to the beds, and the fire extinguisher itself lay discarded on the floor. I held Faraday back as I surveyed the scene in more detail. I heard Lars trampling down the three front stairs and into the cabin.

The second survey found more signs of a serious struggle, now that my phone torch illuminated the scene. Spatters of blood formed an almost artistic pattern on an upper cabinet near the sink, and a trail of crimson drips mixed with the crusty foam. A human tooth, root and all, caked in still-wet blood balanced on the front edge of the narrow countertop as if positioned for a sanguine tooth fairy. Next to an uncapped Sharpie, two words lay in stark contrast to the counter surface. DISOWN SOCK.

I used my authoritative police voice, just as I had been trained. "Lars, stop there. Do not touch *anything*. This is a crime scene, and we need to keep the evidence untouched."

Lars stopped, frozen in his tracks, following my torch beam to the blood trail he straddled. "*Helvete*! What happened here? Where are Higgs and Dot? I have to find them." He started backtracking carefully but quickly, trying to retrace his steps.

"Lars, I need you to focus," I commanded. "Open and look in the two doors as you move backwards. One is the bathroom, and the other is a closet. Make sure there isn't anyone or anything in there."

He didn't question me and did as I ordered. "The bathroom looks normal." A few more backwards steps and then, "Closet is clear too."

I stared in his direction. "Okay, go out your way and come around to the back deck." The gleam of moonlight through the front entrance signalled his retreat, and light footsteps echoed overhead as he trotted across the narrowboat's roof. I wondered why Faraday wasn't pushing on my still-outstretched restraining arm, so I looked over my shoulder to ask what he thought.

I peered back, then had to look down. Faraday was crouched, his hands over his ears as if the silence overwhelmed him. He was quietly, very quietly, whispering to himself. "No. No. Not her too."

Faraday

When Higgs was a toddler, I followed her back and forth through the narrowboat's cabin as it puttered along the canal, and she giggled and squealed at me as she navigated the narrow path between bed, closets, and benches.

When we were 10 and 12, we would angle ourselves on the front bench, reaching our hands forward to be the first to touch the sunlight as we emerged from the Little Ides end of the canal tunnel. Granny Angelina and I had passed through this tunnel on a secret voyage when I was 10, and I remember my hands had been energised by the blazing sunlight. I wanted to share that feeling with my sister.

When I was 16, and she was 14, we would lie side by side on the roof on our towels, taking advantage of rare English sunbathing occasions in the summer. She tried to help me navigate teenage life while I listened and struggled to figure out how to put her ideas into practice.

Last month, I had sat at the cramped table in the main cabin, playing cards with her and her friends. I was aware that they welcomed me as a result of Higgs's invitation, when otherwise I would have barely been tolerated.

On so many expeditions afloat on the canal, I would gaze back from the very front and see my parents chatting, sounds lost in the distance, as they casually directed The Red Fern onward.

But not now. Now they were gone. Mother. Father. Higgs. All taken from us, and we weren't capable of figuring out how. We weren't equipped. Newt didn't have enough power. I was too stupid. The only hope we had was Higgs and her toughness, her willingness to fight. Judging by the havoc in the cabin, she had fought but lost. What flickering hope I had after our discoveries over the last few days were snuffed out like a match in a hurricane.

My vision filled with a shifting pattern of vaguely coloured splotches. My eyes clenched shut. A rush of noise, like a havering wind, was broken only faintly by distant voices. My bones became jelly, encased in muscles that had turned to dry wood. My spine curled, and my head tucked itself between my crouching knees, isolating myself.

I crouched like this for a minute, a day, a week—or was it a year? I couldn't tell. Voices called to me, but from a vast distance. I pushed them to the edge of the world.

And then my sniffer started working.

It had been hiding for so long—detecting smells but refusing to make any impact on me—that I didn't understand it at first. It was like a flame scorched me, and I looked frantically around, unable to find any fire. At first, I couldn't tell that it was a smell. I simply tingled, a message coursing straight to the primitive sections of my brain, and it told me to fight. It told me that the only thing I must do was lash out, to push against the resistance, to use my special talents and follow them, looking nowhere but dead ahead. I smelled my sister, and she told me not to let them steal her from me like this.

I opened my eyes, my ears, and my nostrils and took a deep breath. Lars had somehow materialised beside me, where I crouched on the deck. He was saying to Newton, "I don't care if we can't get through to him! We should leave him here—we have to find Higgs and Dot!" Slung from his shoulder was the small handbag Higgs had been wearing this evening. It dangled in my face, and I could smell her.

"You don't have to leave me anywhere. I'm going to find her." I stood to my full height and looked at Lars, then my brother.

"Thank goodness you're back," Newt began. He looked at me oddly, as if examining something for the first time. "We need you. Higgs doesn't have her phone with her; it's still in her bag. But she left a message for us. For you, really."

The torch beam and his pointing finger directed me to a scrawled message on the counter. DISOWN SOCK.

"She's in Nicholson's Woods. Let's go." Newton looked puzzled. "NICK'S WOODS," I said.

He nodded. "Lars, give me her bag. And you stay here. Don't let anyone in. Is your phone charged? We'll be calling you once we find out more, and you ring us if you hear anything from the girls, okay?"

Lars nodded and stepped onto the back deck to let us pass as we lunged out. He called to our retreating backs, "Call me before anyone else!"

Newton fished out his mobile phone as we ran back toward the polo club. "I'll get some uniformed officers out there now. They can get there before us and start searching."

I grabbed his arm, even though it jarred my throbbing collarbone. "No, Newt. Don't. I can find her. I need to find her. You know that if you bring the police into this and they screw something up and we lose her, it's over for us. We might as well be dead ourselves." He hesitated, still ready to dial. "Newton, only we understand how to find her properly!"

"Oh come on Faraday, how do you always make me throw away my instincts and go along with your plans? You know how things work in the force, I can't just go off on tangents like this!"

I didn't say anything. I just looked him in the eyes, unwavering.

"Dammit. I'm going to regret this." Newton pocketed the phone, and we both started running again.

Our lungs burned as we curved around the polo field's short end, the car now in sight. Breathe, breathe, breathe, Faraday. Disco barked at us. Disco? How did she get here? She ran at full whippet pelt to us from ahead, then did a sharp turn and ran effortlessly beside us. Grover Mann was ahead. He ran on an intercept path, quirking along with his malformed leg, curtailing his speed.

"Hey FurryDay, and FurryDay brother. I was just—"

"No time, Grover," panted Newton as we passed him and left him behind. "Where's Disco's leash?"

"Well, we were playing…"

"Never mind, we'll get it tomorrow."

Sill running, Newton fumbled out the car keys, and we scrambled across the gravel, flinging ourselves into the car. Disco jumped clear across me and settled between us as the car started up and spat gravel. Unable to hold the pull-down handle above the passenger door with my left hand, I clung tightly to the lip of the seat on my right as Newton swung the car in a ragged arc and headed for the exit from the polo club.

Newton drove hard and his brow furrowed in concentration, so I did something I have always wanted to do. I grabbed the magnetic police light and slapped it onto the roof over my head. I had to use my sling-supported left arm, and I paid for it with a grinding feeling and lance of pain, but I will remember that action for the rest of my life.

My awkward hoist included grazing my earlobe as the lamp wobbled past it. Unbidden, an image of Beauregarde's ear stub flashed from my subconscious. "Newt! I remember where I bumped into that Beauregarde Device."

"Who cares? Let me drive."

"You'll care! It's the shape of his ear. I literally bumped into it. In the woods behind the Feynman Centre, when the guy we were chasing disappeared into thin air. Not thin air—it was thick wood. That massive tree stump *was him*. Beauregarde. It was the same height as him, and I bumped my head right against a knobby lump that was *exactly* the same shape as that missing ear of his. I know it makes no sense, but it's time we stopped looking for sense."

"Seriously? I trust your senses, but that's pretty far-fetched."

"I'm getting tingles in my fingers. It feels true."

"One more thing to add to the list of investigations. But focus, Faraday. We need to find Higgs now."

That was the truth. I couldn't go off on a tangent now, no matter how interesting.

We may have caught a little air as the car shot across the canal bridge in the centre of town. We headed for the motorway link road. The electric engine whined as we accelerated toward the roundabout. Newton couldn't risk even a glance at me, he was so intent on the road. He was still recovering from our furious run, so his voice rasped. "Where do we start searching?"

"It's got to be at the inscribed tree where the lorry saboteur lurked. That's the only place that seems relevant. I'm not sure how Higgs knew where she would be taken, but let's start there."

Disco perked her ears up at the mention of Higgs's name. "Yes, Disco, we have to find Higgs," I mumbled to her. She looked like she was listening and tilted her head to one side.

We sped around the roundabout where the motorway link road lay straight ahead, and the road to Nether Ides branched off along the canal side to the right. Rubber screeched. Disco skittered across into Newton's lap and yapped 11 times directly at Newton's driver side window while the tires screeched in protest at our velocity around the roundabout. Wordlessly, Newton shoved her back to my side and sped along the link road, which was mercifully clear of other cars. Disco continued her frenzied barking, now looking behind us.

"Hold on tight," Newton cautioned. "This may get interesting." The tree inscription was on our right, a few hundred yards west on the motorway, but to get there without risking a run across the motorway lanes, we would have to drive to the next junction and double back. Newton apparently had a different plan.

I clutched Disco, who had finally stopped barking, to my right side as Newton slowed a fraction, crossed the link road and ascended the off-ramp slope, hugging the guard rail. We likely had enough room to avoid a head-on collision with exiting motorway traffic, but I prayed we wouldn't see any.

Like most things I hoped for, this too went unfulfilled. A car hurtled past us with a startled looking driver flashing for an instant in our headlights. An SUV followed, slowing as it passed us inches away, snapping off the passenger-side mirror. Disco jerked away from the glancing collision, but I felt strangely unafraid. "Don't worry, Newt. If we get in a crash, you'll have me over here to absorb the impact." He didn't bother to reply. "And Disco can survive anything."

Topping the off-ramp, we sped along the hard shoulder, blue light blazing on the roof. The motorway traffic was light, so cars shifted lanes to give us a wider berth.

"It's right there!" I pointed. The anti-lock brakes did their thing, and we shuddered to a stop, edging onto the grass alongside the hard shoulder. We shot from the car doors as if ejected and headed to the woods. Disco took the quick way out, following Newton, while I lagged as I circled the car. Even from a distance, I could spot the rough carving in the tree bark, emblazoned by moonlight.

CHAPTER 41 -   REDIRECTION

Newton

We both gripped the proper torches that I kept stashed in the glovebox. One, I had instinctively thrust into my pocket as we drove. The beams of light criss-crossed as we approached the spot where the motorway saboteur had lurked what seemed like a lifetime ago. I kept my beam pointed low and in front of me as I ran, looking for any signs of recent disturbance that might indicate someone else's passage. Nothing.

I arrived at the tree several strides ahead of Faraday and shone the torchlight deeper into the woods, looking for lurkers. My brother joined me, and we peered together, scanning the shadowed forest in a semi-circle from the inscribed tree. Still nothing. "I don't know, Faraday. I'm with you on choosing this spot, but I see no signs of disturbance. Could she have meant the helicopter crash site? Now what?"

Faraday pointed his torchlight at his feet, although he looked up and to his left into the moonlit sky. Disco stood at his side, regarding him and sniffing at his leg. "Wait," he said.

"Wait for what? We have to do something!"

There was a pause. "Wait, wait ... wait!"

His head snapped away from the night sky, and he looked at our dog's questioning face. "Disco knows."

"What? What are you talking about?"

"There's another anagram! Disco knows. DISOWN SOCK. DISCO KNOWS."

He knelt and held Disco's head in his cupped right hand. It would have been comical under any other circumstances, but Faraday stared into her eyes and asked, "Disco, can you find Higgs?"

She started barking at once and ran three complete circles around him so quickly I could barely track her. She stopped and stared earnestly at him as he stood.

"Disco—find Higgs."

She sped back to the car at an incredible pace. I tried to follow her course with my flashlight, but I couldn't keep up with her, only illuminating a flapping ear here and a blurred set of pumping legs there. She was scrabbling at the door before Faraday and I had made much progress to follow her.

I popped the doors, and we slid into our seats. While starting the car, I glanced at my brother. "How can Disco know where Higgs is?"

"No idea," he replied, "but she's definitely trying to lead us somewhere." Disco faced backwards, yipping away.

I did a hasty three-point turn, barely avoiding a collision with a swerving curtain-sided lorry. We accelerated along the motorway—in the correct direction for a change—and Disco swivelled to face forward, yipping and urging me to take the exit we had so recently raced up in the wrong direction. We rocketed down the slope and onto the link road, heading back to town.

At the roundabout, Disco started barking at Faraday's window, signalling that we should take the road to Nether Ides. I guess I should have taken the hint the first time when she surged into my lap and almost forced us off the road.

I turned off onto the smaller road and decelerated, but still drove faster than I should. A smattering of small shops dotted the road where we left the roundabout, but shopfronts conceded to houses after that. The whine and whirr of the electric engine echoed back to us as the road narrowed. Disco perched, looking ahead as we sped along the Nether Ides road, canal to our right.

As I approached the pedestrian bridge that led across to West Ides School, Disco scooted across and started scratching at Faraday's door. I edged to the side of the road and pulled over. Faraday scooted from his seat before the car fully halted. Disco lunged off a few car lengths up the road, then turned and waited for us, impatient with a series of small leaps and spins on the spot.

"Is this really going to find Higgs? She can probably smell someone cooking a giant roast beef or something."

Faraday slapped his knee, fire in his voice. "It will work, Newt. We need to follow her."

His newfound conviction was contagious enough for me to trust him and follow along. He caught up to Disco as she turned again. I noticed how dishevelled he looked in his Hawaiian shirt and arm sling, but realised I didn't look much better after the sustained dash.

Disco led us along the street and turned in at a house, ushering us across the lawn with pleading backward looks. In the back garden, Disco slunk up to a darkened basement window and pressed her nose against it. Faraday and I had a look in too, but we couldn't discern much in the deep shadows of the unlit space. Disco sat and continued to stare.

"I don't get it. Why here?"

Faraday was hesitant too, but visibly steeled himself. "Who cares why? Get whoever lives here to the door. And if they don't answer, I'm breaking in. She hasn't led us here for nothing."

"I can't knock on a random person's door and say my dog is on the trail of our missing sister."

"Of course you can, you're a bloody policeman. Find our sister!"

I reluctantly stepped to the back door and rapped insistently with the butt of my torch. "Police! Open up!"

Nobody stirred inside. I knocked again, then turned to Faraday. "Are you really going to break in?"

Instead of answering, he turned and readied his heel to break the small basement window. Before he could act, a light went on inside the back room. I saw someone approach the door, so I repeated, "Police. Come to the door. Keep your hands where I can see them."

It was a teenage boy that answered the door, dressed in a wrinkled T-shirt and track pants. He looked vaguely familiar, but I didn't recognise him immediately. "Um, Newton? Faraday?"

Faraday recognised him and called out in a low, flat voice. "Gregor—you know where Higgs is, don't you?"

His shoulders drooped, and he hung his head. "Dammit. When both of you suddenly appeared up the road, I knew it meant my cover was blown."

I lunged through the half-open door, grabbed him by the collar, and shoved him against the wall, hard. "Where did you take her? Is she here somewhere? Tell me now, or something bad is going to happen."

Gregor's eyes darted between me and Faraday, who was now occupying the doorway. He didn't fight back or try to get me to release him. "Take her? What do you mean, take her? It's only tracking!"

Faraday advanced into the room. "Hang on, Newt, let him go for a sec." He touched my arm with his fingertips, and I let Gregor out of my grasp but maintained my wide stance immediately in front of him.

Faraday continued, an intense gaze locked on Gregor's face. "You said 'tracking'. Are you tracking Higgs somehow?"

"Crap. You *don't* know. Well, didn't know, I guess. Yes, I'm tracking you. And her. I saw your two icons wink into existence up the street, and I figured it was finally turning ugly."

He seemed to forget that he was being threatened by the police and started asking his own questions. "Hey wait, were you just in your car? Did you park over by the footbridge? Now I get it."

I didn't have time for this. "Oi! *We need to find Higgs. Now.* Do you know where she is, or not?"

"Yes, probably. She's not in your car, or at home, is she? If she is, it won't work. Is it okay if I get my phone out? We can find her from there."

"Show me."

Gregor pulled out his mobile phone. It was an expensive new model with an enormous screen. He unlocked it with his fingertip and turned it to show us. "Higgs Redferne," he said, and what we immediately recognised as a map of Middle Ides zoomed in until we could see Higgs's tiny photograph centred on the map. There were a few other pictures in the vicinity, including Dot, whose arrow from her photo appeared to place her in the same spot as Higgs. We could see Lars's icon not too far away.

"This thing is accurate? Higgs and Dot are in the canal tunnel near Little Ides?" I figured it was working, because it showed Lars on the aqueduct, right where we had told him to stay. "How does it work?"

For once, Faraday was uninterested in technology. "Who cares how it works? Let's go get them back."

I grabbed the phone from Gregor, who didn't resist. "You're coming too. Let's go."

The phone was the only link we had to Higgs, so I held it with two hands and passed it to Faraday as if it was a newborn baby. He pressed a button at the map's corner and said, "Faraday Redferne." We were making our way out the back door when he continued. "It's tracking us too, Newton."

Despite being collared doing something very likely illegal, Gregor seemed keen to come with us, so the three of us and Disco hurried to the car. Questions about this tracking business would have to wait—we had higher priorities right now. He seemed mostly harmless.

There wasn't much room on the back seat, so he sat behind Faraday with his legs angled over to the other side, behind me. Disco took up her spot between the front seats, turning periodically with an accusing snaggle-toothed glare at Gregor.

I prepared to scrape the stone wall on the road's opposite side to save wasting time on a three-point turn, but for once things were in my favour. The passenger side, with its missing wing mirror, felt the rush of ivy leaves but must have missed the wall by a fraction of an inch. The electric motor screeched as I put the accelerator flat against the floor and we shot along the Nether Ides road toward the roundabout. There was no way I could drive and make the calls I needed to, so I unlocked my phone with my thumbprint and handed it across to Faraday. He transferred Gregor's phone to his sling-bound hand and did some quick one-handed finger work to open my contact list. "Who first?"

"We promised Lars, so tell him where we're heading, but make sure he doesn't do anything silly. Then the station. And Chronos. We may need his help."

Lars answered the phone before it even rang once on our side. "Newton, did you find her?"

"It's Faraday. And we haven't found her yet, but she's in the canal tunnel, close to the Little Ides end. She's got a tracker on her."

There was a momentary pause, followed by a primal noise of self-criticism. "Argh! Gregor! I should have thought of that twenty minutes ago. I'm such a *dumbom*."

"Wait, you know about Gregor?"

"Yes, we—"

"Forget it. Not now. I have to make more caaaaaalllllls—!"

The car slid sideways slightly on the roundabout before the tires caught and it straightened out again. Faraday hissed in pain and clutched his arm closer to his chest. "But Lars, *do not* go after her yourself. You can sneak across the aqueduct and peek into the tunnel. Check for boats inside, but don't let them notice you. Wait for the police to show before you do anything. We're on our way."

Without waiting for a reply, Faraday hung up and dialled the police station on speakerphone. An officious woman's voice answered promptly. "Middle Ides situation line. State your needs."

I focused on navigating the cobbled high street section while I talked loudly over the vibrating chassis. "Sally, it's Detective Redferne. My sister has been kidnapped, and I believe she is in the canal tunnel a fraction short of Little Ides, possibly on a boat. I need officers—including a tactical unit—to get up there now. She's five foot—"

The voice on the phone cut him off. "I know her. I can do the description. Officers being dispatched now. I'll send a unit to the Middle end and another one up to the Little side."

"And I don't have my radio, so get me on this phone, please. Redferne out."

Faraday called Chronos. "Newt, it's winding down here at the party. I can slink off now. Want to meet me at The Pinnacle?"

"Chronos, listen. It's Faraday. Someone has snatched Higgs from The Red Fern. We aren't sure who, but we think they have her on a different boat in the tunnel. Can you get up to the Little Ides end and meet us there?"

"Damn. Heading to my bike now. I'll tell Ryder, too."

CHAPTER 42 - AQUEDUCT

Newton

"Now it's your turn to talk, Gregor. Why in the world are you tracking your classmates, and how are you doing it?"

I glanced at his face in the rear-view mirror. He looked very alert, but he wasn't getting worked up as he answered. "I treat it as a game or experiment, really. They send me the stuff, and I have to get it onto the people I track. The more people I track, the better they like it. And then we follow them to make sure it's working."

Faraday interjected. "Hang on. Who are 'they' and 'we'? Who are you working with?"

"I don't know. They started calling me four months ago. They pay me to do it, and I get parcels delivered every once in a while with more stuff, and messages in the app from time to time. Initially, they only had me download the app, dab the cream they sent onto the back of my neck, and then test the tracking by having a walk around the neighbourhood without my phone. Once I got home, I checked the app, and it knew the exact route I walked. Then they had me go further and further afield, to work out how far the detection goes. I think it must work almost the same as a mobile phone, because it tracked me around town. It worked from here to Manchester during a family outing. The only place it lost me was when we drove up into the hills to a pub in the middle of nowhere. My dad complained there was no cell coverage, and when I looked back at the tracker, it lost me up there."

"So other people can track us all too?"

"Well, I'm not sure. But I think the app on my phone connects to a centralised tracking system. It's that system that tracks people, not my phone specifically. And after I tested it on myself, they had me track other people."

"So you put the cream on the backs of other people's necks? How?"

"It was easier than that. If I had a tiny smear of cream on my hand, I could touch it to someone, and they'd be tracked. It works most of the time, but not always. I only use a tiny trace, and it seems to depend on whether I get enough on them. Even if it's only on their clothes, it seeps in somehow. I take a photo from the app so that the system knows the latest person to be tracked. Oh—and it's not only the cream. They also gave me a spray, so I use that too, spray it onto people. Leaving a cloud of vapour will get them if they walk through it. I got the two of you that day out in front of your house when I walked home with Higgs. Sorry. I shook your hands, remember?"

Faraday looked at his hand as if he would notice an incriminating blob of cream. "Ew."

"And you have no idea who they are, the people paying you?"

"No. I talked to her twice, and after that, all communication came through the app. She mentioned that I applied to the Territorial Army Officer Training Corps in Northumberland, so maybe that's how they found me."

"She?" I glanced at Faraday. "Well, we'll check the app on your phone. I can get technical forensics to trace which sites the app talks to, and we can triangulate from there. How did you get paid?"

"They sent cash. With the spray and cream shipments."

"Okay, we can check shipping records too. We'll figure out who is co-ordinating this, I'm sure."

"But you know something weird, guys? I couldn't always track Higgs. I never really paid much attention to you two, but it seemed like when Higgs was at home or in the car, she wasn't visible. She kept winking in and out."

Faraday looked again at the phone. "Faraday Redferne … nope, it can't currently find me. Gregor—what's your last name? Okay. Gregor Radzinski … nope, can't find you either. It has greyed out icons on Nether Ides Road where we got into the car. Higgs Redferne … yes, there she is, still in the tunnel. Oh, and what's your unlock code? I'm changing it."

Gregor grinned and nodded to himself. It was like this was only a prank to him. "I knew it! There's something special about your car that interferes with the tracking."

I recalled Dad's notes mentioning the car headlights. Did he know about the tracker? It seemed once again the UPDA, whoever they were, had tainted our lives.

We reached the car park near the aqueduct. I removed the key fob. The aqueduct stretched off to our right, its tall arches casting elongated, eerie moonlit shadows on the floor of the valley. At the far end, where the towpath faded away at the tunnel entrance, the vague outline of a person turned to peer our way, hand shielding his eyes from the moonlight. Probably Lars.

I looked sternly into Gregor's eyes. "Come with us. You're still in a whole heap of trouble, but you can make amends now by helping us make sure Higgs is okay."

The three of us and Disco jogged along the span. Lars must have recognised us and gave us a double-handed overhead wave as if he was directing an aeroplane into its gate at the airport. Disco took off toward him. The speed of whippets and greyhounds running at full tilt had always amazed me, but it appeared Disco had gained an extra gear. She blazed along the path.

I glanced back at Faraday. He ran awkwardly with his left arm hugged tight to his chest and one of Mother's tubes in his right hand. His face was a grimace. I noticed he was on the path's extreme edge, closest to the canal, consciously averting his gaze from the railing that separated us from the precipitous drop to our right.

"Faraday," I said breathlessly as we ran. "Are you okay? Why did you bring that tube?"

"My shoulder hurts. But I'll be okay. And I talked to Iain at the party. He said something that made sense. Maybe Higgs has the key to open the tubes. And if she doesn't, I can always use it to knock some apologies out of whoever took her." He laughed in bitter, descending tones.

I laughed too, but more authentically. "As if you'll hit anyone. That's not you, brother."

"You only know me when our sister hasn't been snatched away."

"True," I said, jogging along beside him and stuffing the car keys into his jacket pocket. "I'll need to stay here for a while when this gets resolved. You can drive yourself home." I surprised myself with my optimism that this would all work out okay.

We reached the widening in the path as the aqueduct gave way to the small basin at the edge of the hill through which the tunnel passed. In hushed voices, we greeted Lars, careful to stand aside from the darkened tunnel entrance so that sounds wouldn't reverberate through and alert the boat crew. The soft putt-putt of an idling narrowboat engine emerged from the tunnel, the only sound other than our own breathing after the run across the aqueduct.

Lars looked anxious. He directed his whispered words to me as if I seemed capable of saving our sister single-handed. "There's a boat in there, Newton, like you said. It's moved slightly, but it's mostly just idled. Did Gregor track Higgs and Dot in there?" He glared at Gregor, accusingly.

Faraday produced the phone. "Look, there she is, still in the tunnel."

Lars examined it. "But Dot's not with her. Look, she's heading back home."

Faraday whipped the phone around to see for himself. "He's right. She's halfway to Pendlethwaite House. She's escaped!"

I slipped automatically into my police persona. They trained us to be decisive and authoritative, and it's amazing how well that worked when you needed to appear competent and get co-operation. "Okay, here's what we'll do. Faraday and I will use the pony track over the hill to reach the tunnel exit. Lars, you and Gregor stay here and keep peeking into the tunnel. Text me if the boat starts moving. I may call you to tell you to shine your phone lights and shout through the tunnel to agitate them if we need them to move out of the tunnel. If I say so, try to make them think you're coming in after them. Police officers should arrive at both ends any minute, so when they do, stay out of the way. And keep Disco with you. We don't have her leash, but you can hold her by the collar for now."

I wouldn't say I was interrupted, because I'd already related the full extent of my plan, but as I looked between Lars and Gregor to make sure they had listened and understood, something unusual happened to the moon. My peripheral vision hinted that the moonlight was changing, so I looked up at it. Then we all looked.

"Oh, come on! Again? Not now." From over the hill's brow rose a densely packed fleet of candle-lit sky lanterns, partially eclipsing the nearly full moon. "Some idiot kids keep releasing these bloody sky lanterns from up here. I could do without that extra complication right now. We don't want them alarming Higgs's captors."

Lars looked at me sidelong, raising one eyebrow. "It's not idiot kids. Those things have magic in them."

I stifled a chuckle, but Lars stared at me intensely, recoiling when I laughed. "Wait. You're serious, aren't you?"

"Yes. Dot told us right before the party. She helped make the spell. It's something about pure thinking, and it's making people hate science and love parsnips."

I held my forehead in the palm of my left hand. Why had all the weirdness piled up at the same time? I was unsure if I could believe this, but Lars seemed convinced.

"Okay, whatever. Let's park the idea of magic floating sky lanterns, Dot casting a spell, and everyone scarfing down parsnips as something to wrap my brain around on another day. Let's focus and make sure the police can rescue Higgs. Are you good with that plan?"

Lars nodded earnestly. Gregor looked up from where he was knotting a piece of string produced from one of his pockets to Disco's collar and gave me a slight nod too. Faraday was ahead of me, climbing the rough path that the canal horses once followed.

The ascent was steep and the path not well used, so it was tough going with a few stumbles over roots that intruded on the formerly well-worn path. The moon cast long and gnarled shadows ahead of us. I reached the flat summit a few steps behind Faraday, who had marched on with determination ahead of me, using the nanotube as a walking stick on the more treacherous patches. The sky lanterns dispersed and gently floated over Middle Ides behind us.

At the skeletal communications tower that perched on the hill, I tugged the back of Faraday's sleeve to get him to pause for a moment. "Hold your horses! Let me call in and check where the backup is before we go to the tunnel exit."

I scanned the next rise, trying to assess the launch position of the sky lanterns, but without success. No more lanterns rose. I couldn't see or hear anyone in the immediate vicinity, although the moonlight gave the bush-covered grass an alien appearance as if the moon was attempting to make Earth look more like the lunar surface. It would be hard to pick out anyone up here unless they broke cover.

While I surveyed, Faraday fiddled with Gregor's phone. He had the camera pointing across the hilltop and zoomed in to the snake of a road that approached the Pendlethwaite Estate. The zoom and the low-light ability of the phone's camera were impressive, but what it revealed was not. Dot Pendlethwaite was being dragged by a man in dark clothing toward the gates of her own home. All I could tell was it wasn't her father, who had distinctive hair and didn't move with the power or urgency of this man.

I called back on the police situation line, and Sally answered again. "Where are the bloody uniformed officers? It's only me up here so far. I don't hear any cars on their way!"

"Newton, get out of there. The whole thing has been c—"

The call dropped. Not just cut off. My phone stopped working entirely, the screen a confusing array of pixelated chaos.

Faraday cursed, and I saw his phone screen was similarly garbled. "Did you hear that?" he hissed.

Trailing tendrils of my brain latched onto something I suppressed while on the call. A sound from further up the hill at the same time as the call dropped. A muffled thud.

"It's another EMP. Someone blew out our tech, like at Chronos' club." He pointed up the slope, where a figure slunk off through the bushes on the rise above us. A small set of sky lanterns rose from that point as if taunting us with a launch right in our faces yet out of reach.

"Did you hear? They aren't sending anyone for some reason. I don't know what's going on, but I know one thing: we need to monitor the narrowboat ourselves now and alert Chronos once he arrives."

Phones useless, and giving up on the sky lantern launcher as a lost cause, my brother and I crouched and descended through the bushes to the Little Ides canal exit.

CHAPTER 43 - SUMMIT

Faraday

I used the metal tube as a makeshift walking stick as I descended the steep and overgrown pathway to the tunnel exit. My collarbone pained me enough without a tumble into the canal. Based on Higgs's last position on Gregor's tracking app before the electromagnetic pulse wrecked the phone, Newton and I must have been right above whatever was happening to her in the tunnel. The stone blocks that framed the tunnel arch hulked just ahead and below us. Why weren't the police coming?

We scrambled down carefully to the arch, keeping a low profile as we perched above the archway. The idling narrowboat's muffled thrum drifted up to us. I whispered into Newton's ear, "Now what?"

Even in his whispering voice, I detected angst. "I don't *know*. They shouldn't have called off my request for backup. I guess we wait and hope that they actually show up. And we have to warn off Chronos when he arrives—there's no way I can let him wade in all heavy-handed."

Silence descended, as palpable as a mist. The only sounds were the muted boat engine and the background music of insects praying to the overhanging moon. Just waiting here infuriated me. We needed to do something, anything. Our sister was a captive, facing who-knew-what. I semi-consciously stroked the wiry fur between Disco's ears to soothe my jangling nerves.

Wait—Disco? Where had she come from? I looked down at where she perched on her haunches. I picked out the white of the string trailing from her collar in the dimness as if it was woven from pure moonlight. I pulled Newt's sleeve and motioned to Disco. "Gregor and Lars aren't doing very well at following instructions."

Although distant, there was a faint metallic creaking, and a glint of movement as one of the imposing gates opened in the Pendlethwaite Estate's walled perimeter. Two figures moved through the opening and turned, looking back toward the tunnel and our position. They couldn't pick us out at that distance, could they? A single headlight appeared in the distance to the south. That might be Chronos on his motorcycle, speeding along the Little Ides road to the canal bridge and the turnoff to the Pendlethwaite Estate. Or maybe a car with one burnt-out headlight. No sound came our way from that direction—it was probably downwind.

The only interruption to our hush was the frantic wing-work of a pair of dragonflies that flitted to and fro along the berry-adorned contours of the bushes to my left. I wondered again about Newton's mention of dragonflies but pushed that thought into the shadows and parked it.

I watched the headlight slither along the road's contours, hoping to catch a snatch of motorbike rev. But I didn't last long tracing its path before events started unfolding in the tunnel.

A weak light shone from the tunnel and lit the black canal waters right below us. The engine's two-stroke beat changed timbre and sped up. The narrowboat turned on its bow light and eased into motion. Then a shouted threat sounded from deeper in the tunnel. "Yeah, you'd better run. We're coming for you!" It was an adolescent-sounding male voice, loud but without the bass notes you would expect from a grown man. And it had a Swedish cadence to it.

"Bloody Lars," Newton spat. "Didn't he listen to anything I said?"

The narrowboat's nose appeared right below us. Newton grabbed my right arm, signalling that he would descend the path to the canal's edge. But if we did that, the boat would clear the tunnel before we made it down. Yes, narrowboats moved slowly and we would catch it, but I couldn't wait that long. It was decision time, and I made one. I jumped.

The tunnel arch was low, so I didn't have much time to accelerate as my feet headed for the front deck below me. Still, I landed hard, my feet and the tube I carried making a booming echo on the metal as I came to a stop in a three-point landing. A rod of pain shot up my whole left side as my sling-hugged arm flailed. I looked up briefly, and Newton stood atop the tunnel archway above me, mouth open but saying nothing.

Disco was already airborne at this point—she apparently thought my idea more sensible than anyone else did, including me. She landed between me and the tunnel arch, her four paws striking in a tight sequence on the flat roof, where her claws skittered and scratched to find purchase. Her calculation of momentum was slightly off, and she slid scrambling over the side. A lungful of breath was expelled as she struck the turf on the canal side opposite the towpath.

The narrowboat's full length emerged from the tunnel, and I glimpsed Newton scrabbling down the last section of path to reach canal level. I still reeled with a red flash of pain as I straightened up and peered over the length of the roof to the narrowboat's rear. Steering the boat from the rear was a shaven-headed man, shouting and pointing my way. "Get him!"

Although he spoke only those two words, I recognised that voice. We had spit from those lips in an evidence bag. I had never wanted revenge on anyone before, but the feeling rose through my spine to my ear tips.

But someone was already following his order. Advancing in a half-crouching stance along the moonlit rooftop, with a grimace of determination marring her face, was a sleekly dressed woman, her long hair and machete catching occasional glints of light. She charged at me, holding the wicked-looking knife aloft.

Newton sprinted too, along the narrow path beside the canal. I raised the tube I held, uncertain of how I should defend myself against a machete attack, but reacting reflexively. She had taken 12 steps so far, and it would only take her 3 more to reach me. I squinted in anticipation of my impending amputation and raised the tube in my right hand a fraction. My left arm hung as useless as a wet noodle in its sling. Disco barked frantically somewhere to my right.

Out of one squinting eye, I watched Newton make a diving lunge for my attacker's legs, an angled jump from the path toward the narrowboat roof. It wasn't very successful. I heard a loud, "oof" as his chest slammed against the boat's side. His leading arm reached above roof level, but all he managed was a quick grasp, snagging the cuff of the marauding woman's pants before he collapsed back to the path.

She stumbled momentarily. One step, another, then she had to throw out her left hand to catch her balance. The right arm shot up the air, the machete's cruel edge ready to slice downward. With more luck than skill or judgement, I swung the tube in a wide arc as she leant in to break her stumble. Her hair swept forward as her momentum slowed, and I noticed that it was a vibrant red. It softened the edges of her cynical face, which bore an alert and apprehensive expression as it tracked the progress of my swinging 'weapon'.

My attack, which hadn't anticipated her stumble, turned out to be perfect. The impact made a hollow *thock* as it struck her left cheekbone. The sound was half-way between the twang of a bowstring and the impact of the arrow striking a canvas target. Her head flicked to the side with the impact, before her body slumped and fell to the path near where Newton lay sprawled. I marvelled at the dent in the metal tube, two-thirds of the way along its length. Iain wouldn't be pleased with the indelicacy I showed the tube, but its alternative use as a weapon was effective. The machete's clatter as it landed on the paving mixed with the sound of a motorcycle engine.

If you have never seen our man James McCann in full action, it's something you should add to your bucket list. He had upped the ante this time around.

The motorbike's aggressive growl preceded its flash past the jumble of Newton and my splayed attacker on the path, its thrumming tires missing them by inches. It happened abruptly—Chronos launched himself from the bike's foot posts straight at the bald man poised at the tiller of the canal boat. He struck the man with the force of a cannonball, making contact shoulder-first and wrapping his target in a staggering rugby tackle.

The man's harsh face and furrowed brow line jerked forward—as did his feet—as our friend's flying form propelled his waist backwards. His body was still frozen in that position as his backside hit the bank.

With no one steering the narrowboat, it continued forward, scraping intermittently against one side then the other, still confined in the narrow single-track that carried on for a scant distance beyond the tunnel exit before resuming its normal two-boat width.

I surveyed the scene. Newton was already fastening the arms of the woman I had so viciously clubbed behind her with a cable tie. Never leave home without cable ties—they come in handy in many situations, improvised handcuffs being one use. Blood streamed from a gash on Newt's chin, making matted clumps in the back of her hair, red on red.

Chronos had his knee in the bald man's back, holding one arm and grinding his face into the grass. "Newton! I need handcuffs over here!" Apparently, he hadn't brought his own cable ties. His captive cried out in throaty anguish. Disco emitted a muffled growl, a jaw-full of the man's calf in her mouth, and she was giving it a ruthless shake. Revenge achieved!

A second narrowboat nosed out of the tunnel. Right at the front, doing his best *Titanic* impersonation, Lars leant in full extension, calling to me. "Is Higgs okay?"

"She's still inside, I think," I replied. My voice sounded as shaky as my hand. I could barely hold on to my precious tube as I tried the handle of the door to the cabin at my end. Locked.

There was a slight jolt and a hollow metallic boom as the two narrowboats collided. Lars leapt dextrously from his boat to the next, landing on the back deck. I wriggled onto the roof, with the tube pinned by my left armpit, my right arm my only leverage. I tried to minimise the movement of my throbbing shoulder. I spotted Higgs inside, tied to a chair that jerked around the floor with her violent struggles to free herself. "This end is locked, but she's there inside, tied to a chair."

I ran the narrowboat's length, noting that it took me 18 strides, while it had only taken the machete-wielding nutcase 15. I gingerly stepped down to the back deck and handed Lars the tube.

"Break the window. We can turn the handle on the inside to open the door."

Glass shards tinkled on the floor inside the cabin. Lars reached in and popped the door open, and we scrambled through the doorway.

"He's getting away!" Higgs shouted at us. And I saw that somebody was indeed leaving—a pair of legs wriggled up and out of the top hatch in the boat's midsection. Across the roof, 5 footsteps echoed and then no more. The fleeing former captor must have jumped to the grass.

"Lars, I'm fine—I'm fine! Just cut this crap off me." Higgs sat strapped to the chair with several loops of packing tape around her torso, her arms and legs taped separately. Cable ties wouldn't help much here, so I engaged in a frenzied pat-down of my pockets for what else I could use to slice the tape. The key fob from my mother's car was round, but I remembered that a traditional key dwelled inside it. I held the fob in my left hand and pressed the recessed release button to free the length of the key, keen to use its jagged edge to cut the tape.

Huh. No key came out. Instead, a truncated integrated circuit with tiny metal connectors dotted on it appeared in the key's place. This wasn't the key to the car—it was the key to the tubes I had found in my mother's lab.

Lars pulled me from my thoughts. "Faraday, what are you doing? Hold the tape so I can cut it. I found scissors in the kitchen."

CHAPTER 44 - CHUKKA

Higgs

Those of us dressed up in our party-going clothes looked the worst. Newton pressed his chin with the palm of his hand, but it was too late to save his blood-splattered shirt, and his jacket had a big rip at the left shoulder. Chronos had a grass and mud skid up the front of his shirt, and Faraday looked completely dishevelled—everything untucked, he hugged his arm to his chest in its sling, and his hair was more tornado than style. I was little better. Bruises had appeared on my arms where I was manhandled during the scuffle in The Red Fern. I also sported tracks of tape gunk around my forearms and calves.

Lars appeared unscathed but sweaty. He presented my handbag, which he must have retrieved from our boat where I had dropped it. His attention was focused on Newton while he held the bag in his outstretched arm. "I know I didn't follow your instructions, but I couldn't stand there doing nothing. I figured Gregor and I could push them out the other end of the tunnel, and the police could grab them at the Little Ides end. Nobody showed up at our side to help, either!"

The two narrowboats floated end-to-end while everyone gathered on the towpath. Gregor had tied off one end of The Red Fern and approached our huddle. "Oh … nice hair, Higgs."

I glared at him. "Listen, everyone," I said with surprising authority in my tone. "Of course you are glad you rescued me—thanks—but Dot is still in trouble." I pointed beyond Beauregarde's fleeing figure to where Dot knelt in the vice of a threatening grip at the gate to her own property. "But first, that man that ordered us to be captured, his name is Beauregarde. And he's one of a group of witches, with who-knows-what powers. We can't just get over there and wrestle him to the ground—he's likely to do something serious in response if we attack him. We need to wait for the police to arrive."

Newton spoke up. "Um, about that. It seems they aren't coming. I called in, and they started explaining something when our phones were blown. I could run to the car and drive to the station to see what's going on, but that would take a while."

"Someone else call them, then!" Lars and Chronos pulled out their phones, but discovered there was no signal.

Faraday gestured to the hilltop above the tunnel. "The EMP must have taken out the cell tower."

I looked across the grassy field to the drive that snaked to Pendlethwaite House. The one-eared man closed in on the gate where his thuggish accomplice held Dot. "Okay, we need to take them out ourselves. But be caref—"

Twelve horseshoes clattered onto the towpath as three riders rounded the base of the hill at speed and came to a stop short of where we huddled. It was three of the Argentinian polo players, still dressed in their formal pants and polo shirts, but each clutched a polo stick under his arm as if they couldn't ride without their normal equipment. "Señor Ryder told us to get over here and help, however we could."

Chronos had righted his motorcycle from where it had slid to a halt near the tunnel entrance and cranked it into life. "You can help me get that man there before he reaches the gate. But be careful, Higgs says he has special powers."

Squealing rubber accompanied an acrid smoke as the bike's back wheel spun on the pavement. Chronos shot past us, followed by a Disco-shaped blur. There was an arrhythmic patter of hooves as the polo ponies shied away from the passing motorbike before the riders wheeled their steeds around and galloped after man and dog. On foot, the rest of us ran after them, heading for Dot's family estate.

The pursuit formed a ragged line at first, with Chronos leading the way. He skidded into a graceful quarter turn before rocketing across the footbridge and into the field on the canal's far side. Disco kept pace with him somehow, and the three horseriders followed not far behind, leaning forward in their saddles with their polo mallets tucked behind them. The five of them fanned out as they surged across the open grass of the moonlit field.

The rest of us took a shortcut, hopping across the narrowboat deck so we could take the most direct route to the gates. We barely started thrashing our feet through the field grasses when something unexpected happened. We fixated on the pursuers, trying to estimate if their quarry would reach the gate before he was caught. It appeared he might; Chronos was not quite closing in fast enough. But then I gasped and a murmur of disbelief washed like a wave over our pursuing party. Disco ran past the motorcycle.

It wasn't like Chronos held back—the bike jostled slightly as he rode but the field was flat and he easily outdistanced the horses. Disco seemed to sense the target now, lowered her head a fraction more and leaned into the run. She didn't only overtake the motorcycle, she *shot* past it. A widening gap opened between her and the bike. She would definitely intercept her target before he could secure himself behind the closed gate.

I slowed marginally and rummaged in my handbag for the gold glasses Granny had given me. There they were! I flicked them open and had a look. My fears amplified. A strong glow of what I realised must be magic limned Beauregarde as he turned to face the streaking Disco. Instinctively, I thought that Disco had magic powers spurring her on in this speed burst, but no glow accompanied her straining silhouette. To my left, another cluster of strong magical glow glimmered from the hills outside the Pendlethwaite Estate, and the last few sky lanterns loitering over the hill behind us twinkled with magical traces. My guts clenched at the thought of confronting this power.

Disco

At first, I didn't know where Chronos was headed. So I followed him. I trotted along beside the motorbike. My horse friends ran too. But I ran faster than them now. I left them in my wake.

Then I understood the goal. We were chasing a man. He ran from us, and he smelled scared. I was determined he wouldn't outrun me. Wait, did I howl? Why would I do that? Maybe it wasn't me, but there were no other dogs around.

I went faster and then faster again. The fastest I had ever run. The rushing air made me nearly close my eyes. The man was not that close when I leapt, but I made a mighty leap. I was airborne for so long that I brought my back paws to line up with my front ones so I could strike him with all four at the same time.

Everything was dust and flying clods of earth after I thudded into his back. He landed on his face and carved a little furrow in the mud, making a satisfying, "Uhn!" I carried on past him, somersaulting three times before sliding to a stop right at the gate. A man stood over me, holding Dot by the hair. He said something in an angry voice and kicked me in the ribs. I yelped as I slid back out through the gate and came to a stop.

The man I had knocked over crouched on all fours, beside a tree that flanked the gate. He held two handfuls of earth as he rose to his knees. From his throat came a terrible noise. Not words. It sounded inhuman, something deeper and darker. I could almost understand it.

He flung the two handfuls of dirt toward the approaching motorcycle. Where the earth hit the road's surface, it turned instantly to frost. A sheet of ice sprang forward from the frost and coated the track. The icy patch shot forward across the field until it met the motorcycle's front wheel. The bike toppled. Chronos slid past me at full speed, motorcycle on top of him. Man and bike hit the stone wall behind me with an ugly crunch.

The bad man stumbled to his feet, heading for the gate. The horses would not catch him in time. I had to protect the pack. I shook myself off, and although my ribs hurt a lot, I launched myself at the man again.

This time I led with my teeth, aiming for his face. At the last second, he put up an arm to protect himself. I felt his hand hit my snout, and he flung me to the icy ground. I slid for a while before I reached the grassy edge and came to a halt. The man struggled the last few steps through the gate, screaming in anguish. Well, not the entire man. I spat out a pinky and another finger—complete with a jewelled ring—onto the grass.

One of my friends reached me and nuzzled me with his long muzzle and warm breath. I signalled to him that I was hurt, but still able to run and bite. He wanted to understand how I ran so fast.

The gate closed, and the man with only eight remaining fingers shouted at the other man. Dot was yelping. I remembered what the stable boy and the horses taught me about jumping. I had an idea.

CHAPTER 45 -   GATES

Faraday

My legs hurt. My shoulder *really* hurt. My breaths came in ragged and shallow bursts, but still, I forced myself to keep running, though everyone else was well ahead of me. Even Higgs, in her dress and low heels, had outpaced me. I clutched the tube in my usable hand as if I could use it to batter my way through the gate ahead and save Dot.

Lars, as ever, was the fastest runner, and he skirted the drive, staying outside the haphazard arc of trees flanking it. He arrived at the foot of the wall to the left of the gate where the wrecked motorcycle lay out of sight of our adversaries. Gregor was only 4 steps behind, crouching for the last stretch to minimise his profile as he glanced sideways at the one-eared man and his over-inflated-looking sidekick.

The polo players had retreated behind the treeline now that the gate was closed, and the puffs of their mounts' breath formed misty cloudlets amongst the trees on the right. Disco limped around their hooves, pacing in agitated circles.

I joined Newton and Higgs, who had their backs to a tree a stone's throw from the gate. It was a majestic chestnut tree, with deeply grooved bark and a cushiony layer of forgotten chestnuts beneath. Higgs took quick peeks around the trunk to where Beauregarde Device and his compadre stood in defiance behind the massive ironwork gates' protective barrier.

I overheard the hushed but disturbing conversation between Lars and Gregor as they attended to Chronos.

"Gods! Look at him. His eyes are moving, but I don't think he sees us," Lars said.

Gregor's tense voice replied. "This is serious, Lars. I need you to focus. He'll bleed to death if we can't slow the bleeding. Here, give me your shirt so I can try to tie off his leg. That's a start."

"Okay – I'll help you tie it tight."

"But we need to get him medical attention right away. Can one of the riders carry him back to the polo club where there's bound to be a doctor and proper first aid supplies?"

"Not with his leg like that. Ew, look, one of the bike's forks is going right through it. Everything's wrapped and crushed around him. We'll have to free him from the bike before he can be moved."

"We can't phone for help, so yeah, if we can't spring him free here, he's going to die, even with this tourniquet."

"I can get you a lever of some sort from the boat. Will that work?"

I heard sprinting footsteps and saw a shirtless Lars pass us, heading back toward the canal. He whistled and gestured, and a polo player cantered across to meet him and help him up onto the horse.

I handed Higgs the small but powerfully beamed torch I had used at Nicholson's Woods as she scooted to the tree trunk's other flank and shone the light onto the wreckage where Chronos lay pinned. Newton and I peered around too. It was a horror show—the bike was folded in two, and Chronos' leg from the knee down disappeared into the twisted mass. His head lolled to face us as Gregor tightened and held the tatters of Lars's shirt above the knee with all the strength he could muster. The torch beam shining on the scraped face of our dearest friend didn't register with him. He lay there, unblinking and twitching spasmodically.

Newton ran to him without a glance back, but Higgs and I couldn't bear to look anymore and spun back into the lee of the tree trunk. After a wordless moment during which we digested our shock, Higgs and I exchanged an intense glance as two voices competed from behind the gate.

One voice was that of an older man, and I recognised it as Lord Pendlethwaite. "My God, man, what are you up to? You're hurting her. Release her at once, you—"

The other voice was a deep bass and spoke in a language that I couldn't understand. The words grated at darkened recesses of my consciousness and thrummed with an anti-musical quality. What in the world was occurring inside?

I felt compelled to discover what was occurring. Higgs and I peeked around opposite sides of the tree.

By the time the torch shone on the scene beyond the gate, Lord Pendlethwaite was sprawled, flung to the ground, and the brute who still held Dot's hair was pressing his face into the dirt with a black boot. Lord P. protested unintelligibly but failed to free himself. Dot stopped crying and regarded her father in shock.

The perpetrator of this violence struck a pose like a ragged but victorious bare-knuckle boxer. Dried blood caked his chin, and one front tooth was missing. His torchlit eyes blazed with anger.

"Give me another shot at that bastard, and I'll finish the job," Higgs hissed.

The other pair of illuminated eyes verged on alien. Beauregarde knelt, palms pressed with outstretched fingers into the earth, and his eyes shone with black radiance as if the pupil wholly engulfed each eyeball. A corrupt language erupted from his mouth as his 8 remaining fingers moved in unnatural sequences in the ground before him.

I heard the polo horses fussing, but the opposite row of trees obscured them, so I couldn't make out why they spooked.

They skittered, and Disco joined in the disturbance, yipping intermittently. Beauregarde kept rumbling the otherworldly words.

Higgs let out a sudden yelp of pain and flicked the torch beam to the back of her calf. A small snake had clamped its jaws onto her leg. Although it was not much bigger than a plump earthworm, it struck with magic-infused determination, and two thin trails of blood descended her leg beneath it. She swiped at it, alarmed, and it released its grip, falling behind her. It didn't fall to the ground, but onto the backs of a wriggling mass of other small snakes, heaving in the pool of torchlight.

We both leapt up and pranced around in a vain attempt to keep both feet off the ground simultaneously. A pair of snakes latched on to my trouser leg, biting the fabric but not finding purchase in the flesh beneath.

We each kicked away several serpents before I bent and made a circular sweep along the ground with my nanotube, sending squirming snakes flying away from us. There were too many to count, which highly annoyed me. With 3 more sweeps a circular patch opened around us, although more snakes advanced from the surrounding grass. I plucked the 2 tagalongs off my trouser leg and flung them by their tails into the general mass of snakes surging toward us.

Beauregarde was raving now, out of sight, as we kicked and swept the snakes away from us. He had returned to his natural voice now, and it rang out with accusations. "I told your grandmother not to marry a Redferne!"

The two remaining horses whinnied, and syncopated hoofbeats signalled their disorderly retreat. They too dealt with the onslaught of serpents. Their riders called out calming Spanish commands, struggling to regain control. In the periphery, Newton also sprang into action, kicking and stomping to protect Gregor and Chronos from the advancing tide of serpents.

"Your grandmother polluted the bloodline and now look what's happened! You were supposed to help us now that we have nature on the rise, not interfere. I hope your damned father burns in hell!"

I felt a tremor of complex emotion, a combination of hopelessness, anger, and the primal urge to run. Higgs radiated rage as she quaked beside me, taking it out on any snake that dared to dart towards us. She took a step out from behind the tree, fists clenched hard. She halted, glaring at the one-eared man, then stepped back and pressed her back against the bark, breathing hard.

I knew I had to act before Higgs did something foolish. It would be better if I took the brunt of whatever damage was on offer here. "Higgs—Iain said that whatever is inside this tube from Mum's lab is likely dangerous. I have the key to open it, so let's see what it can do."

Higgs didn't argue, so I moved in front of her, peeked around the tree, and surveyed the gate area. Beauregarde seemed to be working himself up to further cursing of our family but hadn't yet mustered the words. I knelt and stabilized myself. I didn't know what to expect, so I did my best impersonation of a rocket launcher operator and balanced the tube over my right shoulder, aiming at the gate. "Higgs, help me balance it, It's light, but I can only use one hand here."

My sister stood behind me where I knelt, and I felt her chin press into the back of my hair. The tube steadied immediately. With minor fumbling, the crypto key to the tube emerged from its hiding place in the car key fob. "Ready?"

"Give him hell," Higgs said, venom in every syllable.

My inner anarchist urged me to let the power of our mother's nanotechnology unfold. Worryingly, I spied a few snakes slithering into the circle of light emitted by the down-turned torch. I reached forward and, on the second attempt, slotted the miniature crypto key into the recess on the tube's lid. There was a brief hiss of air being released and an abrupt pop as the lid plopped to the ground ahead of my bent knee, the letters WFS^IS^L facing the sky. I knew from Mum's notes that this was something about whips, flyers, and seekers, but I couldn't predict what might happen.

The result was a definite anti-climax. A slight smell of lubricant and a hint of vapour emerged, but nothing more dramatic. I dropped the tube and rotated back behind the tree trunk. "Okay, sis, we've used up plans, A, B, C, and several more. What's our plan Z?"

"The only thing that springs to mind is running up there and trying to punch him through the gate's bars. But it looks like Disco has a plan."

I followed the line of her index finger to the lane's far side. The two riders had regained control of their horses but had backed several strides away from the trees lining the track. Disco ran a wide arc around them and then sprinted at an ear-flailingly blinding speed on a path toward the high stone wall. It wasn't clear what she was chasing, or if she chased anything at all. Whatever her plan, it looked like she would not change direction in time. A snout-plant into a rough-hewn stone wall was in her immediate future.

But then she jumped.

She was still distant from the wall when she coiled and took a full steeplechase spring into the air. Unfortunately, the wall was formidable—taller even than many trees outside its perimeter. It was impossible for her to clear it. She sprang, flattening her ears back, and sailed in an incredible arc. At the peak, she had a good arm's length of clearance to spare, and she cast a backwards glance over her shoulder at us as gravity finally took hold. The last thing we saw was her vanishing tail as she sailed over the wall to the grounds behind.

I looked at Higgs and said something supremely unintelligible. She widened her eyes and shook her head. But we didn't contemplate the surprise for long, surrounded as we were with an encroaching horde of snakes and a distinct sound of buzzing insects.

The first bees cruised in a few seconds later, congregating at Higgs's feet where we were illuminating our snake-kicking arena. Then several more, and then hundreds. Was this a second biblical plague come to test us because we had dared to diminish the caresses of the snake fangs? One bee stung me in the ankle, then another. I cursed and kicked yet another snake away. The buzzing was all-encompassing now, and I watched an even more menacing cloud of bees zeroing in on us through the scattered beams of moonlight.

Higgs flinched and dropped the flashlight as bees stung us repeatedly. The beam swung in crazy loops before settling on the leaves of the chestnut tree above us. A chaotic maze of bees circled up there. There were now enough homing in on us to cover every inch of us both in a layer at least 10 bees thick. I sank to the ground and covered my head as best I could, using only my right arm and hand.

"Faraday! Faraday, get up! Look!" Higgs wasn't using the tone of voice normally associated with a teenage girl being swarmed by a cloud of angry bees. I raised my head and discovered she wasn't beset by bees as I feared. Instead, they had congregated in their thousands in the leaves above us—right at the spot lit by the flashlight's beam.

We both said the same thing at the same time. "They're swarming toward the light."

She was way ahead of me on the tactical front. "Keep those snakes off me," she said as she set to work. Higgs rotated the torch lens to get the most intensely focussed beam possible. Then she directed it away from the tree, following a wide semi-circle around us on the ground. She stepped past me and flicked the beam to point directly at the one-eared man's figure. She jammed its end into a patch of earthy grass, fixing its beam on him.

This further enraged him, and he screamed in a breaking voice, "I'm going to do what should have been done years ago! I'm ending the Redfernes *now*. Thanks for lighting me up while I do it!"

He broke into a thrumming chant in a wordless language, and his hands moved in a strange dance as if he was pulling an invisible anchor from beneath the ground. Higgs slipped on the gold glasses and peered through the gate. The bees massed overhead as though plotting a revolution but needed a leader to emerge. "Whatever he's doing, it won't turn out well for us. The magic is burning way brighter in him than earlier."

I had never before said a prayer to bees but this seemed like an excellent time to start. "Come on, guys—the light's over there. Do your thing!"

I swivelled my empty nanotube again, scattering several snakes in the grass. The buzzing persisted overhead, more bees joining the dense cloud. Beauregarde's still illuminated one-eared figure stooped with his hands scraping the ground as if readying for the last heave of the invisible anchor. The bees had failed us.

Just as he reached the crescendo of his spell-casting, the thud of a body hitting the ground and the muffled growling of a dog savaging a human arm disturbed our adversary. Beauregarde turned long enough to shout, "Somebody kick that damned dog!" as Disco released his grip on the bloody-faced thug's arm and circled him at a distance, barking. Dot, hair released from his cruel grip, ushered her father away from the threats. He wobbled on his feet, unsteady.

Beauregarde turned to us and resumed his obscene chanting even as the bee swarm sprang into action and sped toward their illuminated human target. Beauregarde's ritual movements concluded with a word something like "Haraii" and an elaborate overhead flourish as if he heaved the titanic anchor over an obstacle. Three squat shapes, wreathed in fire, emerged from the ground and stood poised for a moment before him.

The flames congealed, giving a truer form to the shapes. They coalesced into furious, horn-studded wild boars, composed of iron-tinged patches of molten material swathed in deep crimson fingers of flame. They charged us.

CHAPTER 46 -   BOARS

Higgs

How dare Beauregarde threaten to eradicate our entire family because of a stupid ancient bloodline feud! His membership in the secret society that tricked my best friend into casting a malicious spell was a second black mark against him. Despite his age, he wasn't mature enough to have access to the magic at his fingertips. If there was a proficiency test, he might pass, but on the magical ethics front, he was proving a failure in spectacular fashion.

But there was no time to spend on useless internal outrage. More practical things consumed me. Three magical flaming boars raced toward us, and I had no idea how to halt them. After their release, the hellish beasts surged ahead, slowing only slightly as their fiery forms seethed around the bars of the estate gates until they reformed on our side, leaving behind red hot silhouettes emblazoned on the iron gate.

One boar lowered a tusk-adorned snout and looked off to its right. It peeled off from its two imposing brothers when it spotted Newton, still attending to Chronos at the fallen motorcycle. It made a sound more like a grizzly bear than a boar and hoofed off in that direction. Not only was Newton there, but I noticed that Lars had returned with the third polo rider—he and Gregor were using the narrowboat's anchor to try and open the cruel crush of the motorbike.

If the Redfernes *were* descendants of a magical clan, shouldn't we at least have inherited magical defences? The aura streamed from these three hideous flame-beasts as I watched in horror through Granny's spectacles. Maybe this was why she insisted I take them. But it wasn't helping much to be able to see magic. Every eyeball in the vicinity could see that this snake infestation and flaming animal circus was not normal.

"Argh, Granny! Why didn't you teach me some *actual* magic?" I wailed a cry of pure rage. But the cry dropped into the background, although I knew I still hurled the sound of my anguish full force toward Beauregarde. The sound of crackling flames from the charging boars also subsided, as did the angry buzzing of the overhead swarm of bees coursing at the one-eared man. The only remaining sound, dulled as if I heard it through a haystack of cotton wool, was Newton's voice, pleading with Chronos to stay with us. I could somehow see him, crouched beside our friend, despite not turning my head in his direction. The eerie near-silence was interrupted by my grandmother's disembodied voice, just like that evening in my bedroom a lifetime ago. "Higgs. Remember. You ... are ... a ... tree!"

Damn right I'm a tree! I closed my eyes and concentrated. Tightening the muscles in my trunk, I filled with power and rose to my full height, blocking the onrushing boar's path to Faraday. My arms, raised and pulsing with their own anger, extended as barky boughs, leaves growing around my gold bracelet and exploding from every finger. My roots forged into the earth, shredding my shoes. I roared with wood-rage, a sound audible only to other plants.

My roots sent out my messages to the chestnuts near me and to other trees further afield in the hills above the Pendlethwaite Estate. They awaited instructions and prepared to help.

I formulated three simple instructions for them. But before I could communicate them, the two boars struck. One slowed and tried to calculate how to get around my swinging boughs that shielded Faraday while the other leapt toward where my throat would have been if I wasn't a tree.

The leap was true, and the boar was upon me. I felt the heat of its flaming body. My tree-self reacted with revulsion to fire, and an extra surge of anger coursed through my sap. Its jaws closed around my throat.

Closed but did not clamp shut. The raging teeth stopped a fraction away from touching me. The golden bracelet from Lars's mother's shop became icy and emitted a radiant blue light from beneath its covering of leaves.

The flame-boar's gnarled face recoiled then redoubled its efforts as it tried harder to crush me in its jaws. Its flames flickered and then faded until what remained was a boar-shaped chunk of charcoal. It dropped to the ground in front of me, charred bits scattering around a spent husk.

I ignored the shouting, barking, whinnying, and the thrum of a helicopter rotor that assailed my ears and sent my message out through my roots to the other trees.

Stop the boars.

Open the gate.

Show me the magic.

I swung my fully extended boughs in wide, slicing arcs as a show of force to the boar that circled and threatened Faraday. My brother cowered, seeking a modicum of safety near my trunk as the boar darted in and back out again, evading the vicious swing of my branches. Lean snakes were fastening themselves all over Faraday—he resembled a Live Oak draped with wriggling Spanish Moss.

I still projected my rage toward Beauregarde—or at least, the *shape* of Beauregarde, who now waved his arms ineffectively to repel the throbbing mass of bees covering him from his head to three-fingered hand. As I watched, he collapsed. Behind him, Disco flew backwards through the air after a kick from the bloodied thug. The man's eyes were wide with terror at the bees attacking his master, and his missing tooth and shredded jacket sleeve marked the earlier trauma delivered by my swing of the fire extinguisher and Disco's frenzied attacks.

The other trees obeyed the messages.

A clutch of low bushes, growing unplanned near the motorcycle wreckage, erupted into rapid growth. This caused the boar hurtling toward Newton to skid and change direction. It pawed the earth and swivelled its hideous inferno of a head, looking for a way around the thorny new barrier to complete its mission.

The chestnut trees at either side of the gates to Pendlethwaite House twisted and extended their branches to the gates, entwining the ironwork with shoots and twigs. Flexing powerfully, the branches strained at the gates, ripping them off their hinges and dropping them beside the drive. The two closest polo players ushered their horses into motion, and they swept through the newfound gap. They cantered past the human-shaped mound of bees on the track and made liberal use of their polo mallets on Dot's captor.

Wind from the helicopter ruffled our leaves as distant trees on the hillside above sent me a vision of a group of retreating figures. They wore hooded cloaks and masks, grotesque parodies of animal faces that I recognised from Dot's description of the Drowned Cabal members. One carried a clutch of unlit sky lanterns, bobbling on their wire handles. I couldn't identify the people behind the masks, but one hood lowered and revealed a cascade of well-kept grey hair that framed the sinister stork-faced mask. The bronze mask tilted and scrutinised my host tree as if they sensed the observation. That hair was familiar.

I withdrew my perceptions back to my body and noted that Dot and her father were now safe. They huddled together with a limping Disco as the polo players knelt atop the black-jacketed thug. They nervously eyed the dispersing bees that buzzed away from Beauregarde's thrashing, hunched, no longer illuminated, but still-upright husk of a body.

With a last garbled groan of accusation aimed at me, Beauregarde slumped and fell face-first onto the ground, lifeless. A single thundering toad croak, so low-pitched it was felt more than heard, washed over the scene from the hills behind us, sounding both anguished and victorious.

My rage subsided, and I involuntarily returned from a tree to a girl, shreds of shoes encircling me. What would prevent the remaining two fire-boars from attacking my brothers now?

CHAPTER 47 - CLAMPDOWN

Newton

It was mayhem. I glanced repeatedly over my shoulder as the desperate attempts to stop Chronos' bleeding escalated. I strained at the tourniquet as Gregor and Lars pried at the motorbike body to gain enough space to free Chronos' skewered leg. I was losing hope at the same rate he was losing blood.

My glances showed Disco leaping the wall, the gates being ripped off, the polo players storming into the Pendlethwaite Estate, and the charging flame-beasts. The boar charged around a thicket of intertwined saplings—that couldn't have been there a moment ago—and now bore down on me with menacing speed. I released my grip on my friend and turned to ward off this new threat.

The boar skidded, regained its footing and circled the newly-grown thicket. He would be upon me in a few seconds.

Behind me, Lars shouted, "You can't do that, it'll kill him. I brought the machete to free him, not for—"

Gregor cut him off. "I've seen them do it in movies. If I don't cut it off, we'll never move him from here."

Torn between protecting Chronos from the raging horror in front of me and the unfolding obscenity behind me, I braced myself for impact and turned to see Gregor swinging the machete in an overhead arc that cleanly sliced through

Chronos' lower leg, a few inches below his knee. What was he thinking? The knife wasn't even sterile, and it's grizzly slice was followed immediately by a spray of blood from the femoral artery. Somehow, a helicopter thrummed overhead.

No, no, no! Forget the marauding boar—I dove to my friend's side and clamped both hands over the ragged stump, desperate to stop the flow of blood.

It was no use. Lars hauled on the tourniquet above the knee, but blood oozed and frothed between my fingers. Chronos was long since unconscious, but miraculously still breathing, and his heart was working at full speed.

I prepared myself for the snorting boar's impact, not sparing a glance over my shoulder, but I didn't raise my arms to ward off the attack. Only death could make me release the pressure on my best friend's wound now.

I felt Higgs's hands over mine, even though I couldn't see them. Her voice was urging me, a soundless presence inside my head. "You can't let him die, Newt. I won't let you. Stop the bleeding."

I think I had briefly given up hope, but my sister was somehow there beside me, even though I knew she was a sprint away, with Faraday, and she tapped into a reserve of strength I didn't know I possessed. The warmth of the blood suffocating my hands took on a deeper, smouldering quality and the spurting slowed, then stopped. I felt Higgs's approval and knew that if I took my hands away I would see something miraculous.

"Keep pressing, Newton," Lars screamed. "You can't stop now, he's still alive."

I pulled one hand away, then the other. It was like the wound had been cauterized by my hands. No blood was escaping and the stump had a charred but surprisingly sterile appearance. Higgs had dome something inexplicable here, through me. And then I remembered the hell-boar.

The downdraft from the helicopter was intense—it hovered directly overhead. The boar left its molten hooves and leapt at me, covering the last few yards airborne.

I recoiled beneath a sensation that I felt, heard, and saw fleetingly but simultaneously. At first, I thought it was the onset of death, but it washed over me as I squatted, straining at the tourniquet. The sound reminded me of a generator powering down—a descending electrical hum that began at a deafening level but petered out to nothing. My hair electrified, every strand pointing upward, fleeing my scalp to full extension, before slashing back down again as if blown by a gale-force wind. I had the impression of a large, glowing cargo net emerging from beneath the hovering helicopter, draped over the entire area. Its red fibrous squares grew ever smaller and more tightly packed as it descended until it passed over me—through me—and sank into the earth around us.

After the energy net descended, there was scant sign of the flaming boar, other than shards of unidentifiable black residue scattered around me, a clod of it stuck to my left shoe. I heard later from Faraday that he experienced the same thing, watching the glowing net descend from the helicopter to banish another demonic boar making its last charge on him and Higgs.

The net also disabled a massive swarm of nanotech-infested bees that Faraday had created almost by accident. Their black-and-yellow bodies lay heaped on the unrecognizably bloated form of Beauregarde Device. Occasional whimpers were the only sign that he was still alive.

After releasing the mysterious net, the helicopter swivelled and came to a swift landing in the field between the remnants of the Pendlethwaite Estate gates and the canal tunnel. A small squad of military-clad figures jumped out and cleared the downdraft. A detachment trotted off toward the narrowboats while others fanned out and approached our position. They wore military helmets and an array of combat and communications gear.

Although the unit that approached us walked with purpose and an authoritative posture, the other members of our own raggedy team reached my location first. It was a relief that everyone survived, although this was the most dishevelled array of characters I had ever been a part of.

The polo players were the most presentable. Marco Antonio didn't look any worse than he would after a match as he rode off to join his two teammates who had Beauregarde and his associate under control. Dot still looked impressive in her party outfit, with her ruby dangling around her neck, but she had clearly been dragged across a field, and her hairdo hadn't survived the rough tussling. Her face was a mess, with mascara icicles decorating her cheeks and eyes red from crying. She cradled a curled up Disco in her arms, and a stunned looking Lord Pendlethwaite leaned on her for support.

Lars and Gregor stood ruffled, Lars shirtless and Gregor splattered in blood. My brother's clothes asked for a direct trip to the garbage bin when we got home, and inexplicably he had three small snakes dangling by their fangs from his good forearm. He didn't brush them away, oblivious. His pallor was grey, and his grimace suggested considerable pain.

Higgs was a wreck. When I had last crouched behind the tree with her, she was slightly unkempt from the run across the field, but still appeared ready to hit the dance floor. Somehow, in the last few minutes, she had lost both shoes, become covered in bee stings, had acquired puncture marks in her calves with trails of descending, congealing blood, and her dress fluttered in tatters. But her gold bracelet shone with a faint internal glow, and her disarrayed hair still managed to look impressive. It was as if a hairdresser had strategically positioned a fashionable array of autumn leaves, so they peeked out from her short spiky crop.

At the sight of the incapacitated Chronos, two of the helicopter troops ran forward, one unslinging a bulky backpack emblazoned with a red cross. "Medics! Give us room!"

We surrendered access to our fallen friend and they busied themselves treating him. Gregor's mouth hung open and his shaking hand dropped the machete, as if he only now became aware of what he had done.

Two camouflage-wearing and carbine-wielding soldiers accompanied another medic toward the gate. Three soldiers approached us at the ready, flanking the unit's leader. She removed her helmet and shook her head at us before speaking. It was Scarlett Thorisdottir.

"You don't know what you're doing, any of you, do you?" She said this calmly but firmly as if it was an established fact.

I opened my mouth, gestured at Chronos and then at the gate, trying to formulate a sensible reply, but Faraday cut me off. "We'd know a lot more about what we were doing if you hadn't killed our father!"

She let out a truncated, scornful laugh. "Come now. Templeton and I worked side by side for the UPDA. There's no reason for me to kill him, and no way I could get away with it. They track us all continuously. He died in a car accident, not by my hand. Don't be ridiculous."

She approached Dot, saying officiously, "Miss Pendlethwaite, you need to correct what you have done. Close your eyes and start thinking pure thoughts. But this time, think purely that there is absolutely nothing wrong with science, and that it would be brilliant if more people took an interest—especially girls. We need that."

Dot was buzzing with agitated energy, swivelling her gaze between Scarlett and Higgs, shaking arms hugging herself. "But you can't undo it with just me. Can you?"

"We can do a lot that might surprise you. You look like you're in no state to compose your thoughts. Let me help."

Scarlett approached Dot and cradled her cheeks. "Close your eyes. Listen only to me." She leaned in and began to murmur in Dot's ear. After thirty seconds, Dot let her arms drop to her sides and she rolled her head in gentle circles. After another minute, Scarlett motioned to one of her squad to bring her something. "Tell me when you are ready, and then fill this bag with one giant exhale." She offered something considerably higher-tech than the paper bags of the sky lanterns—a thick-sided, flattened plastic sac with a breathing tube and elaborate valve at one end.

Dot kept her eyes closed, drew a series of protracted deep breaths. Everyone went very quiet, and I held my breath until she announced she was ready. Scarlett handed her the bag, and with a final pronounced lungful, she exhaled, expanding the sac to an impressive volume.

"Thank you. That will clear things up nicely," Scarlett said to Dot as she took it back. Dot's eyes fluttered open. She glanced dismissively at Gregor. "And Radzinski, I'll deal with you later."

"Magic is just science underneath," she said, holding the sac aloft and giving it an appraising stare. "Or maybe science is magic. We're not fully sure yet. Your dad was figuring that part out."

Finally, my police brain started lighting up. "What even *is* the UPDA? And how did you arrive here, now? Are you spying on us with those dragonfly drones?"

She surveyed our motley array of friends. "I can't talk to you here. You three kids need to come with me. Only you three."

She beckoned to us to return with her to the helicopter, but none of us moved.

I retorted sharply to her half-turned back. "I'm not going *anywhere* without Chronos … er, McCann."

Her head turned, and she locked her piercing gaze on me. With an impatient wave, she gestured to her compatriots. "There is another helicopter coming momentarily. He can travel in that one with the medical crew." The medics had been busy. Blood packs and saline were already administered and they were working on his stump, sanitising and wrapping it in compression bandages.

It was Higgs's turn to stamp her angry authority on the question. "He comes with *us*. Get him to the hospital, and you get us too."

With an exasperated shrug that seemed to imply acceptance, she turned and strode to the helicopter. The medics lifted Chronos' unconscious form onto a field stretcher with the help of Lars and me. This was not a man that was easy to lift. Hustled to the helicopter, we slid him into the open passenger space. The medics continued to attend to him, administering a rapid series of injections, and connecting him to a field medicine monitoring device.

Disco jumped on board just as the helicopter lifted off. Dot stood with Lars and Gregor outside the buffeting of the downdraft and watched us pass another incoming helicopter and depart the battle scene.

As we rose and rotated to point back toward the town, Scarlett was busy. She took the plastic pack full of Dot's exhaled breath and attached its valve to a squat machine that looked like a cross between a portable heater and an industrial vacuum cleaner. Its corrugated hose escaped the helicopter body through a porthole in the fuselage. Once we reached an altitude where the pilot put the nose down and sped over the hill separating Little Ides from Middle Ides, Scarlett activated the machine. Dot's counter-spell pumped through the hose to undo the earlier influence on our townspeople.

Without the headsets sported by the military team, there was no way to talk over the ferocious noise of the helicopter's flight, but the questions were piling up. My siblings and I exchanged glances, shrugs, and eye rolls. Higgs cuddled Disco, who nestled in the lap of her torn dress.

Scarlett busied herself with a second task. She pulled a scanning device with a protective, ruggedized shell from a latched flight case and ran it over us. The red line illuminating the target area under scan passed once over Faraday and me, but she did several passes over Higgs, dwelling twice on her gold bracelet. A raised eyebrow was Scarlett's only reaction.

She scanned Disco almost as an afterthought but spent even more time with her. Whatever she was looking for, Disco seemed to have in abundance.

As the military staff continued to work with clinical efficiency on Chronos, the helicopter traveled in an arc over the town, venting Dot's burning, spell-laden breath. Our path ventured as far as Nether Ides before a final, tighter circle during the approach to the hospital. Touching down on the helipad bulls-eye, the doors rolled back and a waiting medical crew took great care in transferring Chronos onto a hospital trolley.

I moved to step out and follow him, but Scarlett grabbed my arm and motioned me to stay. She closed the door and signalled the pilot to cut the engine.

CHAPTER 48 -   SEEING RED

Faraday

Being confronted with Scarlett Thorisdottir was a confusing mix of curiosity, accusation, and suspicion. We each had a raft of questions floating at the top of our minds, and Newton barely began his questioning before Scarlett cut him off with a sharp gesture.

"Look, kids." I felt Newton at my side bristle with umbrage at the belittling reference, but he remained silent. "I can tell by your reactions and apparent misinterpretation of what's going on here that your father didn't tell you much about his work with the Unusual Powers Defence Agency. Is that right?"

I nodded. "We only recently discovered he worked for the UPDA. Didn't even know what it stood for until now."

She gave only a hint of a nod. "Got it. His specialty was scouting out pockets of magical activity, both in the United Kingdom and abroad. He had particular … *skills* that made him suitable for the job. I was responsible for the cases he worked. And I also cover other threats and unusual powers, including potential misuses of nanotechnology." She gestured at Disco, who lay curled up beside the inactive machine that dispersed Dot's pure thinking over the town. "Anyone want to explain what's going on there?"

"We think she got accidentally exposed to a tube-full of nanotech. She seems healthy, but it's somehow given her unnatural speed and jumping ability. It happened when the tube cracked open during a *car accident*. Want to explain what went on *there?*"

Scarlett glared at me. "And why would I have any information about a local car accident? That's got nothing to do with unusual powers—hardly seems like something UPDA should concern themselves with. Although now that I see it involved tubes of rogue nanotech, maybe we should have paid attention."

"I know how you—"

"You know *nothing*. Listen, all three of you. The things that happened here, both the magic and the nano, stop now. The unfortunate Mr Beauregarde Device—who you will soon hear died peacefully at home, not at the pointy end of a swarm of nano-infested bees—was the only one here who had any grip on how magic works. Those other mask-wearing amateurs will wilt now that he's gone. And we have a nice collection of nanotubes in our possession now, both from the lab and, more recently, from your car. I don't expect any more nonsense like that, right?"

She didn't pause for an answer. "I'm deeply sympathetic about the loss of your parents. Templeton was a trusted friend. But you three need to stop fooling around with things you clearly don't understand and get back to sorting out your actual lives. I don't want to have to come back to this godforsaken town. Ever."

There was a blur in front of me, and my palm stung. With startling calmness, given that I had just slapped Scarlett's face, hard, I heard myself say, "This isn't over until I tell you it is."

She returned my stare as I snatched the door open and jumped out.

Higgs, still barefoot, backed out after me, staring at Scarlett the entire time, unblinking. I looked away, committing every detail of her voice and face to memory. But Newton wasn't finished yet. I could see his nostrils flaring as he turned back to the helicopter to confront her.

"This won't stop for you. Just wait until the investigation of these events gets underway. We'll find out what you really did!"

She shook her head and smirked, a reddening palm print blossoming on her left cheek. "Investigation? Really? Is that going to work better than when you called for backup at Little Ides? Are you going to get more answers than when you asked your Detective Inspector to find out what UPDA was up to? I can twist your backwater police force around my little finger without even raising it. And don't bother trying anything with Gregor Radzinski—you'll find that's a dead end too."

I had nothing else to add, so I stepped out. She slid the door closed, and the rotors lazed into their spiral. She didn't turn away from our three accusing stares, seeming to look each of us in the eye at the same time. Eventually, we had to relent and scampered from under the helicopter.

CHAPTER 49 -   CAKE

Disco

My ribs hurt. I felt them crack when I was at the gates. That guy who kicked me deserved to have his arm bitten. But I could run fast now. And jump high. Wait until I saw the horses again. They could race me!

I wondered when Templeton would come home. I snuck to the basement and curled up under his desk. When I woke up, my ribs felt perfect. No pain at all. The house was silent, and it was dark down here. Not total silence. I heard that scritch sound again. The one I heard up at the shed behind Granny's house. I walked to the back wall. Yes, definitely coming from behind that wall. I must still protect the pack.

Higgs

It took two or three days before the three of us shared every finer detail of our various ordeals. Not that we intended to hide anything from each other, it was just that a lot had happened, and we kept remembering to share fragments as we realised which of us had missed out on each chaotic event.

"Everything would have made more sense if we shared this information earlier."

Faraday nodded. Newton replied, "Agreed. I know you want to fight your way out of this crap pile of a year, Higgs, and Faraday wants to solve the riddles that we uncovered. And I can't seem to get organised enough to get our lives under proper control. But you're right. If we had only communicated better, events wouldn't have escalated like this. Magic, the secret nanotech lab, they are so tempting to abuse. We're lucky nobody was killed. Chronos, nearly, and Beauregarde didn't look too pleased when we last saw him, but I'm not losing any sleep over him."

"Let's make a pact: no more secrets." I held out my right hand, palm up.

Faraday hesitated, his hand moving with a tremor of uncertainty toward Netwon's and mine. "You know how you kept your first tinglings of magic from us because you were afraid we wouldn't believe you? Especially me?"

"Well, you are famously rooted in facts, Faraday," I said.

"More than anyone, except maybe Dad, I would have believed you. I haven't told anyone this because I have trouble believing it myself, but I saw Granny do some major magic. Up at the canal when I was still at Giant Grove School—the day we found Disco. She saved my life when I was ten, but it's been ridiculously hard to get her to confirm the events, and seeing her with rings of energy forming around her hands was so fantastical it seemed like a dream. Let's get her to tell us all about it, next time we see her."

I locked eyes with him and nodded very slightly. That was enough. His hand completed its brief journey. Our three hands clasped, then five. I unslung Faraday's left arm, and we made it six. Disco extended herself into a standing stretch position, accidentally adding her two front paws into the mix. The three of us smiled and spoke in unison. "No secrets."

Faraday's new phone pinged with an incoming text message. He read it. "Okay, let's start now. This message is from Iain Vanderkamp. He says he made a discovery in Mum's lab notes from the book I salvaged up at the Ides Giant. It mentions something about *another* nanotech lab. He also took his nanotech scanner to Mum's grave on a hunch, and says he has some unusual results."

"Tell him we'll *all* meet to hear about it," I said.

* * *

I organised a group visitation for everyone to see Chronos. Normally, the hospital limited visitors, but it was his birthday, so I persuaded them this was a special case and deserved an exception. We assembled in the corridor outside his recovery room and entered together.

Every remaining Redferne was there—I pushed Granny in a wheelchair with a contented Disco hidden under the fleece blanket on her lap. Dot and Lars came with us, as did Emeline Grey—she and Newton were leaving from here to go out for the dinner they had arranged what seemed like an incalculable number of days ago.

I led the way, pushing the wheelchair into the room marked 'James McCann'. Maybe a little too enthusiastically. I almost dumped Granny onto the floor at the foot of Chronos' bed, but she held on as I recovered our balance. Everyone else piled in behind me.

"Happy birthday!"

Chronos beamed. "Hey! My goodness, check out you lot! You're looking *way* better than you did at Little Ides."

A burst of chatter started spontaneously, with a barrage of questions aimed at Chronos. I had been to visit twice already, so I wheeled Granny back and let the others make the hospital bed the centre of attention.

I smiled and observed the camaraderie. Teens, new adults, my grandmother, chatting and laughing. It was as if this was all a charade, and Chronos would leap out of bed at any moment and run a few laps around the hospital.

Granny stroked the mostly concealed Disco under the blanket and beckoned me closer with her other vein-riddled hand. "I thought Templeton would have told you more about our family history. How *everything* goes back to Pendle Hill. The Redfernes stood against Elizabeth Southerns, the Device family, and the Greys, but if you knew your grandfather, he would have told you tales about how the Redfernes were snarled up in the witchery too. Old scores should have been left behind as the families intertwined. Heck, I'm part of the same Device family tree as Beauregarde, and married a Redferne! But that poor man ultimately couldn't leave behind events from four hundred years ago. Something reached across the centuries and laid a fresh chip on his shoulder. But you felt it, didn't you Higgs? I watched you. I told you that you were a tree."

Finally, a confirmation! I shook my head, but with a smile on my face. "Why Angelina Redferne, you are full of secrets, aren't you?"

"Secrets? I don't have any, dear. It's you that has secrets."

"Is that magic? What happened to me? I tried so many times on my own to conjure up any special powers, but it never seemed to work."

Granny's expression softened. "It takes practice, my girl, practice. And I feel your brother has to be there to let it fly from you."

"What, Faraday is part of the magic?"

Granny laughed out loud. "He refuses to really believe magic when he sees it first hand! No, not Faraday. It's Newton that I sense you need."

I looked up through misty eyes, overcome by the new and invisible bond between us, and noticed that I needed to rescue everyone from Lars, who was performing a violent re-enactment of Gregor's field amputation, one bent arm raised overhead holding an imaginary machete. "I didn't want to look, really. But I did! My eyebrows were on the back of my head when I saw what Gregor was going to do. I don't think he knew what he was doing but he sure had the guts to do *something*. You were squirting blood all over the place. I'm not sure he knew what he was doing, but he took aim then raised up the … hacker?"

This was a little too much, so I intervened. "It's called a machete, Lars. And I don't think we need a full repeat performance."

He got the hint. "But Canny was unconscious… I haven't even got to the part where Newton saved him … I was just … Oh, I see … I'll get the cake!"

He slunk off to open the covered cake carrier from the hamper he had brought, and Emeline organised the side plates and forks. I had a sneaky peek at the back of her grey hair tied in a loose ponytail. Was it dyed that colour, or was it naturally grey? As she lit the candles, I couldn't help but wonder how that hair would look under a hooded cloak with a bronze stork mask pulled over her face.

Our family's closest friend, who would risk and sacrifice life and limb for us, blew out the three token candles. "That was a complicated wish I just made. Even if I could tell you, it would take a while," he said, as slices were plated and doled out.

Chronos was already devouring his oversized slice of cake. A few crumbs of sponge littered his blanket, and a blob of vanilla icing awaited clean-up at the corner of his mouth. "This cake is amazing, Lars. Your mother made it? What flavour is that?"

"Yeah, she's a really wonderful baker. It's a parsnip cake." I watched Newton and Faraday put their plates aside, although they hadn't been served yet.

Dot leaned in and whispered in my ear. "Well, Scarlett only said to reverse the anti-science thoughts. I didn't hear her say anything about parsnips. Did you? Oh, and I'm pretty sure you don't need to get your hair cut very often. It will look fabulous to people around here no matter what you do."

LAST WORDS

Thank you for reading *Sky Lanterns Over Nether Ides*. If you enjoyed the story, leaving a review is a good way to let other readers know how to follow in your footsteps. I appreciate your feedback.

Higgs, Faraday, Newton, and Disco will return in *Shadow Over Loch Ghuil*.

When a rash of violent crimes spreads from London and a sinister organization blackmails the Scottish parliament, the Redferne siblings must consider the unthinkable to preserve the nation - joining forces with the woman involved in their parents' deaths.

The twin threats of magic and nanotechnology are stirring, combining to elevate The Tartantula, a conspiratorial organization that will stop at nothing to seize control of Scotland. Faraday must set aside his accusations long enough to solve the puzzle of murderous teenage girls. And will Higgs's newfound talents be able to stop the *death clock* and protect her friends from otherworldly magic in the remote Glen Ghuil? Not if the forces arrayed against them flex their overwhelming powers. Join the Redferne family and their colourful adversaries in *Shadow Over Loch Ghuil*.

Join my mailing list and find more at
www.pattisontelford.com

Pattison Telford lives in Toronto, Canada, with his wife, two quietly magical sons, and snaggle-toothed dog. Previously living in Scotland, England, and Australia has armed him with a considerable range of slang words and insults. He grew up playing basketball and has spent far too much time sitting in front of computer screens in his job as a Microsoft IT Consultant.

Lightning Source UK Ltd.
Milton Keynes UK
UKHW011927060821
388460UK00001B/214